"So what kind of sex do you need to have?"

The curiosity and humor in her tone were what made Zach open his eyes. Kiera had turned to face him and had one leg tucked up underneath her, her elbow on the back of the couch, her head in her hand.

And he wanted to make her breakfast in the morning.

Not a no-go-ahead-and-keep-it travel mug of coffee on her way out the front door. Real, made-from-scratch pancakes. In his kitchen. With his mom's recipe. After they'd cuddled late into the morning in his bed.

He sighed. "Up against the wall, hard and fast and loud. And over in one night." He made sure to add that at the end. Just in case she was feeling cuddling-with-pancakes too.

Kiera seemed fascinated by his answer. "And you can't have that with me?"

She wasn't being coy; she wasn't flirting. She was truly curious, and Zach shook his head. "No." Because he wanted the against-the-wall stuff, but he also wanted to take about three hours to kiss her from head to toe before he did anything else.

He definitely liked her. *Damn.*

ACCLAIM FOR ERIN NICHOLAS

"Heroines I love and heroes I still shamelessly want to steal from them. Erin Nicholas romances are fantasy fodder."
—Violet Duke, *New York Times* bestselling author

"Sexy and fun!"
—Susan Andersen, *New York Times* bestselling author on *Anything You Want*

"Erin Nicholas always delivers swoon-worthy heroes, heroines that you root for, laugh-out-loud moments, a colorful cast of family and friends, and a heartwarming happily ever after."
—Melanie Shawn, *New York Times* bestselling author

"Erin Nicholas always delivers a good time guaranteed! I can't wait to read more."
—Candis Terry, bestselling author of the Sweet, Texas series

"A brand new Erin Nicholas book means I won't be sleeping until I'm finished. Guaranteed."
—Cari Quinn, *USA Today* bestselling author

"Reading an Erin Nicholas book is the next best thing to falling in love."
—Jennifer Bernard, *USA Today* bestselling author

"Nicholas is adept at creating two enthralling characters hampered by their pasts yet driven by passion, and she infuses her romance with electrifying sex that will have readers who enjoy the sexually explicit seeking out more from this author."
—*Library Journal* on *Hotblooded* (starred review)

Completely Yours

ERIN NICHOLAS

FOREVER

NEW YORK   BOSTON

Copyright © 2016 by Erin Nicholas
Excerpt from *Forever Mine* copyright © 2016 by Erin Nicholas

Cover design by Elizabeth Turner. Cover illustration by Blake Morrow. Cover copyright © 2016 by Hachette Book Group, Inc.

Forever
Hachette Book Group
1290 Avenue of the Americas, New York, NY 10104
forever-romance.com
twitter.com/foreverromance

First Edition: December 2016

Forever is an imprint of Grand Central Publishing. The Forever name and logo are trademarks of Hachette Book Group, Inc.

The publisher is not responsible for websites (or their content) that are not owned by the publisher.

The Hachette Speakers Bureau provides a wide range of authors for speaking events. To find out more, go to www.hachettespeakersbureau.com or call (866) 376-6591.

ISBNs: 978-1-4555-3964-2 (mass market), 978-1-4555-3966-6 (ebook)

Printed in the United States of America

OPM

10 9 8 7 6 5 4 3 2 1

For Nikoel, my geeky girl. For everything.
And to Liz and Lindsey. Just...thank you.

Completely Yours

$\mathcal{C}$HAPTER ONE

$\mathcal{T}$hey're estimating up to twenty thousand were inside when it came down."

Zach Ashley stared at his crew leader, Troy. "Twenty *thousand*?"

Troy nodded grimly. "If a ceiling in an exhibit hall is going to collapse, it's gonna collapse during Comic Con, right?"

Zach scrubbed a hand over his face. It was going to be a long day.

The ambulance screeched to a halt outside the Seaport World Trade Center, and Zach bailed out of the back, yanking his bag up onto his shoulder. His crew members were right on his heels as they started toward the front doors. But the going was slow through the throngs of people. And Zach was trying not to simply stand and stare. Creatures and characters in all shapes, sizes, and colors had been evacuated from the convention center and now covered the sidewalks and streets. It was a sight to behold.

"This way!" A member of the Boston PD waved them forward, clearing a path through the crowd.

They made it inside a moment later, and Zach had no idea what he was looking at. The general panic and confusion that went along with any catastrophe were multiplied by the thousands. A big crowd was always a difficult scene to work, but this was insanity. The convention boasted an attendance of nearly fifty thousand each year, so Zach knew it could have been worse. But twenty thousand potential victims inside a 115,000-square-foot exhibit hall where a sixth of the ceiling had come crashing to the floor? That was holy-shit-chaotic stuff.

"Worst of it's in the center," Troy called to them, holding his radio to his ear. "There are three crews already on-site treating vics as they dig them out. Start out here and triage as you work to the middle."

Fortunately, most of the building had been evacuated. Besides the rows and rows of booths that sold everything from comic books to jewelry to tech gadgets, the huge exhibit hall was empty of all attendees able to walk out on their own and not bleed along the way. The only people remaining inside were the emergency workers and the injured con goers.

Zach and the other guys spread out, stopping and examining anyone they came across.

"You're good to go," Zach told a woman and her son a few minutes later after checking out a wrist sprain and a few scrapes and cuts. "Ice, rest, and call your doctor if anything worsens."

He moved on to a guy who was limping toward the front doors. A few minutes later, he applied an ankle splint and told the guy to head to the ER. And so it continued over the next half hour. One injury at a time. One person at a time. That was what he needed to focus on. Even though everything in him itched to storm toward the center of the hall to help dig through the debris himself.

The people on the periphery were hurt too. They needed to be checked over too. Zach's job was to treat and help those he came into contact with. But the need was greatest in the middle. His crew should have been first on the scene. He should be in there with the worst of the worst. He should be doing everything he could, including search and rescue, instead of applying Band-Aids and ACE wraps. But they hadn't been dispatched first. They hadn't been the closest. It had taken them longer to get there than squads two, six, and seven.

Still, Zach hated being on the periphery of anything.

"Sir, I'm going to have to ask you to remove your... scales." Zach was proud of himself for hesitating only slightly as he addressed the man he was kneeling next to.

Of course the man, who was dressed as what Zach could best describe as something half man, half alligator, didn't look impressed.

"They're not scales. They're body plates," the man said.

"Is there a difference?" Why had he asked that? He didn't care one way or the other.

"You're born with scales; you *apply* body plates."

Right. "Well, I'm going to need you to remove them so I can get your blood pressure," Zach told him.

The alligator man exposed a spot on his arm for the blood pressure cuff, and Zach worked on focusing on one thing at a time. Regardless of how the victims were dressed, they all had actual human blood, bones, and organs inside that needed attention. But the injured here presented a challenge Zach hadn't encountered on any of the crazy calls he'd been on in his five years as an EMT in Boston. It was hard to tell which red streaks were blood and which were stripes of paint, which protruding appendages were broken or dislocated bones and which were horns or dorsal fins or extra arms or legs. It was even hard to tell if victims were male or female, if they were young or old, and how tall some of them were—he'd just assisted a guy who had been on stilts underneath his long black wizard's cape. Or had he been a warlock? Hell if Zach knew.

"Hey, need more hands on deck in the middle. How are things out here?"

Zach looked up to find Troy at his side. "Good. We've cleared a bunch out."

"Great. Let's go."

He was more than ready to get into the thick of things. "Blood pressure is good." Zach released the alligator man's arm. "You're not bleeding anywhere. You don't have any tenderness except on that rib. I'm guessing you have a crack. You need to get to the doctor to be sure."

"You're not taking me?"

Zach glanced around and then gave the man a look to say, *Are you kidding me?* "There are going to be a lot of people not able to get themselves there. You should be grateful you're not one of them." Zach shouldered his bag and turned to Troy. "Ready."

As they started toward the center of the convention hall, three figures went running past, almost tripping Zach. They were short and wore identical wigs of shaggy brown hair and had capes flapping out behind them.

"Munchkins?" he asked. He'd seen that movie. Probably.

"Hobbits," Troy said.

"Ah." He'd heard of them. He was pretty sure.

"You have to know hobbits," Troy said with a laugh.

"Some kind of dwarves, right?"

"Jesus, don't let any of them hear you say that," Troy said. Then he gave Zach another grin. "And go to the movies sometime."

"I go to movies." Well, at one point he'd gone to movies. But yeah, it had been a while. Sitting still for two hours straight was not his thing.

"Go to a movie without a sports theme," Troy said.

"You saw the hobbit movie?" Zach asked.

"All six of them."

Zach glanced over at his friend, his mouth open to reply, but his gaze landed just beyond Troy's left shoulder. Words deserted him, and every thought evaporated but one—*I could be a Trekkie for one night.*

Because the woman who could make him care about all of this was standing one hundred feet away.

She was on her feet—and her own two feet without the help of stilts or platforms—but she was yanking on the skirt of her dress, trying to pull the bottom from under a pile of debris. Her attention, however, was on two women talking with other EMTs. One woman, dressed in purple from head to toe, was sitting on the ground, wincing as one of the EMTs pressed fingers into her side. The other was in white, with streaks of blood red. Literal blood red from the gash on her head.

Zach immediately started in the direction of the woman who had first caught his attention.

"Zach, hey!"

He glanced back at Troy. "Got somebody." He gestured toward the woman.

Troy looked over. "Looks like Steve and Reed have this."

Zach shook his head. "She needs me."

As he approached, Zach's gaze worked from her feet up. Well, the one foot he could see, since he could see only her right side. She wore a flat gold slipper on a tiny foot that connected to a delicate ankle that connected to a smooth calf that led to a toned thigh. Her leg wasn't long, but the inches of smooth skin he could see still made his heart thump. They peeked from the slit in the skirt of an emerald-green dress that flared below her hips but hugged her waist and breasts. Her shoulders were bare, and she had a gold necklace around her throat that connected to the light-green cape draped down her back. Her long brown hair was held away from her face by a circle of gold adorned with green gems that caught the sunlight as she moved. She had small ears and a small nose, but large round eyes.

She was cute. That was the best word.

And most of all, she sparkled.

Literally.

From her cute forehead to the sweet breasts behind the bodice of the dress to the top of her petite foot, every inch of skin he could see was gold. Not gold*en*. Gold. Shiny, gold-coin gold. Like the coins in the leprechaun's pot at the end of a rainbow or a pirate's treasure chest.

Clearly it was some kind of body paint, but the fact that it had him thinking about leprechauns and pirates made Zach wonder if it wasn't a little magical too. Because he really wasn't a leprechaun or pirate kind of guy.

He was the kind of guy to wonder just how committed she was to that body paint, though. Had she painted only the skin that would show, or had she gone all in and painted *everything*?

Just then she looked around, and her gaze connected with his.

And Zach suddenly couldn't remember how to breathe.

Those big eyes in that cute gold face were outlined with thick black lines, surrounded by elaborate, sparkling green, white, and black swirls almost like a half mask, and her lashes were twice the length of normal lashes. But in spite of all of that, Zach could focus only on the huge black pupils surrounded by a deep French roast–coffee brown...and the fact that they were filled with worry.

Sparkly gold breasts might get his heart pumping, but that look in her eyes sent a streak of protectiveness through him that was stronger than any feeling of lust.

She straightened quickly. "Oh my God, can you help me get free? I have to get to my friends." She yanked on the skirt of her dress.

"Definitely." He was prepared to do whatever this woman needed.

"We were together, but I hung back at this booth and then the ceiling came down and things went flying and they were hurt and I don't know what's going on." She was talking fast, her cheeks pink with adrenaline.

Out of instinct, Zach stepped close and took her upper arms in his hands, making her focus on him in an attempt to calm her. "Are those your friends?" he asked, gesturing toward the women in purple and white.

She nodded. "Maya and Sophie."

"Which one is in purple?" he asked.

"Maya." Her voice shook as she answered.

Zach bent his knees so he could look into her eyes, realizing as he did it that she was nearly a foot shorter than his six foot three. "Hey," he said firmly and evenly. "I'm going to help."

He had a lot of experience dealing with accident scene anxiety. He understood the pounding of the adrenaline that yanked oxygen from lungs and obliterated rational thought. Too well. But because of his own past experiences, he was the best victim communicator in Boston. It wasn't as big a deal as being a hostage negotiator or something, but the jobs involved a lot of the same skills. Being firm and thinking fast, but staying calm and reasonable at the same time.

The woman's gaze clung to his with something he was very used to seeing at scenes—a combination of gratitude and hope. But that usually happened with little kids. The ones who looked at him as if he were one of the superheroes who had brought people here today.

She started to nod her head. "Okay. I'm good. Just get me loose."

"Alright," he said calmly. "Are you hurt?"

He'd looked her over pretty thoroughly. Not necessarily with a professional eye, but he would have seen any major wounds or blood.

She shook her head. "No. I don't think so."

"You didn't get hit in the head or anything?"

"I'm fine."

"Okay. Hang tight."

He crouched beside her, proud that his gaze danced over her sparkly bare leg for only a moment before examining how her dress was caught. The bottom of it was sandwiched between the floor and a huge piece of metal. A huge piece of metal that had missed cracking her in the head by only inches. Zach felt a shudder go through him before he focused again. It didn't do a damned bit of good to examine a scene with an eye to all the things that *could have* happened. He needed to deal with what *had* happened.

He pushed against the metal beam, but quickly confirmed that he wasn't moving the thing by himself. If it had been on someone's leg or something, he would have recruited help, but this was a skirt. He withdrew his pocketknife and slashed the bottom of the skirt, parting the material and freeing her within seconds. If she was upset about her dress...

The woman took off at a run the moment she was loose.

"Hey!" Zach followed.

She ran toward the two women being treated. "Maya! Sophie!"

His buddy Reed was the EMT working on one of the woman's friends. Zach strode forward. Reed saw him coming.

"Check her out? For something?" Reed gestured toward the golden goddess.

She was fussing over the woman in purple. She was readjusting the ice pack Reed had put on the woman's shoulder and was kneeling directly next to the woman's injured arm. In Reed's way. The look he gave Zach said, "Just get her out of here."

"I can check her out," Zach offered, pointing to Maya.

That was ridiculous, of course. Reed had already assessed her and had been cleaning a large gash on her forearm. Still, for some reason Zach wanted to give Maya his attention instead.

The woman was dressed in tight purple leather and was

beautiful. And she didn't stir him a bit. *That* was ridiculous. What guy wouldn't respond to a beautiful woman in tight leather? But no, the woman who made his body hum was the one in green velvet and gold body paint.

"I'm good here," Reed said. "She needs to be assessed."

He gave a pointed look at the princess, who suddenly popped up and rushed to kneel next to the woman in white. Sophie. She was lying on her back and had a laceration above one eyebrow and a goose egg already starting to show.

The princess was talking to her friend rapidly and trying to blot at the cut while Steve, another paramedic, moved around them, trying to determine if there were other injuries. The least Zach could do was help his fellow EMTs. With a sigh, Zach went over and took the princess by the arm. He tugged her to her feet.

"Hey!" She pushed against his hand. "Stop it."

"I need to see if you're okay." When he started walking away from her friend, she dug her feet in, but Zach was twice her size. And not overcome with emotion.

Curiosity and attraction weren't really emotions, were they? And he couldn't really be attracted to her anyway. He didn't even actually know what she looked like because of her face paint and makeup.

"I'm fine." She struggled against his hold.

She continued to try to peel his fingers off her arm until he got a few feet away and turned so her back was against the side of a still-intact vendor booth. He pressed her against it and got right in her face, somehow ignoring the gold breasts that were now rising and falling rapidly only a few inches below his chin. And mouth.

Holy shit. Who knew that he had a thing for the color

gold? Because that had to be it. He did *not* have a thing for girls who wore capes or for girls who went to Comic Cons. It had to be the shiny gold. Maybe he'd been a pirate in a past life and he had a centuries-long desire for sparkly treasure. Because pillaging and plundering suddenly sounded good.

He itched to run his hands all over her. Not to mention the tingling in his tongue. And even if they hadn't been in the middle of a trauma situation that needed his attention on things other than how gold-painted skin might taste, she was a victim. He couldn't mess around with a victim. That was Emergency Management 101.

But then he caught a whiff of her scent, and the sweet smell only intensified the desire to taste. She smelled like candy flowers.

Jesus. Candy flowers? Really?

"You need to stay out of the way and let the guys do their jobs," he told her firmly. "You're not helping anyone right now."

Her gaze flickered to her friends. Her mouth tightened.

"Breathe," he told her. He ran his hands up and down her arms once, then immediately stopped because dammit, that gold skin felt really good.

Her eyes locked on his. She nodded. And breathed.

"Zach, what is—" Troy came up behind them. "Oh."

"We have a little situation. No big deal," Zach said calmly, not taking his eyes off the woman.

"I see." Troy sounded surprised. Maybe even amused.

Zach didn't care. "Surprised and amused" was better than what *he* was feeling. Considering he was feeling aroused and protective and confused and worried all at once about a woman he'd just met. Who wore a cape.

"While the guys are checking your friends over and treating their injuries, I'm going to make sure you're okay," he told the woman.

"I'm *fine*," she insisted.

Just because she wasn't feeling any pain at the moment didn't mean she wasn't injured, though. Adrenaline did crazy things.

"Good. But we still need to be sure. How about we start with your name?"

She swallowed and licked her lips, and Zach figured he deserved a freaking medal for not watching the motion of the tip of her tongue. For more than two seconds.

"Kiera," she finally told him.

"Is that your—" He let his gaze move up and down over her costume. "Elven name?"

Kiera lifted an eyebrow. "Elven?"

Okay, not an elf. "Your enchantress name?"

Her other eyebrow went up. "Strike two."

It was a limb, for sure, but his chance of getting this right was a billion to one anyway. "Your hobbit name?"

She snorted at that. Actually snorted. And it was the cutest thing he'd ever heard.

"You think I'm a hobbit?"

"Nope, pretty sure you're not. But I don't know what you are."

"Kirenda. Warrior princess of Leokin." The corner of her mouth curled slightly. Also very cute.

But the word *Leokin* made him want to groan. He knew World of Leokin. It was the new worldwide online gaming phenomenon that had sucked his sister in and turned her into an antisocial near zombie over the past few months. Zach hated that game more than anything.

Of course the first woman he'd been attracted to in far too long was into WOL and dressing up for Comic Con. That was exactly how his luck had been going lately.

He swallowed his bitterness and focused on her. She was a victim, and he needed to assess her status. "And while you're...dressed up...do I call you Kiera, or is it strictly Your Majesty?"

She narrowed her eyes.

Apparently he'd miscalculated his charm on that one. He'd messed up somehow, but he wasn't sure if it was the *dressed up* part or the *Your Majesty* part. "What'd I say wrong?"

Just then an ambulance came bumping down the main aisle of the convention center.

"Who needs transport?" someone called.

"Over here!" Reed yelled to them.

Zach felt Kiera stiffen under his hands at the words. Clearly one of her friends was getting a ride to the hospital.

"Kiera!"

At the sound of a woman calling to her, Kiera slipped around him and ran back to her friends.

Dammit. Zach followed, wanting to be there when they told her about her friends' injuries. It had nothing to do with her gold breasts. But it might have had something to do with her big brown eyes.

He caught up with her as she rounded the back end of the ambulance.

"Is she okay?" Kiera asked Reed.

"She's got a nasty gash on her arm," Reed said. "And I'm concerned about her side there."

He pointed to her right side, and Zach knew he was worried about her spleen or a kidney.

"They'll want to do X-rays and tests, and I'm sure they'll keep her at least one night for monitoring," Reed summarized.

Zach leaned so he could see Kiera's face. "You okay?"

She looked up at him. The worry in her eyes made him want to pull her into his arms.

Whoa. What was that? He'd been in a lot of emergency situations, and that was definitely a first.

But she nodded. "I'm fine."

"Need another hand!" Zach heard someone call. He immediately ducked around a pile of metal and plastic. They were getting ready to roll Kiera's other friend onto a backboard.

An EMT was kneeling with the board while another stabilized the woman's neck. Zach got into position, knowing exactly what they needed. One of the EMTs made sure her spine didn't move while Zach knelt and slid his forearms under her hips, and they slowly shifted her onto the board.

Once she was secured, Zach stood back as the others picked the board up.

"Her neck hurts," the EMT at her head filled Zach in. "But she can move all of her extremities and feels touch and pain."

It wasn't a bad report. Neck trauma was never good, but the fact that she could move and feel things was positive.

"Oh my God!"

Zach's attention snapped to Kiera, who had followed him.

"We've got her, Kiera," he said in a firm, soothing voice. "We're going to take care of her." He stepped in front of her, willing her to look at him instead.

As the EMTs started for the ambulance with Sophie, she said Kiera's name.

"She can't turn her head to look at you," Zach said. "You can get close so she can see and talk to you."

Kiera swallowed hard and moved beside her friend. She took the woman's hand. "Soph, I'm right here."

"I have a guy coming to check the lighting at the theater on Monday."

Kiera frowned and squeezed her hand. "You'll be okay by Monday."

She glanced up at Zach, and he felt her clear desire for reassurance like a punch to the gut.

He swallowed and nodded. "I'm sure you'll be feeling a lot better by then." But he had no idea if she'd be out of the hospital or back to work.

"Just promise you'll remember to go down there for me if I can't," Sophie said.

"Yes, of course I promise."

"You swear you'll remember? It's at two p.m."

Even from where Zach stood, he could see the dubious look Sophie was giving Kiera.

"I will absolutely try my very hardest to remember," Kiera said.

"I'll call you to remind you," Sophie told her.

Kiera sighed and looked at Steve. "Her ability to nag is a good sign, right?"

Steve chuckled. "It is."

They loaded Sophie into the ambulance, and then Maya walked over with Reed's support.

"Are you okay?" Kiera asked, the worried expression immediately back.

"This is just precautionary," Maya said. "Or so I'm told." She winced as she climbed up into the back of the rig with Reed's help. "Reed here doesn't get that margaritas can fix anything, and that free margaritas are the best kind."

"Where were we going to get free margaritas?" Kiera asked.

"Well, they'd be free for me. You totally owe me for dragging me down here for this."

Kiera flinched, and Zach felt the stupid desire to come to her defense. But that was ridiculous.

"This is what you get for making me leave the house," Kiera said.

Her tone wasn't totally lighthearted, but Zach saw the smile Maya gave her.

"Touché," Maya said with a nod.

They started to slam the back door.

"Hey!" Maya stopped the door with a hand on the window. "You," she said, pointing at Zach.

He stepped closer. "Yeah?"

"Take care of her." She pointed at Kiera.

Zach turned to the warrior princess. "You got it," he promised Maya.

"Can't I...," Kiera said, watching them shut the back door of the ambulance and start weaving the vehicle back out of the hall.

"No room, Princess," Zach said gently. "Nonvictims don't get to ride in the cool trucks with the sirens."

She was still watching the ambulance, and she nodded absently. "Okay."

He moved in front of her and crouched to get on eye level. "You can go right over and see them at the hospital. Mass General. If you're not family, they might not be able to tell you much, but if you can get in touch with their families, they can come and sit with you, right?"

She nodded again, but Zach wasn't sure she'd heard him. He really wanted to know that someone was going to be there with her. Shock in survivors wasn't uncommon. The that-could've-been-me thing could kick in at any moment if it hadn't already. But there was nothing like seeing someone you cared about hurt.

He put his hands on her arms again, this time rubbing up and down and just ignoring how good her skin felt against his rough palms. Mostly. He needed to comfort her more than he needed to worry about how *she* made *him* feel.

"Do you know where Mass General is?" He didn't love the idea of her driving herself over there. She was clearly overwhelmed.

Kiera nodded. "Yes."

"You can get there?" he asked.

She nodded again.

Okay. So...

"Zach! Let's go!"

Zach glanced over at Reed. His coworkers needed help, so he was going to be here for a while. He couldn't be messing around, obsessing about a woman who liked to play dress-up. "Kiera, I need to go, but..."

"Yeah, of course." She shook her head and looked around. "You go."

"But..." But nothing. She was fine, and he was needed by people who weren't fine. "Okay."

He had the fleeting thought that he wanted to kiss her good-bye. But that was crazy. They'd just met. In the middle of an emergency. No way should he kiss her.

Finally he let go of her and stepped back. But not touching her didn't do a thing to make him not *want* to touch her. He forced himself to turn away and head toward Reed, trying to clear his mind of green and gold sweet-smelling flowers as he went. But when he got about twenty feet from her, he glanced back.

And she was still standing there. Hugging herself. Looking lost.

Fuck.

"I'll be right there," he told Reed.

Reed glanced back. "Dude…"

"I know." And he did. He needed to not be distracted. But the only way that was going to happen was if he knew for sure that Kiera was taken care of.

He jogged back to her side. "Hey, Princess, what's up?"

She looked at him, and her look of confusion cleared. That made him feel stupidly good.

"I don't have a way…"

She trailed off, and Zach frowned. "You don't feel up to driving?"

"We brought Sophie's car, and her fob thingy is with her."

Ah. A little issue. "You have someone you can call?"

"I didn't bring my phone."

"You can use mine."

"No one's home. I live with Maya and Sophie," she said. "Obviously they're not… there."

Her voice wobbled, and Zach worked on not grabbing her and hugging her.

They'd just fucking met. Hugging and kissing wasn't appropriate. *Dammit.*

"How about a cab?"

"I don't have any money."

He looked her over again, revisiting the curves he realized he'd already memorized. He could give her money for a cab, of course. He could get her home. But she'd be home alone. He could get her to the hospital, but they wouldn't talk to her and she'd be stuck in the waiting room for God knew how long. Alone.

And leaving her alone was simply something he could not do.

"You need to come with me." He reached out and snagged her hand before he could tell himself that holding her hand was a bad idea.

Because it was. Her hand felt good in his, and the way she curled her fingers around his tightly and followed him without question felt good. And the idea that he was going to get to spend more time with her felt good. And all of that was bad. And yet he pulled her along with him through the convention hall and into the heart of the chaos.

"What are we doing?" she asked.

"I need to go help with some more injured. And I need you to stick with me."

"Me? Why?"

He looked over at her. Her cape floated behind her, and for the first time, he noticed the golden sword swinging at her left hip. Damn. That was kind of hot. "Because you're a gorgeous kick-ass warrior princess, and the people in here are gonna need some gorgeous kick-ass stuff."

She looked at him with surprise, but as he held her gaze, he saw something that turned him on even more than her smelling like candy—a spark of determination. She pulled up straighter as she walked, and he felt her hand tighten on his.

"Kick-ass. Right. I can do that."

He smiled. "And I could use some help from an interpreter."

"An interpreter? I speak some Spanish, but that's about it."

"You don't speak geek?" He hoped he wasn't committing a faux pas in calling her, and all of this, geeky.

But she actually gave him a half smile. "Oh, *geek*. Yes, I'm fluent."

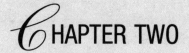

CHAPTER TWO

Zach grinned at her. "That's what I need."

Kiera felt her heart flip. That grin. *Dang.*

She immediately recognized what it was, of course—pure adrenaline. But that didn't make the flip any less strong. But it wasn't throw-me-over-your-shoulder-and-take-me-to-bed adrenaline. It was throw-me-over-your-shoulder-and-carry-me-out-of-here adrenaline. This guy had come striding confidently through the dust and confusion and had freed her. Of course she was projecting feelings of affection and attraction on him.

But adrenaline-fueled fantasy or not, that grin was lethal. She even felt a little dizzy looking at it. And nauseous. Kiera frowned. No, not nauseous from his smile. Just...off balance. Or dazed. Or something.

Zach squeezed her hand, and she took a deep breath. She really loved his hands. When he'd held on to her and when he'd run them up and down her arms, she'd felt reassured. His touch had been warm and steady, and she'd needed it in those moments. He'd known exactly how to make her feel safe in the midst of the chaos, and it was definitely working now too. Zach was a big guy. Well, big in the over-six-foot, big-hands, big-feet, big-grin way. He had a wide chest and shoulders, but his stomach was flat, his legs long, and his butt tight...

Kiera frowned. When had she had time to notice his butt?

When he squatted next to Sophie to help lift her up.

Kiera was not going to analyze what kind of friend that made her.

As they moved deeper into the convention center, there was more of everything—more mess, more people, more noise, more problems. Kiera crowded close to Zach. So what if it was a shock reaction? Being close to him made her feel better.

Zach stopped next to another man in uniform. "Where do we start?"

"Anywhere," the other man said grimly.

"Got it." Zach tucked Kiera closer to him. "Stay close, okay?" he asked her.

She nodded. "Absolutely no problem." When she'd been standing alone, the ambulance driving off in one direction and Zach walking away in the other, she'd felt so discombobulated. She was really not herself at the moment, and he was the only steady thing around her.

Zach glanced from side to side. "We don't often manage such a huge scene, but I promise we don't need superpowers or capes to get our jobs done."

Yep, that calm assurance was definitely sexy.

"Your uniform is kind of a superhero outfit, though," she said.

He looked down and grinned. "Yeah?"

"It tells people that you're here to help and gives them a sense of comfort."

He seemed a little surprised, but he said, "Well, I'm glad to hear it."

"And you saved me with just a pocketknife," she said, trying for a lighthearted tone. She felt his hand tighten around hers.

"Yeah, we're just regular guys." He paused. "Okay, really awesome, strong, and smart regular guys."

She smiled. "I won't argue with any of that. You're making me feel better."

She cringed even as the words were barely out. That sounded clingy. She blamed the whole one-of-us-could-have-died-today thing. But the big, solid body moving against hers wasn't helping. She *wanted* to cling to him. Her head hurt, and it still felt as if the room were spinning at times. She needed something to hang on to. Or someone.

"Well, that's definitely pumping up my ego. It's not every day I get to rescue a beautiful princess."

Don't let that get to you. He's placating you. He's just flirting to keep you calm.

He tugged her around the stretched-out legs of a couple of people already being tended to. "I'm guessing you take care of most of the mass disasters that occur in your kingdom, though, right?"

"We don't have mass disasters," she said, completely straight faced. Maybe if she tapped into Kirenda a bit, she'd make it through the rest of this without sounding pitiful. She might sound crazy, considering Kirenda was a fictional video game character, but crazy was preferable to pathetic. "But I do lead troops into battle when necessary."

"Battle, huh?"

"Yep."

Princesses in Leokin weren't just figureheads. Kiera had made sure of that. Of course, when her friends Pete Candon and Dalton Sagel had first come up with World of Leokin in a dive bar just off campus six years ago, she'd never imagined the guys would eventually turn those scribbled notes and beer-infused ideas into the fastest-growing video game franchise in history. But they had, and they'd used all of Kiera's beer-infused input too. Which meant that even though she was a princess, she got to participate in a good battle once in a while. Lopping the head off a troll or two was a great way to work out pent-up frustration. Even if their heads did grow back during the next full moon.

Zach grinned. "You probably don't even need to unsheathe your sword to get most of the opposing army to surrender," he said.

"Why do you think that?"

"Unless all the men in bordering kingdoms are stupid, they'd *want* to be captured by you."

Oh, he thought he was so smooth. Kiera fought the smile that threatened. As far as diversions went, he was pretty good.

"I'm not their type."

"No? I find that hard to believe."

"The trolls would rather feed me to their dragons, and the centaurs on our eastern border only mate with their own kind."

Zach studied her for a moment as if trying to decide if she was messing with him. Then he said simply, "Glad I'm not a troll or a centaur."

Yep, definitely smooth.

He was playing along. That was nice. But she kind of hated feeling like a little kid he needed to play along with in the first place.

Still, maybe thinking about how everyone in Leokin got six lives as long as they lived them with virtue and honor was better than thinking about how her friends were at the hospital right now.

Zach stopped next to a tall man sitting with his back against a wooden booth that had survived the collapse. He was easily in his sixties, with a long white beard that was clearly real. He was clutching one arm with the other and was very pale.

Zach dropped Kiera's hand and squatted next to the man. "Sir? I'm Zach. I'm an EMT. Can I help you?"

The man looked up but seemed to have some trouble focusing. "My arm."

"Did something hit you or did you fall?" Zach asked, opening his bag and pulling out a blood pressure cuff.

Kiera stood to the side, hugging her arms across her body, watching. She felt a little cold without Zach right against her, and yet there was a definite heat from watching him do his EMT thing. He had a deep voice, and he kept it soothing and calm as he checked the man over for injuries.

The man didn't answer. He was staring past Zach's shoulder.

"Sir? Can you tell me what day it is?"

"The attack came out of nowhere," the man mumbled. "We weren't prepared."

"Sir, can you look at me?"

The man wore a floppy black hat that covered most of his skull, and Kiera realized that any head injury would be hard to assess with the hat in the way. Zach reached up to remove the hat, but the man jerked away.

"You cannot touch a sorcerer of Relmand."

Relmand. One of Leokin's allies. Kiera grinned. Of the two of them, Zach might be the all-knowing healer, but this man needed a little geek first. She was definitely a little geek. "Your Greatness, I have word from the king."

Zach pivoted so quickly that he almost fell over. Kiera ignored him, not wanting to smile or, worse, feel like an idiot, as she knelt at the sorcerer's feet and addressed him.

The man focused on her, and something changed in his face. He went from overcome to earnest in a flash. "You are from Leokin."

"I am," she said with a nod. "We were also caught unaware. But our king fights alongside yours to defend our kingdom, and they have enlisted the help of these men to tend our fallen."

She felt Zach staring at her. She knew it was in part the lilt she'd added to her voice and probably also that she was gazing back at the man in black as if all the things she was saying were real and...not crazy.

"These men are sent from the king?" the older man asked.

"They are," Kiera assured him.

The man looked at Zach. "They don't look like much."

Kiera smiled quickly but hid it before the man looked back at her. "Sir, I—" she started.

But then Zach said, "Our powers are well hidden so the enemy doesn't capture us and use us on his side."

Oh my God. She had to work to not stare at him, mouth hanging open. He was going along with this? In character even? Really? Why? And how could she *not* like him now? Emotional trauma or not, she might be in trouble here.

Kiera was completely composed—on the outside, anyway—by the time the older man looked back to her for confirmation.

With the man's head turned, Zach did take the opportunity to inspect the back of his neck, but Kiera knew that Zach needed to see everything that was still covered as well.

"Sir, can you tell me what the date is?" Zach asked again.

"It's day three of the great battle," he said. "We're going on the eighth hour."

Okay, well, it was day three of the convention and about eight hours since the doors had opened that morning. She gave Zach a quick nod.

Zach actually shook his head. Did he think she was weird? It didn't matter. The injured man was the priority. In fact, the weirder Zach thought she was, the less likely it was that he'd keep flirting and charming her. And that was a good thing. Because hot guys who didn't know anything about Leokin or wizards or any of the other things she adored were firmly and forever *off* her to-date list.

"You need to rest," she told the older man. Kiera moved closer and put a hand on his shoulder. He let her guide him to a supine position on the floor, and as she did, she slipped his hat from his head and laid it on his stomach. "He has everything you need," Kiera said, gesturing to Zach. "Your care is in his hands. As ordered by the king," she added.

Kiera met Zach's amazed gaze. And winked at him.

Why did you wink at him?

His eyes went hot as a grin stretched his mouth.
Oh, that's why.

* * *

Suddenly Kiera was on her feet and backing away. Zach frowned. She couldn't leave. Zach started to stand, but the man chose that moment to say, "The Leokinese are a beautiful people."

Um…yes, they were.

Zach got back to work, but he kept track of Kiera out of the corner of his eye, grateful she hadn't gone too far.

Ten minutes later, the man had passed all the general assessments. He had a huge bump on his head but he was otherwise fine. Then he started talking about wizards.

"So you have wizards in your world?" the man asked him.

They did. They played basketball in Washington, D.C.

"Yes."

"Ah." The man nodded. "A well-trained wizard can be an asset to any kingdom."

"Are they different from you and other sorcerers?" Zach was proud that he didn't even look around to see if his buddies were within earshot to hear that question.

"In our world, wizards are made—through study and training—while sorcerers are born," he said.

Well, Wizards on the courts in D.C. didn't get there without study and training, that was for sure. "I would say it's the same for us," Zach told him.

The man gave him a big smile. "Then you are fortunate."

"Seems you are too," Zach said, leaning back on his

heels. "Minor cuts and scrapes, no indication of internal bleeding, no fractures." He grabbed a cold pack from his bag, snapped it in the middle to mix the cooling chemicals, and pressed it against the bump on the man's head. "But you're going to need to have your head checked."

The man gave a low chuckle. "My kids have been telling me that for years."

Zach grinned at this first glimpse behind the veil. "I wouldn't seek treatment for anything but this lump," he told the older man sincerely.

He meant it. The man wasn't doing anything but enjoying a few hours in a world that made him happy. He wasn't hurting anyone.

"Thank you, Zach," the man said, holding the cold pack to his injury. "You've been very kind."

Because of Kiera. He was kind and caring to all his patients, but he knew that without her he would have grown frustrated with this guy's role-playing, and no way would he have gone along with it. Zach glanced over to where Kiera was standing, watching them.

"Um…" He forced himself to look back to his patient. "I'm going to put you down for transport to the ER. But it might be a bit. There are others who will be more critical."

The man nodded and reached under his robe. "I'll just call my daughter. She can take me."

At the sight of the cell phone, Zach smiled. "I didn't realize Relmand had cell service."

"It's spotty in the woods and over the Calanthe Mountains," the wizard said, grinning. "But if you stay in the villages, it's not bad."

Zach laughed and got to his feet. "It was nice to meet you."

"You too. Go to your princess."

He wanted to do exactly that. More than he should. He headed in her direction, and when she saw him coming, she gave him a big smile that sent his heart thudding against his ribs.

"How's our wizard?" she asked.

"Sorcerer," Zach corrected without thinking.

She lifted an eyebrow. "Very good."

"You were testing me?" He wanted to reach out and pull her closer. He gripped his bag tighter instead.

"Maybe a little."

There was a twinkle in her eyes now that had nothing to do with the sparkly eye shadow surrounding them. And he decided that they were more the color of rich chocolate brownies. One of his favorite things.

"He called his daughter on his cell phone for a ride to the ER."

"Ah." She looked pleased. "That's good."

"Thanks for your help back there." He moved a few inches closer. "That was pretty great."

"No problem. Escaping reality is a specialty of mine."

His first reaction to that was *Damn*. He lived very firmly in the real world. His second reaction, however, was surprising and went along the lines of role-playing and costumes in the bedroom.

He cleared his throat and gave her a grin he was sure worked in any universe. "Reality can be good."

She looked up at him with a thoughtful expression. "That has not been my general experience."

He had to admit it hadn't always been his either, and he was tempted to see what it would be like to spend more time escaping the real world with Kiera. Even if it would lead to an evening of her regaling him with stories of quests for hidden treasure or something. Because being regaled by Kiera seemed like a hell of an idea suddenly. And yeah, maybe *regaled* meant something different in his world.

"You okay sticking with me for a little longer?" Not only had she been helpful, he was enjoying having her around.

She took a deep breath. "Yes."

"Great."

It didn't take long to find someone who needed him. Zach knelt and immediately started his assessment on a woman with a bloody foot, but he glanced up. It was always a good idea to keep an eye on other people at a scene. If one of them fainted and fell, they could turn into another patient quickly.

Kiera looked pale.

"Kiera," he said sharply, "sit down."

She plopped to the floor on her butt. She was still staring at the woman's foot. Clearly the warrior didn't do well with blood. Real blood, anyway.

"Hey," Zach said to her softly, but firmly.

Kiera looked at him.

"Gorgeous and kick-ass, right?"

Her eyes widened slightly as she processed his words. Then she nodded and pulled in a deep breath. "Right."

"Are you Felicity Smoak?" Kiera asked the woman as Zach began his assessment.

The woman turned her head toward Kiera with a small smile. "Yep."

"I always liked Felicity the most of all of Oliver's women," Kiera said.

They chatted about what Zach surmised to be a television show called *Arrow* while he determined the woman had no other significant external injuries. He started to clean the wounds on her ankle and foot. She needed to get to the hospital to be assessed for internal injuries.

"So I'm clearly missing out by not watching *Arrow*," he commented. If he could get Kiera snuggled up next to him on the couch, he might just be willing to turn his TV away from ESPN for a night. Or two.

Then he shook that thought off. He didn't have time to be cuddled up on the couch for anything or with anyone. The last thing he needed was another woman in his life to worry about. The amount of concern and protectiveness he'd already felt for Kiera was more than he needed to take on for anyone outside his own messed-up family.

"Felicity Smoak is an ally and love interest of millionaire playboy Oliver Queen, aka Arrow," Kiera said. She turned to the other woman with a smile. "And you look just like her."

Zach carefully began splinting and wrapping the woman's ankle, and she sucked in a quick breath and gritted her teeth.

Kiera leaned in. "Did you watch *The Flash*? I love how they did the crossovers with *Arrow*."

The woman opened her eyes and smiled at Kiera. "I did. I was so happy it got renewed for another season."

He finished wrapping her up and radioed for transport as Kiera distracted her. A few minutes later, he helped load Felicity into the back of a rig. As they drove off, he turned to Kiera. He might not have time to watch TV with her, but he was impressed and intrigued by her, and he liked to think it was about more than her breasts. And the dress that showed flashes of smooth, toned legs. And the way her hair fell down her back in silky waves that made him itch to touch. And the sword that was surprisingly sexy. "Thanks again for the help."

"My pleasure." She frowned, seemingly puzzled by that. "It was nice to be able to help."

He smiled. The hero thing was addictive. He knew well. "I have some more work to do."

"Yeah, you'll be here for a while."

"Do you..." He cleared his throat. "Would you stay?" he asked. "I know nothing about *Arrow*. God knows what else I'm going to run into here." He wanted her to stay so he could keep an eye on her and make sure she was okay. At least that was part of it.

She laughed and nodded. "I can stay."

They worked together for the next hour and twenty minutes. She helped calm a Teenage Mutant Ninja Turtle while Zach splinted his arm. She talked about some Ryan Reynolds movie with a teenage girl wearing a T-shirt that read "Save a broom, ride a wizard" while Zach cleaned a deep cut around her eye. She talked Batman sequels with a man with a significant crush injury to his leg while Zach started an IV and gave him a shot of a painkiller while waiting for the ambulance. Zach helped start an airway, hooked up three more IVs, and cleaned more cuts and scrapes than he could count. And all the while, Kiera was there, talking to the patients, handing Zach supplies, and generally just making everyone feel better.

Maybe especially him. Big disasters were tough on the first responders and rescue workers too. There was no rest while patients were still in need. There was no break. And there were higher odds of not being able to help some victims. Zach didn't deal well with not being able to help people.

Kiera looked exhausted and still a little pale as he walked with her toward the front of the convention center an hour and a half later.

"How about I let you tell me all about Princess Kirenda over dinner?" he heard himself ask.

Why had he done that? He didn't have the time or energy to date anyone. Too many other people in his life needed his attention right now.

But he did have to eat.

And eating while listening to Kiera go on and on about…whatever…would be better than eating and *not* listening to Kiera go on and on. As long as he could be sitting close enough to smell those candied flowers and maybe touch that gold skin and start inching that emerald-green dress down a little farther—

"And you're going to tell me all about the brachial plexus and how the tibia and fibula connect?"

He pulled his gaze from her cleavage to her eyes. She knew the brachial plexus?

"I read books," she said to his unasked question.

He moved closer and dropped his voice. "Well, I can tell you about any body part you're interested in."

He saw the interest flare in her eyes, whether she wanted him to or not.

The corner of her mouth curled slightly. "Is that right?"

"Absolutely."

Zach watched Kiera consider the invitation for a few seconds.

"I should warn you," she finally said. "I'm immune to charm."

"You got a shot or something?" he asked. She amused him. He couldn't help it.

"You're right. More likely it's an allergy," she said thoughtfully.

He felt his mouth quirk. "An allergy? To charm?"

"Yeah, my stomach feels a little funny."

He gave her a slow grin. "Oh, those are butterflies, Princess. And that's a *good* symptom."

* * *

Kiera gave a little huff of laughter. Which was amazing after the day she'd had. She'd never seen anything like the convention center. Her head was throbbing, and she felt a little woozy, as if she could sleep for the next fourteen hours straight. Plus she was worried about Maya and Sophie. But she'd felt as if she'd truly helped a lot of people today. She'd bonded with people over her interests in World of Leokin and comic books and superheroes before, but today that bond had felt…important. It had helped some people through a pretty horrible experience.

And she'd met Zach.

Which was noteworthy. Because he was right. Those were most definitely butterflies. And she hadn't felt butterflies over a guy in forever.

But Zach's grin said that he'd fully *expected* her to have butterflies around him. That should annoy her. Instead it made the damned things swoop and swirl even faster.

She was responding to cocky.

She *never* responded to cocky. Anymore.

Confidence was attractive for sure, but there was a difference between cocky and confident. A subtle but definite difference.

Zach Ashley had both. Not to mention the hero thing.

But she'd bet nine and a half out of ten women got a few butterflies because of the hero thing. That wasn't a concern so much as it was something to be careful about. She wouldn't let herself get too caught up in the way he could clean and bandage a wound with sure, steady, strong hands, all the while smiling and joking and putting off this air of I've-totally-got-this.

Especially because he was also alarmingly good looking. Denying that would be like denying that the North Star was in the northern sky.

But he didn't know wizards from wombats. He didn't know anything about *Arrow*. He couldn't have picked Felicia Day out of a lineup of kick-ass gamer girl redheads.

There was no way she could think for two seconds about even having dinner with him. Not to mention developing a completely over-the-top, blushing, giggling, butterflies-in-her-stomach crush on him.

She'd been there. *So* been there. And had no desire to go again.

Plus she was twenty-seven years old, for God's sake. Blushing and giggling and butterflies were in her past. She was a mature, intelligent, professional woman. Who dressed up as a warrior princess on the weekends.

She sighed.

At one time she would have downplayed her interests and laughed it all off so that Zach didn't think she was weird. But she'd done that once and had still gotten her heart broken. She'd then spent a period hating herself for trying to change for someone and then hating herself for hating herself for that.

She wasn't going to change for anyone ever again.

Including the hot hero who was really cute about not

knowing anything about wizards but who had played along
with a scared, hurt old man anyway.

"I can't," she said. "But thanks."

"You can't?" he frowned. He probably didn't recognize
a woman turning him down for … anything.

"My two best friends are in the hospital. I have to go
check on them."

She did. She'd been trying to put Sophie's and Maya's
injuries out of her mind so she wouldn't freak out or break
down and be no good to anyone here. But the truth was,
she had no idea how they were.

"Holy shit." Zach was staring at her. "You're right.
Fuck. I can't believe I forgot that." Then he grimaced.
"Sorry about the *fuck*. And the *holy shit*. And forgetting."

She smiled. "Not offended. And don't worry about it.
You've been preoccupied."

His eyes roamed over her face. "Yeah, I have. But
maybe not by what you think."

Goose bumps danced up and down her arms. "Anyway,
I should get to the hospital." Besides, the idea of food made
her queasy.

"You definitely should," he agreed. He grabbed her hand
and started toward the front of the convention center again.

"Where are we going?" Kiera asked.

"I'm getting you to the hospital." With the hand not
holding hers, he pulled his phone out and started swiping
his thumb over the screen as he walked.

Well, that would be a way of extending their time together without it being a *date*. Or whatever dinner would
have been. He hadn't let go of her hand yet, and he still
didn't when he paused just inside the conference center's
doors.

He pulled her around to face him. "I confirmed that Sophie and Maya were both taken to Mass General."

"You did?"

"Texted a buddy in the ER."

"Oh, great. Thanks."

He reached into his pocket and tugged his wallet free. He did let go of her then to pull a twenty from it. He handed it over, and Kiera's cheeks got hot again. He was giving her money for a cab. *Damn.* She suddenly didn't want him taking care of her. She didn't want him to see her as just another person he was being paid to help.

"I'll pay you back," she said quickly. She did need it. Or she'd have to walk to the hospital.

"I was hoping you'd say that." He gave her a grin. "That means I'll get to see you again."

Okay, he was a hot guy who saved lives and had a grin that made her tingle. Big deal.

"No, I can mail it. Just give me your address." She reached for the money.

He pulled it back out of reach. "I'd rather have a personal delivery."

She couldn't meet his eyes and focused on his collar instead. She wasn't a mess—she really wasn't—but in spite of her warrior princess outfit and her sword, she knew she'd come across that way today. Hell, her outfit and sword—spray-painted foam board, of course—probably made her seem even more pitiful, like someone who could be tough only when she was pretending to be someone else.

"It'd be better if I mailed it," she said again, finally lifting her eyes to his.

He frowned slightly and handed her the twenty. "Okay, I'll text you my address. What's your number?"

She couldn't help it. She smiled slightly. He was smooth. "Nice try."

"Then I'll give you my number. You can text me for my address, and I'll text you back. But that seems less efficient."

"Probably the easiest thing would be to mail it to you at work," she said.

"You don't know that address."

"I can look it up."

Finally he gave up with a shake of his head. "What am I missing here? I'd like to see you again and thought you'd feel the same way."

She swallowed her pride, which wanted her to say, "Nope, don't feel the same way, thanks all the same," and told him the truth. "I like you. You made today...not horrible."

Okay, part of the truth. He'd made today pretty damned great.

He gave a quick laugh. "Not sure I've ever had a woman describe time with me as *not horrible*."

She could imagine.

"I just..." Dammit. She took a breath and blew it out. "I'm a geek, Zach. I love to cosplay. I game every single night. All of my friends are into this same Comic Con stuff. I go to every Marvel movie on opening day. I read fantasy and sci-fi. I spend ninety-eight percent of my time on the computer—both for work and pleasure. I'm addicted to *TableTop* and Felicia Day is my idol."

Zach looked at her for a long moment. Then, just as she thought he was going to say, "Yep, you're right, this will never work" or even "What the hell is *TableTop*?" he reached up, cupped her face between the two big, capable hands that had been helping and healing all day, and pulled her in for a kiss.

No, not *a* kiss, Kiera corrected herself three point two seconds later. The. Best. Kiss. Ever.

It was not a meeting of lips. It was a full contact we-were-made-to-do-this fusion.

It literally made her head spin.

And then her legs got a little wobbly.

And the next thing she heard was, "Kiera!" just before everything went black.

CHAPTER THREE

*H*aving a woman fall into his arms sounded like a compliment. But having one actually pass out while kissing him? That was new.

Zach strode into the emergency department at Massachusetts General Hospital with Kiera cradled in his arms.

"You can put me down now."

He didn't respond. His jaw was clenched too tightly.

She'd been unconscious for only two minutes, but he'd already been on his way to the ambulance with her when she'd awakened. He'd found the huge goose egg on the back of her head and made her confess that she'd had a headache and felt dizzy and a little groggy the entire time she'd been with him.

A little groggy? She'd been amazing, helping him with patients and keeping everyone, including him, calm. And she'd been groggy during all of that? Damn. He wondered what she'd be able to do at full capacity.

"Zach! What's going on?" Sheila, the emergency department's receptionist, came around the front of the main desk.

"Comic Con. Concussion. Brief loss of consciousness," he said.

"Bay four," Sheila said. "Tom's around here somewhere."

The place was crazy. It was usually busy, but the majority of the serious Comic Con injuries had been brought in here, so the activity level was now frenzied.

"Thanks." Zach started for the fourth curtained area in the room. Tom Watson was one of Zach's favorite ER docs. He was glad Tom was going to check Kiera over.

"Kiera?" a female voice called out.

Zach turned to find Kiera's friends, Maya and Sophie, in bay two. Sophie was on the bed and Maya was in the chair next to the bed, but she sprang to her feet when she saw Kiera in his arms.

"Oh my God, what happened?"

She was across the floor and in front of him before Zach could blink.

"Nothing. I just have a little headache," Kiera told her.

Zach frowned. "It's not nothing. She has a concussion. She was hit in the head at some point but didn't tell anyone. She fainted."

Maya looked up at him. "Not really what I meant when I said you should take care of her."

He scowled, but Maya didn't look impressed. Or intimidated. She crossed her arms and frowned right back at him.

"Yeah," he said shortly.

He felt the same damned way. It wasn't his fault. He didn't need to defend himself. But *fuck*. He couldn't shake the feeling of panic that had hit him when Kiera had gone limp in his arms. She'd been with him all day and he hadn't noticed anything. But he should have. This was what he did for a living. He took care of people. Hell, his job was who he was—a lifesaver, a hero. At least until six months ago when his sister had been killed and his world and family crumbled around him. Now it seemed he couldn't get a fucking thing right. Not even recognizing a head injury in a woman he'd spent a solid two hours with.

Yeah, he was doing a bang-up job at the hero thing.

Kiera wiggled, and he tightened his hold. That streak of panic was probably why he hadn't let go of her since she'd fainted. That and needing to prove that he could take care of her. And he wasn't letting go of her yet. He wasn't putting her down until there was a bed under her and a doctor looking her over.

"Zach—" Kiera started.

"Give me another minute," he told her firmly. Of course she didn't need him to carry her. This was all about him. He'd gone through the concussion protocol in the ambulance. He'd put an ice pack on her head. He'd brought her here. That was what he could do. That was what he would have done for anyone with a head injury.

But it didn't feel like enough.

He headed for bay four, Maya right on his heels. He could feel the protective mama bear vibes coming off her, but he wasn't going anywhere. Not until he heard the doctor say Kiera was fine. He put her down on the bed and made himself take his hands off her and step back. He didn't want to. He wanted to keep touching her, as if, somehow, that would ensure she was alright.

Kiera looked up at him with wide eyes. "Are you okay?"

He laughed humorlessly. "No."

"*You* didn't hurt me, Zach. And I'll be fine."

"But I didn't—"

Tom Watson strode through the curtain just then. "Zach, what's the situation?"

"Concussion." He rattled off her assessment scores and recounted her symptoms and how long she'd been unconscious.

"How'd it happen?" Tom checked Kiera's pupils, then had her turn her head so he could see the lump.

Zach shook his head. "I didn't see it. It was before—"

Tom looked over at him. "I was asking Kiera."

"Right." Zach shut up, but it was hard to just stand there.

"I don't remember," Kiera said. "I was too busy worrying about getting to Maya and Sophie. I saw them both get hit, and I guess it just blanked my own injuries out."

"It's not uncommon to have a temporary loss of memory, particularly of the injury, with a concussion," Tom told her.

"I just have a headache," Kiera protested. "I'm fine."

"Kiera," Maya said with a frown. "Stop it."

"I'd like to get a CT," Tom went on. "Since no one saw the injury, and based on your assessment scores, I'd like to do it just to be sure."

"But—" Kiera started to protest.

"Kiera, let him do his job." The softer appeal came from Sophie, the curvy blonde who had made her way to Kiera's bedside.

"You shouldn't be up," Kiera protested when she saw her friend.

"I'm okay to walk five feet," Sophie assured her. "My neck is fine. That was the main concern."

"I'll get the CT ordered," Tom said, and stepped beyond the curtains.

Zach resisted the urge to follow. What would he ask him? He knew everything Tom knew at this point. But he felt as if he needed to be doing something.

"I hope this doesn't take long," Kiera said to her friends. "You guys have already been here for so long."

"It's been a madhouse," Maya said. "They really just got both of us fully admitted and evaluated and everything. We've both had X-rays and CT scans too."

"But you're okay?" Kiera asked, concern lacing her tone.

"They're moving us upstairs for observation overnight, but mostly yes," Sophie told her.

Kiera looked on the verge of tears as she took that in. "God, you guys. I'm so sorry."

"It's not your fault," Zach heard himself say.

Everyone turned to look at him.

He frowned. "Well, it's not." But why did he feel the need to jump in and defend her?

"I talked them into going to Comic Con today," Kiera said.

"Well, it was Maya insisting that you get out of the house that prompted it," Sophie said with a smile. "If she hadn't nagged you, you'd still be up in your room working."

Kiera shot a look at Zach and then frowned at her friend. "Okay, that's . . . all we need to say about that."

"You're the one that said she had to pick a place with more than five other people and had to stay out longer than two hours," Maya said to Sophie.

"You guys," Kiera protested, her cheeks pink.

"You were the one that didn't check the calendar. If you'd seen the date, you would have known she'd pick Comic Con," Sophie told Maya.

Maya sighed. "True. But Comic Con shouldn't have counted as social anyway," she said. "That was basically work for her."

"You didn't say it couldn't involve work," Sophie said. "You just said it had to be out of the house and in clothes other than her *Galactic Renegades* pajama pants." She grinned at Kiera. "She's definitely not in her pajamas."

"You *guys*," Kiera said, her voice firmer. "Enough."

Zach couldn't help it. He was intrigued.

Someone arrived just then to take Kiera for her CT scan. Zach stepped forward as she started to get up from the bed to move to the wheelchair. He took her arm and more or less lifted her into it.

She gave him a sweet smile that made him want to kiss her and insist on going along with her. Hell, part of him wanted to carry her to the test. All of which was ridiculous. When he stepped back, he caught Maya and Sophie exchanging a look.

He was making an ass of himself. Terrific.

As the tech rolled Kiera down the hall, Zach took a deep breath.

"You don't have to wait around," Maya said to him. "We'll be here. And Rob can come and pick her up."

Rob? Who the fuck was that? Zach relaxed the scowl he felt on his face before he turned. "I'm good. I think I'll stick around."

"Just to be sure she's okay?" Maya asked.

"Yeah."

"You give such personal service to all of the people you bring to the hospital?"

Zach realized what was going on. These were Kiera's best friends. They were checking him out. But he couldn't explain to them what he was feeling. Responsible? Sure. But it was more than that. As an EMT, he typically dropped people off at the ER and headed out again. So hanging out to see how things turned out for Kiera would be unusual.

He didn't care. "Nope," he said simply.

Maya nodded. "Okay."

While Kiera was being scanned, Zach figured he'd run down to the locker room and change. He was off duty now and would head out as soon as he knew Kiera's status. He didn't have time to be hanging out in the ER all day and night. Hell, he shouldn't still be here now.

He not only didn't have time for another relationship in his life, he didn't have the energy for it. Relationships took work. He'd learned that the hard way when he'd lost his sister Josie. He hadn't been there for her. He hadn't been paying attention. And now she was gone.

He was trying to give his other sister, Aimee, the time and attention she needed, but he felt as if he was losing her too. Not physically, maybe, but emotionally. No, physically too. She holed up in her room on her damned computer for all her waking hours. She gamed and slept. She didn't go out, she didn't eat anything but cereal, she didn't even shower some days. So yeah, physically she wasn't doing so well either.

He barely had energy left for his parents, who weren't doing much better than Aimee. Zach had plenty of people he needed to help. He didn't have the time for a warrior princess, no matter how kick-ass and gorgeous she was.

By the time he checked out with Troy and changed and grabbed his stuff, Zach had convinced himself not to stop back in the ER to check on Kiera. Her friends were there. She wasn't his responsibility.

He got halfway down the hall before he amended the plan. He'd check on her quickly and then get the hell out. But the moment he stepped into the emergency department and Kiera looked up and smiled at him, he realized he was screwed. He couldn't walk out. He was here for her until…hell, he didn't even know. Until he was sure she didn't need him anymore, he supposed. Maya and Sophie were there, each in a chair by Kiera's bed, but still he strode to her bedside, planting himself there for the foreseeable future.

"How are you feeling?" he asked her.

"Like everyone is fussing over me," she said.

"Good," he told her. "That's kind of the point."

"Kiera isn't very good at being the center of attention," Sophie said. "I can't get her onstage at the theater for anything."

Kiera rolled her eyes. "You should appreciate that I'm not trying to steal the spotlight from you."

Sophie laughed. "You've got me there."

Theater. Something else Zach knew very little about. But the mention of being onstage made him think of his sister. Josie had loved the spotlight. She'd been doing a show with her band the night she'd been killed. Her love of the stage had been the reason she'd been on the road so late.

He cleared his throat. "How's your head?" he asked, focusing on Kiera again.

"Hurts," she admitted.

"That might be like that for a few days," Tom said, stopping at the end of Kiera's bed. "But your scan is clear."

Thank God, Zach thought.

"You have a moderate concussion," Tom went on. "And

it could progress over the next seventy-two hours. We'll need to keep an eye on you, and you'll need physical and cognitive rest."

Kiera slumped back against her pillows, but Maya sat up straighter. "What's that mean?" she asked.

"Concussions can be tricky. The next couple of days will require monitoring so we know what we're dealing with. You need to avoid anything physically exerting," Tom said. "For the next twenty-four hours, you'll need to be pretty quiet in general. No jogging, jumping, sports of any kind."

"Not a problem," Kiera muttered.

"And cognitive rest means just what it sounds like. Nothing that involves much focus or concentration, nothing stimulating. With kids and teens, we keep them out of school for a few days. You'll need to take a couple of days off work. At least."

"Awesome," Maya said brightly.

Kiera frowned at her. She focused back on Tom. "What's 'at least' mean?"

"It means it depends on your symptoms. You need to be symptom-free before you're back to full activities. You can slowly work back up to full time, but you have to pay close attention to how you're feeling—headache, dizziness, nausea, feeling slow or groggy, trouble focusing. We'll give you a guide that outlines some of the things you might experience and what to do and not do."

Kiera was chewing her bottom lip, looking thoughtful, and Zach wondered what was going through her head.

"We'll be sure she doesn't do anything she's not supposed to do," Sophie told Tom.

"We'll absolutely keep her away from work and the

computer," Maya added. "We're completely on board with that."

"Hey," Kiera said. "He didn't say I had to stay away completely."

"She works fourteen hours a day, every day, on a computer," Maya told Tom. "Her work is very creative and stimulating and takes a lot of concentration. She sleeps weird hours—like two or three hours at a time and then is up again for a few hours and then sleeps again. She eats cereal for at least fifty percent of her meals. And she hardly exercises or socializes or does anything non–work related."

Zach had been watching Kiera's eyes during Maya's recitation. They'd grown progressively wider as her friend listed her behaviors for the doctor and, at the end, her mouth even dropped open.

Zach was torn between being amused and thinking, *Of course.* It wasn't that she was a workaholic. That he understood. He loved his job and was totally committed. But the never leaving her room, wearing pajamas all day, and eating cereal all the time was too familiar. The woman he'd been unable to walk away from all damned day did all the things that made him nuts with Aimee? Yep, of course.

"Kiera, it's very important that you take care of yourself during this recovery period," Tom said. "The first seventy-two hours are when we can see a progression of symptoms, but patients can experience residual effects from a concussion up to a year, sometimes longer."

Kiera frowned at him. "A year? Or *longer*?"

Tom nodded. "You should recover completely. On average it takes about a week. But sometimes there are issues that linger."

Zach felt his stomach knot. He knew everything Tom was saying, but watching Kiera's eyes fill with worry got to him. "If you take it easy, you can minimize the chances of it getting worse or lasting," Zach said.

She looked up at him. "Fine," Kiera finally agreed. "I'll stay off the computer for a day or two."

"And if you don't, I'm telling Pete," Maya said.

Who was Pete? Zach felt a frown form.

Kiera's eyes widened again. "No!"

Maya nodded. "Yes. If you don't take some time off, I'm going to tell Pete what happened and that you can't work for a while. And I'll tell him about the fourteen-hour days stuck in your room."

"Maya—" Kiera started.

"I'm serious, Kiera," her friend said. "I know that Pete needs you and wants you working on this new stuff, but he won't like that it's *all* you're doing, and you know it. I haven't said anything so far, but this better be a wake-up call. You take care of yourself or I'm telling Pete that he needs to get you help."

"He doesn't," Kiera protested. "I can do this. I want to do this."

"I know. So show me you can be a responsible grown-up who works normal hours and has a life outside of work and I'll leave it alone."

Kiera sighed heavily and leaned back on her pillows again. "You're such a bitch."

Maya grinned. "I know."

"Okay, so you'll need someone with you for the next twenty-four hours," Tom said. "I'd like them to wake you every four hours throughout the night to reassess."

Kiera looked at her roommates.

Sophie frowned. "You're keeping us for observation," she reminded Tom.

He nodded. "Yes."

"Can Kiera stay with us?"

"I don't have a reason to admit her," Tom said. "And we're filling up with all the Comic Con folks. I'm sorry."

"So she has to go home," Sophie said.

"But no one's there to be with her," Maya said.

"Rob can come over," Kiera said.

"You can come home with me." Zach heard the words come out of his mouth before he'd really thought the offer through.

Still, as he looked into Kiera's eyes, he knew that this had been inevitable. He'd insisted on keeping her with him all day at the convention center, and that was when she'd simply been alone and shook up. As far as he'd known, anyway. Now that she was actually hurt and in need, there was nothing else he could do but take care of her.

"You do *not* have to do that," Kiera said. "I'll be fine."

"You can't even drive home," he told her.

"I have twenty bucks I can use for a cab," she said, lifting her chin.

He couldn't help but smile. She had his twenty bucks.

"I'm taking you to my place for the night. If you need references, I know everyone in this ER. And my sister lives with me, so we won't be alone."

"That's perfect," Maya said before Kiera could protest again. "Not only will you be with her, but you're an EMT so you know what to look for and what to do if things get worse."

All true enough. But he didn't miss the twinkle in Maya's eyes.

"This is ridiculous," Kiera said. "Zach and I just met. He can't take on the responsibility—"

"I want to," Zach interrupted. "If you're uncomfortable coming home with me, I get it. Your call. But I want to do this. It's not an imposition."

That was all true. He did want to take care of her. He shouldn't. But that was a whole other story.

He watched her thinking it all through and wished she'd stop turning the wheels in her mind, trying to find another solution. Her brain needed to rest. And she needed to come home with him.

Kiera looked at her friends. "I can just call Rob," Kiera said.

"No." Zach said it firmly. He didn't even need to know who Rob was.

Kiera looked over again, eyebrows up. "Rob is—"

"Not necessary." He didn't give a shit who Rob was.

She crossed her arms again. "I'm not helpless."

"No, you're hurt," he said. "And helping hurt people is what I do best."

* * *

Kiera followed Zach to the elevator in his building. She couldn't believe this. She was going home with Zach Ashley.

This was such a bad idea.

But it felt good to have Zach taking care of her. And that was so uncharacteristic that she actually wondered if whatever had hit her in the head had, indeed, knocked something loose.

"Come on in." Zach unlocked the door to the apartment

and swung it open, standing to the side so she could pass by him.

She took a surreptitious deep breath as she did. Yep, he smelled good.

He followed her in, tossing his duffel bag to one side.

Kiera took in the living room that opened directly off the entryway. There was a huge stone fireplace, a couch and a love seat, a coffee table and a big-screen TV. In other words, it was a very typical living room. But she still felt a little jumpy being in *Zach's* very typical living room. Hanging out with him at the convention center had been one thing. There had been lots of other people and commotion. They hadn't been alone. Now, in his living room, with only one table lamp glowing and no one else around, it definitely felt different.

"Your sister lives with you?" she asked.

He nodded. "Aimee. But she spends all of her time in her bedroom." His expression tightened, but he didn't say anything more. "How's your head?"

"Better." They'd given her medication for the pain at the hospital, and since it had kicked in, she'd been feeling a lot more like herself. She still felt as if her thoughts were coming a little slower than usual, but the dizziness and nausea had passed. She did not love the idea of being away from her computer for a couple of days—or longer—but she had to admit that the thought of looking at a computer screen right now made her wince.

"Are you hungry?" he asked.

She shrugged. "Maybe."

"I have cereal," he said. "Three different kinds."

She smiled. "Well, why didn't you say so? I would have agreed to come home with you right away."

He didn't smile. "I suppose you should know that I have this...thing about saving people."

No kidding. "A hero complex."

"No." Then he sighed. "Yeah. Kind of."

"Your natural reaction is to insist on helping people. That's nice," she said. "I admire that. But you don't have to take care of me. I can call Rob."

"Okay, who the fuck is Rob?" he asked with a scowl. "Tell me he's your brother."

"Only child. He's our neighbor."

"Yeah, no Rob," he said.

That hint of possessiveness made a butterfly or two flitter. "Okay, I'll stay."

He visibly relaxed at that. "Okay."

She scratched her arm. The body paint was starting to itch. "Would it be okay if I took a shower before cereal?" she asked.

He cleared his throat. "Yes. Sure. Of course."

"I don't have any other clothes with me. Could I borrow something? Just for tonight?"

"Um, yeah, absolutely."

He headed across the room, and she followed him through the kitchen and into the laundry room. He reached into a basket and pulled out a folded shirt and shorts. "These are Aimee's. They should fit."

She held the pale-blue T-shirt and hot pink running shorts up. These would work. It was far better than wearing one of *his* T-shirts. Even though she'd kind of hoped that would be what he offered. "Thanks."

He hesitated, as if he wanted to say something more, but then he just said, "Bathroom is the first door on the left upstairs. Towels are in the closet."

Kiera nodded and headed for the shower. And the solitude. She just needed a chance to breathe. Alone.

As she pulled out a fluffy, fresh-smelling towel and ran the water in the spotlessly clean shower, she realized she was going to be using Zach's soap. That seemed very intimate, and she just stood, breathing, for a moment.

She didn't really do personal relationships. Even with Maya and Sophie, she held herself back. Not because she didn't like them. She did. They accepted her for exactly who she was—when they weren't worried about her turning into a hermit—and shared many of her unusual interests. They would help her out with money, transportation, probably even an alibi. But Kiera didn't let people close. She'd had a fairly solitary childhood—an only child raised by parents so wrapped up in their work that she'd never known anything other than being alone with her books and games and imagination. And eating cereal twice a day.

Only twice in her life had she let someone get close. Once had been in third grade when she'd met her best friend, Juliet, the first person to want to hear Kiera's ideas. The other had been just after college when she met Mitch, the first guy to make her feel special. And both times she'd gotten hurt.

Now Kiera wasn't close to anyone. It was easier, and safer, that way.

So sharing towels and soap with a guy was not a normal thing in her life, and the fact that she was doing it now with Zach made her fidgety.

They weren't in a relationship. They weren't sleeping together. She wasn't even going to see him again after Maya and Sophie were released from the hospital. She was putting way too much emphasis on how protective he'd seemed. She needed to not let that all go to her head. Or her heart.

For both their sakes, she needed to get out of the dress and the gold paint and the whole warrior princess thing and just be her geeky self. And nothing more.

It took a while to get her skin back to its normal color, but she finally stepped out of the shower smelling like Zach's citrus-scented soap. She hadn't even bothered to try to wash the gold stripes out of her hair. That would take more shampoo than she could comfortably borrow.

When she tried to pull her hair up into a high ponytail, it tugged on the bump on the back of her head. *Damn.* The ache had dulled considerably with the medication and ice, but with pressure right on the spot, it throbbed and sent streaks of pain over the top of her skull. She'd have to leave her hair down.

As she started to dress, she realized she had another little problem. She didn't have a bra. The bodice of the dress had a built-in bra so she didn't have to worry about straps. She was only a B cup anyway, so she didn't need a ton of support, but the thin cotton of the T-shirt was a different story from the thick bodice and bra of the dress. And Zach's sister was almost her size. Almost. She apparently had smaller hips and bigger breasts than Kiera, so the shorts were a little tight over her butt and the V-neck of the shirt gaped.

Finally Kiera focused on the mirror in the cabinet over the sink. She was going to go downstairs and face Zach with her hair brushed and her face clean. Zach was going to see that she was just a plain girl with a bunch of geeky interests and that they had about five minutes' worth of things to say to one another. She had promised herself she was never going to downplay her interests or hide her passions ever again. This was her. For better or worse. But she definitely felt exposed.

With a deep breath, she grabbed her dress and cape and sword and pulled the door open.

The butterflies from earlier were suddenly back. Rather than flitting and fluttering, this time it felt as if they were running laps. Hard, fast laps.

She wet her lips and descended the steps. As she stepped off the bottom step, Zach looked over from his seat on the couch, a sports show on TV. He hit a button and the TV blinked off, then he leaned to put the remote on the coffee table as if in slow motion, his eyes never leaving her as she walked toward him.

He stood as she came close. He had changed clothes at the hospital. The jeans and T-shirt should have made him seem like a normal guy. Out of uniform he shouldn't have made her heart trip. But it wasn't working that way. At all.

She stopped when they were face-to-face.

"Well, damn," he said, almost under his breath.

She lifted an eyebrow as the butterflies started kicking against the inside of her stomach. Little bastards. "You liked the dress better, I take it." She laid the garments and the sword on the coffee table.

"I really liked the dress," he said with a nod.

"Me too."

In the dress and full makeup, she had been showing him her sexy fighter side. Now he'd see her stayed-up-too-late-on-the-computer and I-don't-get-enough-vitamin-D side.

"But this is so much better."

She looked up at him. "Excuse me?"

"The costume was stunning, but I like the real you."

"Oh." She didn't know what else to say.

If she doubted his words, the look in his eyes was unmistakable. The heat was there. And it had been turned up a few degrees. Zach apparently liked the all-natural, slightly sleep-deprived, very sun-deprived look. Okay, well...

He reached out and circled her wrist with his hand, pulling her toward him. "I've been wondering about the real color of your skin all day." He ran his hand up her arm, over her shoulder, and up to cup the back of her neck. "And the real feel of your skin."

The butterflies suddenly decided to waltz instead of kickbox in her stomach, and she appreciated the switch. "Oh," was all she managed to respond with. Again.

His thumb stroked up and down over her throat.

"You still want to kiss me?" she heard herself ask.

"So much."

She swallowed. "But you don't like wizards." She was definitely saying that more for her own benefit than to remind him.

"I can make you not care about wizards for a few hours too, Kiera," he said huskily.

She felt the corner of her mouth curl. "I don't know, I really like wizards."

"I, apparently, really like warrior princesses."

A butterfly did a somersault/backflip/triple twist in her stomach.

"Just a few hours?" she asked.

"That's all I've got to give."

She could see regret in his eyes, but she did appreciate his honesty. He wasn't promising her roses and romantic dinners. He was telling her that he was interested, but that there were limits to what he could offer.

"I can't possibly forget about wizards for longer than that anyway." And that was true. She wouldn't, *couldn't*, turn away from the things that were important to her.

"You have close friends who are wizards or something?" he asked with a smile.

"Something like that." Pete and Dalton had been called wizards on more than one occasion.

"Then we're on the same page." Zach pulled her even closer.

They were if his page included him kissing her again... and whatever else they could get to before the sun came up. "I think we are."

*C*HAPTER FOUR

*K*issing this woman was his new favorite thing.

Though he'd first met her dressed up as a fictitious character from a place that didn't exist, he felt as though Kiera's reactions were the most real of any woman he'd been with in a very long time. She gripped his biceps, went up on tiptoe, and arched into him as if she just needed to be closer to him.

There was something incredibly hot about that.

When he ran his tongue over her bottom lip, she sighed, and that sweet sound tightened his gut. The sigh was simple and heartfelt and, yes, *real*.

Zach moved his hand to the side of her face, tipping her head slightly and then urging her mouth open with his tongue. She moaned quietly, and he was suddenly curious about how her moans would sound when he put his tongue in all the other places he wanted it.

She was so sweet. And soft. Her previously gold skin was actually a light peach color and as soft as silk. And she smelled like his soap. As if he'd rubbed his body all over hers in the shower, mingling their soap bubbles...and lots of other things.

The thought was very sexy, and he slid his fingers into her hair, deepening the kiss.

Her next gasp was not one of pleasure, however. She jerked back as his hand ran over the goose egg at the back of her skull.

He pulled his hand away quickly, looking down at her with concern. "Dammit, Kiera, I'm sorry."

What was he doing? She had a concussion, she was here so he could take care of her, and he was thinking about throwing her over his shoulder and heading upstairs? He took his hands off her and stepped back.

She winced and touched the back of her head gingerly. "It's okay."

But there were several inches of space between them now. That didn't feel okay.

"How do I keep forgetting important things when you're around?" he asked. He kept his tone light, but he was pissed at himself. He tucked his hands in his back pockets to keep from reaching for her again.

"It's okay, Zach," she said. "You got...caught up." She shrugged. "I kind of like that."

He didn't. He didn't get caught up. He was focused and on top of things. Always. "I definitely was caught up."

She smiled, and he wanted to get caught up all over again.

Jesus. He needed to get his shit together.

He couldn't get consumed with this woman.

She must have seen something in his face because she frowned slightly. "Are you okay?"

"Not really."

"*I'm* okay, Zach. Honestly."

"I'm glad. I just...need to not touch you anymore."

She frowned as if confused. "But I want you to touch me."

Zach felt the bolt of heat shoot through him, and he pulled his hands from his pockets, clenching them at his sides to keep them to himself. "You're hurt."

"I have a bump on my head. But there are lots of other places you can touch me."

If he'd been attracted to the big brown eyes that made him think of melted chocolate bars, then her self-assurance and the way she owned her attraction to him made him absolutely positive that one night wouldn't be enough. Some time with someone who didn't *need* him, who was strong and sure on her own, would be very welcome. Kiera's confidence made him want her even more than the silky skin and sinfully delicious lips and caressable curves.

Kiera took his hand and led him to the couch, then pushed him down onto one of the cushions. She followed, straddling his thighs.

"I'm going to kiss you now," she told him. "And if you stop it, it better be because *you* want to stop, not because you think *I* should stop."

She put her hands on his shoulders and leaned in.

Zach gripped her hips as her mouth touched his. With the curve of her ass under his fingertips, and her breasts—her braless breasts with the hard little centers—pressing into his chest, Zach let himself sink into the sensations.

Kiera opened her mouth, sweeping the tip of her tongue over his bottom lip, and Zach felt the jolt of electricity clear to his toes. He brought her hips forward, rocking her against his hardening cock and relishing her moan. He stroked his tongue into her mouth, tasting her fully and yet hungry for more at the same time. Her arms were wrapped around his neck, pressing their bodies together from lips to thighs, and it wasn't nearly enough.

Zach ran a hand under the hem of the T-shirt to find warm, silken, bare skin. She sighed and slid her hands into his hair. His scalp tingled, and all he could think was that he wanted her hands on lots of other parts of him. She arched closer to him as he ran his hand up her back, his middle finger trailing over the bumps of her spine.

He had to touch more of her. He wanted to make her feel the waves of heat and want that were rippling through him. Zach rubbed up and down her back a few times, loving the goose bumps he felt in the wake of his touch, before stealing around to the front. He stroked over the curve of her waist and her ribs, feeling her stomach muscles tense. But she didn't pull away. In fact, she pressed closer, grinding against his cock.

He ripped his mouth from hers, tightening his hold on her hip and stopping the motion. It had been a long three months since he'd last had a woman in his bed. And he wasn't sure if any woman had felt as good against him as Kiera did. If he didn't want to embarrass himself, he needed to get a grip. "Easy, Princess."

Her pupils were dilated when she looked down at him, blinking in confusion. "Are you okay?"

"I'm so okay that I'm about to be *too* okay."

She still looked confused.

"You feel too damned good," he said. "You grind against me like that for another minute or so and it's all over."

Understanding dawned. Her lips curved into a smile, and she started to move forward on his lap. He clamped down on her hips. "Not until you're *too okay* too," he said.

"I'm so okay with being *too okay* too." She leaned in to kiss him again.

The kiss was hotter somehow this time, and Zach felt his body begging him to let her grind away. He slid his hand up her side to her breast, his fingertips skimming the underside. Kiera gasped and arched closer.

He took the hint.

He cupped her breast in his hand. It fit perfectly against his palm, hot and soft, the nipple hard and tight. He ran the pad of his thumb over the tip, and she broke the kiss with a gasp.

Resting her forehead against his, she groaned softly. "Zach."

He put one hand against her lower back and arched up, his cock pressing against the hot, sweet spot where he knew she needed him, but it wasn't enough. He wanted more of those sounds, more of her skin, more of her hands on him.

He pivoted them both, laying her back on the couch and starting to move over her.

But the moment her head hit the throw pillow on the end of the couch, she winced and sucked in a quick breath.

The bump on the back of her head. *Dammit.* How did he keep forgetting that?

Zach froze with one knee on the cushion, his other foot on the floor, twisted toward her but holding himself away. "Son of a bitch," he muttered. He grabbed her hand and leaned back, pulling her up to a sitting position. "I'm sorry. Fuck. What's the matter with me?"

She held the back of her head with her hand and gave him a little smile. "Caught up."

"Yeah." Zach ran a hand over his face as he sat back. This had to be a sign that they should stop, or something.

Kiera swung her legs over the side of the couch to sit next to him. "Why do I get the feeling that you're not going to agree to let me just get back in your lap?"

He groaned and tipped his head back. "Can't do it, Princess."

She settled back beside him. "Okay."

He looked at her out of the corner of his eye. "Okay?" That was it? "Not going to try to talk me into it? Not even a little?"

She smiled. "You should probably tell your ego that it's not you, it's me. I don't beg."

He shook his head and closed his eyes. "Dammit."

"You're upset that I'm not trying to seduce you?"

"Upset that I can't have the kind of sex I need to with you." That sounded worse out loud than he'd expected. But it was true. He wasn't looking for a relationship. He wasn't looking for a girlfriend. At most he wanted a quickie one-night stand that meant nothing and that he wouldn't think about again when it was over. Zach dug the heels of his hands into his eyes.

"So what kind of sex do you need to have?"

The curiosity and humor in her tone were what made him open his eyes. She had turned to face him and had one leg tucked up underneath her, her elbow on the back of the couch, her head in her hand.

And he wanted to make her breakfast in the morning.

Not a no-go-ahead-and-keep-it travel mug of coffee on her way out the front door. Real, made-from-scratch pancakes. In his kitchen. With his mom's recipe. After they'd cuddled late into the morning in his bed.

Fuuuuck.

He sighed. "Up against the wall, hard and fast, and loud. And over in one night." He made sure to add that at the end. Just in case she was feeling cuddling-with-pancakes too.

Kiera seemed fascinated by his answer. "And you can't have that with me?"

He looked into those eyes, dropped his gaze to her mouth, and took a deep breath that was scented with the smell of his soap, which was somehow sweeter on her. "No, I don't think I can."

"Because of my head?"

He gave her a small smile. "You have no idea how much I'd love to use that excuse." It wasn't as if being pressed against the wall would be *good* for her head.

"But you can't?"

She wasn't being coy; she wasn't flirting. She was truly curious, and Zach shook his head. "No."

"Okay."

He frowned at her easy acceptance. "Because I have a bunch of messy family stuff going on right now." And because he liked her, a lot, and she deserved more than a quickie against the wall of his living room.

And because he wanted the against-the-wall stuff, but he also wanted to take about three hours to kiss her from head to toe before he did anything else.

And because he also wanted to wake up with her in the morning and start all over on the head-to-toe kissing.

He definitely liked her. *Damn.*

"Okay," Kiera said again.

"I just can't start anything major right now. My sister,

Aimee, is living with me because she's having a hard time, and I really need to focus on her."

"Okay. I understand."

Zach gritted his teeth. She could act *a little* disappointed.

"But I'm not asking to move in or have all your attention, Zach," Kiera said. "Not for more than a half hour or so, anyway."

He couldn't help it. He laughed. "I think I'm offended."

She grinned, as if pleased to have amused him. "Don't be. I would really look forward to those thirty minutes."

He knew, somehow, that those thirty minutes would turn his whole world upside down. "The thing is," he finally said, "I just can't make pancakes for anyone else right now."

She tipped her head. "Are the pancakes metaphorical or actual?"

"A little bit of both."

She smiled at him, and Zach rolled his eyes. When had he turned into such a sucker? And since when had brown eyes been so enchanting? And when had he started using words like *enchanting*?

"Well, I have good news for you," she said.

He could use some, that was for sure. "Like what?"

"I'm not really a pancake kind of girl."

He looked over at her. "No?"

"I'm more of a cold cereal girl."

He smiled at that. "So I gathered."

"Because it's simple. No fuss. Pancakes are...messy. Lots of ingredients and bowls and griddles and stuff."

Zach turned toward her. "Are these pancakes metaphorical or actual?"

"A little bit of both."

He huffed out a short laugh. She wasn't wrong. Pancakes, of all kinds, could be messy.

They sat, neither speaking, for several long moments. But Zach finally couldn't take it any longer. He wasn't a sit-in-silence kind of guy. "It's okay if you have questions."

He wasn't used to spilling his guts. But only because he rarely had anything to spill. His life was good, even keel, no drama, no issues. Or so he'd thought.

But Zach liked to get personal. He liked involved. He liked talking things out and getting into the nitty-gritty stuff.

"Questions about what?" Kiera asked.

"My messy family stuff."

"Oh. I don't have any questions."

He looked over at her. "Really?"

She lifted a shoulder. "It's *your* messy family stuff."

He was curious about her family, and she hadn't even hinted at any messes. "You don't like to talk about personal stuff?"

"No."

No qualification. No apology. Just no. "Really?"

"Really." She tucked her hair behind her ear. "But I am going to tell you some things about me that will help you."

"Things like what?"

"I'm going to tell you all about the things I like and the way I spend my time."

"And that's going to help me?"

She nodded. "And you'll tell me the things you like and how you spend your time too. And we'll realize that we're not actually interested in spending our time together, and this attraction will fade."

She was damned cute. He couldn't get over it. She had no makeup on, and she was wearing a borrowed T-shirt— and no bra, he couldn't forget that—with gold paint streaked in her hair. She'd been whacked in the head after seeing a ceiling crash down on her best friends. Yet she was really cute. And he wondered if she liked chocolate chip or blueberry pancakes best.

"You want the attraction to fade?" he asked.

"Don't you?"

He did. Or he should.

It was worth a shot.

He turned so he was leaning against the arm of the couch, his legs stretched out along the cushions. She followed his lead, taking the same position on the opposite end, facing him. She shifted to put one throw pillow behind her and hugged the other one to her stomach.

He crossed his arms and studied her. He loved being able to see her eyes clearly without all the makeup and glitter around them. "So you're really into the dressing-up thing."

"Cosplay. Yes," she said. "And gaming."

He frowned. Of course she was. He fucking hated video games. He'd never really gotten into them himself, but it wasn't until his sister had disappeared into them that he'd developed a true loathing.

"You don't like gaming," Kiera guessed, clearly reading it in his expression.

"No."

"Okay. What do you do for fun?" she asked.

"Run, bike, play basketball. Watch basketball. Watch more basketball."

She grinned. "See, this is working."

"Me liking basketball is making your attraction to me fade?" he asked. Because, dammit, her liking gaming should repel him, but it wasn't working that way.

It took her a few seconds to respond, but finally she shook her head. "No."

Zach dragged a big breath in. He shouldn't be happy about that. That wasn't good.

"Is it true that you spend fourteen hours a day working in your room in your *Galactic Renegades* pajamas and eating only cereal?" he asked.

She narrowed her eyes. "No. Of course not."

He sighed. Okay, that was good. Maya had been exaggerating so the doctor would insist Kiera take care of herself.

"I have other pajamas than the *GR* ones. And I don't eat *only* cereal. I eat bananas and ham sandwiches and cookies too."

He sighed again. This time not with relief. "But you do spend an insane amount of time on the computer, holed up in your room and not going out of the house?"

She nodded. "I'm a graphic designer, and my bosses are...a little eccentric, and...I work when I'm inspired. As long as I can. I sleep when I'm tired. I eat when I'm hungry. That just doesn't always happen on a schedule or at an 'appropriate' time according to the clock."

"Sounds brutal."

"It's my dream job," she said with a smile. "I get to do what I love, with people I like and respect. No commuting in Boston traffic, no meetings, no shoes."

"Shoes?" he asked. "That's a big deal to you?"

"Absolutely."

He laughed. It was a little strange, but he couldn't help

it—he still liked her. And he hated that she was missing out on the real world going on right outside her door. But he shut that thought down quickly.

He was already trying to get his sister out of her virtual world—with no success. Kiera wasn't someone he needed to worry about or fix. She was a grown-up. She was confident and intelligent and fairly well adjusted, and as long as her concussion symptoms didn't worsen in the next twenty-four hours, he could say good-bye to her, knowing she was fine.

He needed to stop talking to her.

"Is *Arrow* on Netflix?" he finally asked.

She looked surprised for a moment but nodded. "Sure is."

He reached for the remote. "I think I need to see what all the fuss is about."

* * *

Kiera opened her eyes and tried to figure out where she was.

But the hard body pressed against her back and the heavy arm around her waist and the big hand on her breast reminded her quickly.

Zach.

How they'd ended up spooning on the couch, she wasn't sure. She wasn't really sure when she'd fallen asleep. She did know that she had been on the other end of the couch.

Not that she was complaining. This hard body was her new favorite thing to be up against. Even if he couldn't give her orgasms or pancakes. Or *wouldn't*, anyway.

Heck, she should lie here and enjoy being against him as long as she could, considering her time was limited.

But she could have sworn she'd awakened because she'd heard someone walk through the living room. She listened carefully and, sure enough, she heard a kitchen drawer rolling open, then a cupboard door shutting, and, most significantly, someone humming the theme song to World of Leokin.

It had to be Zach's sister. Aimee.

Kiera didn't have one-night stands, so she wasn't sure of the etiquette around meeting the younger sister in the middle of the night, but now that she was awake, she had to go to the bathroom. And she was thirsty.

Yeah, that was it. It wasn't curiosity over the "messy family stuff" that was keeping Zach out of other personal relationships. Because that didn't matter to her at all. A personal relationship with Zach was a terrible idea.

Kiera shifted against him, wondering how she was going to get loose. That made him tighten his hold on her breast and press against her butt more firmly.

Dang he felt good.

She gave a little shiver, remembering how Zach had touched her, how he'd kissed her, how his body had felt against hers. It had been a long time for her, but she knew with absolute certainty that she'd never touched that much hard, hot muscle at one time.

She held her breath and slid his hand away from her breast. Her nipple missed the touch immediately, but Kiera tamped down her lusty thoughts. She moved his hand down her side to her hip until she could push it back gently. Zach gave a soft grunt and then rolled back slightly. Kiera slid off the edge of the couch to the floor, crouching for a moment on all fours. He didn't wake, so she stretched to her feet.

Turning toward the kitchen, Kiera moved carefully

through the living room. Knocking over a lamp or stubbing her toe wasn't part of the plan here.

When she made it across the carpet without any incidents, she took a deep breath and held it as she pushed the swinging door to the kitchen open.

The light was on, and she blinked against the sudden brightness.

The girl standing in front of the fridge swung around in surprise, a jug of milk in her hand.

"Um, hi. I'm Kiera."

The girl frowned. "Hey."

"I'm, um...here with Zach." That didn't sound the way she'd wanted it to.

The girl nodded. "I figured."

She'd figured. Okay, so maybe a strange woman in the kitchen wasn't unusual around here. It was ridiculous that Kiera hated that idea. But she did.

Aimee turned back toward the counter and the bowl of cereal sitting there.

"You must be Aimee."

"Yep." Aimee poured milk into the bowl, then boosted herself up onto the countertop and grabbed a spoon.

Aimee was gorgeous. Because of course she was. She was related to Zach. She had straight blond hair and long legs, and she was built like a Barbie doll.

And then there was the most remarkable thing of all. She was wearing a World of Leokin tank top under her short robe.

Aimee stopped with her spoon partway to her mouth, looking at Kiera warily. "Why are you staring at me?"

Kiera shook her head. *Do not gush about Leokin. Do. Not.* "Sorry. Sleepy."

"Sorry I woke you up." Aimee took the bite of cereal.

"No, don't be. It's not your fault we fell asleep on the couch. Watching TV," she felt compelled to add at the end. "I have a concussion."

Aimee tipped her head. "I'm...sorry?"

Kiera gestured toward the living room. "That's why I'm here. Zach agreed to keep an eye on me since my roommates are both in the hospital."

"Your roommates are all in the hospital?"

"Yeah."

"And let me guess," Aimee said. "Zach did something incredible and saved all your lives, risking his own in the process. Then he carried you all to the hospital on his back, uphill, in the driving rain."

Kiera looked at the girl with surprise. She thought she could actually see the sarcasm hanging in the air. "Um."

Aimee sighed. "Sorry. That was bitchy. Zach's just so..."

"Amazing?" Kiera supplied.

That got a smile. "I was going to say *annoying*."

"Well, Zach did help us," Kiera said.

Aimee rolled her eyes, and Kiera had to laugh. "Well, he did. My friends were hurt when the ceiling came down at the convention center earlier and—"

"Oh my God, you were there?" Aimee interrupted. She set her bowl down. "I saw that on Twitter. Holy crap."

Kiera nodded. "Yeah. It was crazy. And scary. But your brother helped a lot of people. Including me. So...that's why I'm here." She wasn't sure why she felt the need to sing Zach's praises.

"You were at Comic Con?" Aimee asked.

"Um..." *She's wearing a Leokin shirt. She won't think*

you're weird. And you don't care if she thinks you're weird, remember?

She did remember that. Most of the time.

"Yes." She'd been there because she loved Comic Con and because World of Leokin was represented in a bigger and bigger way every year and she loved to see that. "My friends and I cosplay."

Aimee's eyes went round. "Seriously?"

"Seriously."

"Oh my God, what did you go as?"

"Kirenda, actually. From WOL."

Aimee straightened. "Shut up." Then she leaned closer, studying Kiera's face. "Wait a second. You said your name is Kiera?"

Kiera nodded.

"Kiera *Connolly*?"

Shock rippled through Kiera. "You know who I am?"

"Oh my God," Aimee gushed, jumping to the floor. "Yes. I'm sorry I didn't recognize you right away. But what are the chances that you would be in my house? With *my brother*?"

"Well, I..."

"Holy crap." Aimee came forward, still looking at Kiera in awe. "Does Zach know who you are?"

"You mean as Kirenda?" Princess Kirenda was one of the six members of the royal family. Maybe Aimee thought Zach would recognize her character. Heck, she was in the center on most of the posters, T-shirts, and other merchandise. "Yes. He met me while I was in costume. He knows I cosplay," she said with a shrug.

Aimee grinned. "That's...amazing."

"It is?"

"That he's hooking up with a gamer?" Aimee laughed. "Oh my God, yes."

Kiera started to assure her that they hadn't "hooked up," but Aimee had seen them tangled up on the couch with Zach's hand on Kiera's breast. She wasn't sure what the term for that was…so she decided to change the subject.

"He's really not into all of it? Not at all?" She supposed she'd been hoping that he had a secret addiction to Call of Duty or even Mario Bros.

"*Really* not into it," Aimee said. "Hates everything about it. Especially Leokin."

Kiera had quickly figured out that Zach didn't know much—or anything—about her gaming world. But she'd hoped that his dislike for it was more just a disinterest. Hate seemed strong.

It was, however, another very good reason for her to not care that he wasn't interested in a relationship. She wasn't either. She didn't have the time for a guy in her life. Leokin was moving to the big leagues. They had investors now, who wanted a huge expansion in time for Christmas. A project that Kiera was eager to dive into. Pete and Dalton were finishing up the initial work and would be passing it off to Kiera for designing next month. She was preparing for at least two months of very long days during which she barely left her room.

Besides, she'd just gotten her life where she wanted it— dream job, feeling rewarded and as if she was doing something good, not answering to anyone, reveling in the things she loved unapologetically. She wasn't going to push any of that aside for a relationship. Especially one with a guy who didn't get any of it.

"But does Zach know that you're one of the developers of World of Leokin?" Aimee asked.

Wow, Aimee really did know who she was. "No. It hasn't really come up," Kiera answered. "He just knows about the costume. He was the EMT that helped me and agreed to look after me for the next twenty-four hours because of my concussion."

Aimee nodded. "That sounds like Zach. And don't worry, I sure won't tell him who you are."

Kiera looked at her in surprise. "No? Why not?"

"Because then he might not keep hanging out with you."

Kiera wasn't sure what to say. For a split second, she felt the urge to agree that Zach should not know what she did for a living. But that was the old Kiera. The Kiera who had downplayed her own interests to make a man happy and then had gone so far as to start to neglect the things, and people, that were important to her to get involved with his interests and friends instead.

"Zach and I don't have plans to see each other after this anyway," she told Aimee. "This was just a favor he's doing until my friends are better."

Aimee looked thoughtful. "Uh-huh. Well, I saw how you were cuddled up on the couch together. And Zach has pretty much focused everything he has on me for the past six months. So something made him make an exception for you. Maybe I'll get lucky and he'll keep seeing you."

So much information in that short explanation, Kiera thought. "Why has he been so focused on you for the past six months?" Kiera asked.

Aimee grabbed her bowl and headed for the wooden table that sat in the nook by the window. "You want some cereal?"

She did. They had Fruity O's, her favorite. "Sure."

"Help yourself."

Aimee sat down at the table, and after Kiera had a bowl of cereal in hand, she took the chair across from Aimee.

"He thinks I spend too much time on the computer, in the game," Aimee said when Kiera was settled. "He wants me to be out and doing stuff with 'real' people." She included the air quotes. "He doesn't get it."

Well, she and Aimee had even more in common. Maya's insistence that Kiera get off the computer and get out of the house wasn't anything new. The concussion had just given her a great reason to push it hard.

"What do you love about WOL so much?" Kiera couldn't help but ask.

It was market research. At least that's what she told herself. She and Pete and Dalton and everyone involved in WOL were as stunned by the popularity explosion as anyone and were constantly trying to understand what it was about Leokin that attracted people.

"The people in my clan," Aimee answered immediately.

Kiera nodded. That was something they'd heard over and over. Clans in Leokin truly became like family. It was beyond anything they'd purposefully designed into the game.

"But that's what bugs Zach the most," Aimee said. "He doesn't understand how you can get to know someone and care about them when all you've done is talk online."

A lot of people didn't get that. "I'm sure he's just being protective of you." Zach exuded protectiveness the way he oozed testosterone—in great, obvious quantities.

"But you know he's wrong," Aimee said. "You know there's nothing to be worried about."

Kiera could see exactly where this was going. She'd been cuddled up with Zach. Which would seemingly indicate that Zach liked her. Zach didn't like WOL. But if Zach liked Kiera and Kiera liked WOL, maybe she could convince him it was great.

She was not going there.

"Well, you have to be careful online no matter what," she said. "Even in WOL."

"My clan members want to get together in real life," Aimee said, stirring her cereal around in her bowl. "They've been talking about meeting for a little while now." She looked up. "Do you think that you can get close to someone and really trust them without ever meeting them face-to-face?"

Kiera nodded. "I do. Two of my closest friends live in California, and we only see each other twice a year. But we talk online every day. I'm as close to them as I am to anyone."

Aimee smiled slowly. "Pete and Dalton, right?"

Aimee was really into Leokin. Kiera needed to remember that. Pete and Dalton were the public names and faces associated with WOL. They were the ones who gave the interviews and showed up at the Comic Cons, usually. If Aimee knew who Kiera was, she definitely knew who Pete and Dalton were.

"Yep."

"I read the article that included your interview with Pete and Dalton in *Geeks and Gaming*. I know how you started WOL back in college and that you did the initial drawings of all of the main characters and creatures. And..." She paused as if she wasn't sure she should continue.

"Go on," Kiera said, amazed and impressed at the same time.

"I know that you originally made Kirenda blond with big boobs, but Pete said that he wanted you to model her after yourself and that you argued about it until you both agreed to put it up for a vote in a focus group."

Kiera knew she was staring. She'd met Leokin fans before. But she wasn't sure she'd ever met someone who knew that story. Pete had told it to a blogger on an obscure blog two years ago, before Leokin was the sensation it was now.

"I was shocked when the brown-haired, brown-eyed, shorter, less well-endowed princess won unanimously," she told Aimee.

Kiera had adjusted to seeing her image in Kirenda on the small screen and didn't think about looking like one of the most popular animated characters in the world most of the time, but she still wasn't used to seeing the caricature of herself on posters and big screens at cons.

"I think she's perfect," Aimee said.

"I'm amazed," Kiera told her honestly.

Aimee gave her a huge smile. "I love everything about Leokin."

"Then you need to know some insider secrets, don't you?" Kiera asked.

Aimee nodded eagerly. "Yes!"

"Well, Pete still does his initial brainstorming on napkins, just like we did in the beginning," Kiera said with a grin. "And Dalton has recently discovered that dabbing peppermint oil behind his ears helps him focus."

Pete and Dalton were brilliant, creative minds and had all the eccentricities that went along with that.

Aimee grinned. "Oh my gosh, that's awesome. Dalton is *so* cute."

Kiera laughed. She'd heard that a time or two as well. Dalton had been a child prodigy, completing college when he was only eighteen. He was the easy-going charmer in interviews and public appearances. Pete was the brooding genius. Yet in spite of their different personalities and the five-year age difference, Pete and Dalton were best buds. "How old are you?" Kiera asked Aimee.

"Eighteen next month."

She and Dalton were only four years apart.

"Well, I can't wait to tell them I met our biggest fan," Kiera said.

Aimee gave a choked little squeal. "You're going to tell them about me?"

"Of course. We all love hearing how passionate our fans are."

"Oh my gosh!" Aimee was nearly bouncing on her chair. "I can't believe it. My brother finally brings a girl home and she is the coolest girl I've ever met. I did not see that coming."

Kiera *really* wanted to pursue that. What kind of girls did Zach usually bring home? What did *finally* mean?

"Can I hug you?"

"Uh…" Before Kiera had decided how she felt about it, Aimee was out of her chair and Kiera found herself enfolded in an enthusiastic embrace.

She didn't know how to respond. She patted Aimee's back, but it wasn't until the girl straightened and focused on something behind Kiera that she realized they weren't alone.

She turned toward the kitchen door.

Zach was looking at them with resignation. "I take it you discovered your shared love for the World of Leokin." His grim tone made it clear how he felt.

"You saved a member of the royal family today," Aimee said. "There is a great reward for you."

Kiera heard the mild humor in Aimee's voice, but she was still looking at Zach. He looked damned good rumpled and sort of sleepy. And then his expression went from puzzled to surprised as he watched his sister. Kiera glanced at Aimee. She was grinning at him.

"Like money or something?" Zach asked.

"Probably jewels," Aimee said thoughtfully. She looked at Kiera. "Or gold? I'm sure Peter and Dalton would pay any price to the brave soul who ensured your safety."

Kiera started to answer that they'd probably try to get by with an invitation to a huge feast or something, rather than doling out actual treasure. But Zach spoke first.

"Who the hell are Peter and Dalton?"

Kiera looked at him and found him scowling. Scowling? Really?

"Her friends who—"

"The king and prince of Leokin," Kiera said quickly over the top of Aimee's answer.

Why? Why don't you want him to know that two of your best friends developed this amazing thing? Why don't you want to claim your part in it?

Aimee nodded. "Exactly."

"Characters in the game?" Zach asked.

Well, they were...technically...

"Yes," Aimee said. "Her brothers. In the game."

That was true. In the written Leokin history, King Peter was the firstborn of the brothers, and she'd become their adopted sister when they'd rescued her from the trolls. Pete and Dalton were like her brothers in real life too.

Zach's focus rested on Kiera. "Can I talk to you?"

Why did she have a feeling she was in trouble for something? "Of course."

"I'm going back upstairs," Aimee said quickly. "It was great to meet you, Kiera."

Kiera smiled at her. "You too. This was fun."

Aimee and Zach passed one another as he came farther into the room and she headed for the doorway.

"Hey, Zach?" Aimee said.

"Yeah?"

"She's awesome."

"Yeah, I know," he said, sounding exasperated.

"Coolest girl you've *ever* dated," Aimee added.

Kiera waited for Zach to explain to his sister that they weren't dating. And tried to put her twinge of disappointment aside.

Instead, though, he said, "Yeah?"

"Definitely," Aimee answered. "So don't screw it up, okay?"

There was a long pause before Zach said, "Go to bed."

Kiera could hear Aimee's sigh from across the room. "Whatever."

As soon as Aimee was out the door, Zach turned his attention back to Kiera. "Go to my parents' party with me."

Kiera frowned. That hadn't been anything near what she'd been expecting him to say. "What?"

"My parents are hosting a party. I'd love it if you'd come with me."

Oh boy. "Like a date?"

He shrugged. "We can call it a favor. It's a big night

for my family, and Aimee has been fighting the idea for months. She doesn't want to go. But I think if you were there, she'd come. Which would mean the world to my mother. Which would mean the world to me."

She couldn't have explained it for anything, but that made her want to say yes. Zach was all about other people. She'd known him for only a few hours and she knew that. Asking someone for something was a big deal for him.

But seeing him again... She wasn't sure that was a great idea.

"Because Aimee thinks I'm cool and doesn't want you to screw this up?" she asked, using Aimee's words.

Zach pulled in a long breath, then nodded. "Yeah. Basically."

"But there's nothing to screw up."

"I've been screwing *everything* up with her," he said. "For months. She's so unhappy. The smile she just gave me, the lighthearted joking just now? I haven't had that from her in months. I want to get that girl back. And that girl showed up with you. She hugged you. She laughed with you. She hasn't done that with anyone in what feels like forever. So please go to the party with me. Hell, go everywhere with me until she's back to normal."

Kiera felt her eyes widen. The intensity of emotion from Zach made her heart pound. "What?"

"If we're dating, then you'll be around. If you're around, Aimee will be much more likely to emerge from her room. My family might just figure out how to be a family again."

Kiera hesitated. She didn't know what was going on with Zach and Aimee, but she did know she didn't want to get involved.

"You told Maya you'd cut back on your work and get

out more. Just spend some time with me and we'll make everyone happy," he said. "Let Maya know you're taking her concerns into consideration. Let my sister believe that you think I'm awesome for a little while."

Her heartbeat stuttered. She did think he was awesome. And his sadness and worry tugged at her emotions in a way that nothing had in a very long time. She'd thought she had the force field around her heart firmly in place. So how was Zach Ashley getting through?

"I don't want pancakes," she said. "I'm a cereal girl, remember?"

This all sounded beyond complicated and emotionally tangled.

Zach stepped closer. "Yes, I definitely remember. You don't know how attractive that is."

She smiled. She imagined that Zach might need and appreciate more *simple* in his life. In that case, she could be good for him.

"Why doesn't Aimee want to go to the party?" she finally asked.

"It's a long story. She and my mom have been having a hard time lately. This night is supposed to be about us as a family, but Aimee feels like we haven't really been a family over the past few months, so she feels like it would be a lie."

She should not do this. But she asked, "How much would we see each other between now and then?"

Zach looked surprised. "As much as you want, Princess."

She wanted to see him all the time. That was a definite sign she should just walk away now. But this could work for her too. A plan was forming in her mind. Was it just a great excuse to see more of Zach and not worry about getting hurt? Maybe. But it really could make a lot of people happy.

Kiera stood and faced him squarely. "Fine. I'll go," she finally said.

Zach started to respond, but she cut him off.

"But we have to go out at least three times a week." That would keep Maya happy and keep her from telling Pete to cut back on Kiera's work. She wanted the work. She wanted to be part of the force behind World of Leokin's success. It was the most rewarding thing she'd ever done.

"You got it," Zach said without hesitation.

"And then we break up the night of the party."

That he didn't react to quite as quickly. "Why?"

"I have a huge project starting next month. I can't do anything but work then for the next two months. I need Maya and Sophie to leave me alone about going out and being social during that time. So you and I make a show out of this—dating, spending time together—then we break up on the night of the party. I'll need at least two months to recover from the broken heart," she said with a smile. "Being holed up in my room, not wanting to go out, not wanting to see anyone will make perfect sense."

Once she'd said it out loud, Kiera realized this was a brilliant plan.

"But you'll actually be working," he said, clearly not enthusiastic.

She nodded. "I'll have to throw myself into work to keep my mind off of you."

Zach seemed to consider that. "You're willing to lie to your friends?"

"It's not a lie. We'll be going out. And we'll stop going

out that night. And I won't want to leave my room for two months afterward." Yes, this really was brilliant.

But Zach shook his head with a small smile. "I can't break your heart, Princess."

That made her melt a little, she had to admit. "You have to," she said. "I have to retreat from the real world for two months. That means falling hard and having you rip my heart out." She gave him a grin.

He shook his head, his smile growing too. "No way. I'm too nice a guy to do something like that."

She laughed. "I'm guessing you've broken plenty of hearts, Zach."

"I don't think I've ever ripped one out, though."

"Oh, well, this is going to be a crazy-mad love affair unlike either of us has ever had," she told him flippantly.

But Zach paused. There was a moment of silence that felt far too real, their eyes locked on one another's.

Finally Zach said, "Okay. There's only one little problem."

"What's that?"

"Aimee will hate me if I break your heart."

Kiera's smile faded slightly. "Oh, right."

"So she'll have to think that you broke my heart."

Kiera's chest tightened. "Then she'll hate me."

"Guess we'll just have to stay together then," he quipped.

She knew he was trying to lighten the mood, but Kiera started shaking her head immediately. "No. We can't do that." She wasn't in the market for a boyfriend. Especially one with messy family issues. And a sister that Kiera already liked. "I seriously have one month."

"Okay, Cinderella, we'll be sure you don't turn into

a pumpkin. I'll just be grateful it's not over at midnight tonight."

She relaxed slightly and smiled. "Sorry. This work thing...it's just everything right now."

It really was. She'd promised her full commitment—her time, attention, and energy—to Pete when he'd been freaking out about the investors and their expectations. And she was looking forward to it.

The past eighteen months had been an amazing ride. The game was everywhere now and the growth showed no signs of stopping. Yes, it was a video game. But it was more than that. She was a part of something successful that stimulated her mind and her heart, something that was gloriously nerdy and influential at the same time. She was one of the five most important people to the World of Leokin franchise, and she couldn't express how much that meant to her.

"I get it," Zach said. "My family is everything to me right now."

Kiera nodded. "Okay. Then we're friends who are helping each other out. And after a month we'll realize that we're way too different to make it work long-term and we'll stop seeing each other."

Yeah. This would work. Because the people closest to them would already see clearly that they had nothing in common.

But it didn't feel as if they had nothing in common.

"Great. Friends." He paused. "So does that mean no more kissing?"

She frowned. "Why would that mean no more kissing?"

"You sure that's a good idea?"

"It's kind of a perk of this plan, isn't it?" she asked.

"You think we should keep fooling around?"

She really wanted to. She understood that it could be dangerous. It was hard to keep emotions apart from the physical stuff sometimes. But they had outlined their plan clearly. "You need Aimee to go to that party. I need Maya and Sophie to stop nagging me and let me work. Do you expect either of those goals to change because we make out a little?"

"No."

"And the party happens in one month. My work project takes off in one month. Nothing is going to change that timeline either, right?"

Zach grinned, and she was absolutely certain that she wanted to keep kissing him over the next month. As much as she possibly could.

"Right," he agreed.

"So I think we're good," she told him.

"Then there's only one more thing you should know," he said.

"Okay."

"If we go back to the kissing, there's not going to be anything 'little' about the making out."

He stepped close, with something in his eyes that made her heart rate quicken. He ran his hand up and down her arm, then slid both hands up to the back of her neck and tilted her head back. He kissed her softly at first, teasing her with his lips, brushing back and forth lightly. Then he pressed a little harder, drawing on her mouth. Then, finally, with a groan, he opened his mouth on hers and kissed her. Fully. Hungrily. Until she was gripping his forearms and was up onto her toes as far as she could physically get.

His tongue was demanding in a way he hadn't been before. It felt as if he was seeking something, desperately. To feel better. To feel connected. To have something *real* happen. Whatever it was, she gave it back to him. She pressed close, wrapping her arms around his neck, moaning for more. Which seemed to fire him up even further. He turned them both and started to walk her back to the wall, but at the last minute stopped and pulled his mouth from hers.

He stared down at her, his breathing ragged.

"I remembered this time," he said huskily.

She thought hard. What was he talking about? What had he remembered?

He gently ran a hand from her neck to the back of her head.

Oh yeah. Her head. She'd almost forgotten she had one. All of her attention had been focused a bit lower.

"Right," she panted. "Right. Good job."

He gave her a quick, small smile.

God, she wanted him to smile. To be happy. She wanted to *make* him happy.

And she hated that. She didn't want to be emotionally tangled up with him. That never ended well for her.

CHAPTER FIVE

I like the new troll spell and the expanded fairy kingdom, but what happens if you get through the forest without finding any gems?" Aimee asked.

"You'd have to avoid all of the paths to *not* find one eventually," Kiera pointed out.

She and Aimee were sitting in a coffee shop about four blocks from where Aimee and Zach lived. It was officially twenty-four hours after her concussion, and Kiera was feeling good as long as she kept ibuprofen in her system. They'd agreed to meet here while Zach worked. Maya and Sophie had been, predictably, thrilled when Kiera had told them she was going out for the afternoon. They didn't need to know that she was spending the time showing Aimee some of the new Leokin designs she'd been working on. Though Kiera had to admit that getting someone's reaction in real time, in person, was actually pretty fun. And when it was a hardcore Leokin girl like Aimee, it was also very helpful.

"But the witches and even some of the elves would be able to avoid the paths and make it through the whole forest," Aimee said.

Kiera nodded. Aimee had a point. She typed a note about Aimee's observation into the chat window she had open with Dalton.

"Dalton says we could distribute the gems with the moonsky flowers in the forest," Kiera read to Aimee a moment later. Witches and elves were the only ones who could see moonsky flowers and benefit from their powers.

"That would work. But the gems will be too big to be hidden in the moonsky flower bushes," Aimee said.

Kiera typed another note to Dalton, then made a few tweaks to the gem graphic. She sent it to Aimee, who opened it in her e-mail program immediately.

"Yes, that's perfect."

Kiera grinned at her. "Awesome." She typed, "Aimee approved" into the chat window. Dalton sent her a thumbs-up.

"I can't believe it," Aimee said, sitting back in her chair.

Kiera looked up. "What?"

"I'm hanging out with Kiera Connolly, chatting online with Dalton Sagel, and giving input into new Leokin stuff. This is awesome."

Kiera was flattered by Aimee's admiration. But she was also worried. On the one hand, she didn't want Aimee to get too attached to her. This whole thing was going to be over in a few weeks. On the other hand, if Aimee was more open and friendly with Zach because he was dating Kiera, then it was a good thing.

Ignoring all of those confusing thoughts, Kiera gave Aimee a smile and focused on her work. Leokin was always the answer when things got confusing in the real world.

Her phone started buzzing, and she glanced over. Zach was calling. She frowned and reached for the phone.

"Hello?"

"Hey, Princess."

His deep voice made shivers dance through her. "Hi."

"Where are you?"

"At the coffee shop near your place."

"What are you doing?" he asked.

Kiera narrowed her eyes. "Talking to your sister."

"Great. I thought I'd swing by after my shift and say hi."

She knew that Zach had told Aimee he'd be by around four. She'd been hoping to see him. She leaned back in her chair, trying to make her tone nonchalant. "Okay."

"Everything going well?"

"You're checking up on us?"

"No. Just thinking of you and wanted to say hi."

She wasn't sure she believed him, but she couldn't help that her heart flipped a little at that idea. Still, she didn't want to encourage quick calls "just to say hi." She hated talking on the phone, and unimportant phone calls interrupted her work flow, and, most of all, this whole thing with her spending time with him and Aimee had been his idea. If he felt he needed to check in all the time, they needed to rethink their plan.

"You still there?" he asked.

"Yep."

"And everything is okay."

"Yes."

She was sure the short, one-word answers drove Zach crazy. He was a talker. But she wasn't.

"You're not very talkative," he commented a moment later.

She smiled in spite of herself. "No, I'm really not. I don't like talking on the phone."

"Oh." He sounded confused. He probably was, she thought, her smile growing. Zach was clearly an extrovert who didn't get introverts.

She heard him sigh.

"So if I want to check in, say hi, make plans..."

"Text me," she said cheerfully.

She imagined the exasperated look she'd already seen a few times from him.

"Okay," he finally said. "But I will see you later. And you'll talk to me in person, right?"

"Within reason," she agreed, wondering if her grin was evident in her tone. She wasn't sure why it was fun to poke at Zach. Maybe because he seemed so sure that he knew exactly how things should always go. She liked shaking up his expectations a little bit.

"Right. Okay." He sighed again.

"See you later," she said.

"Yep. See you."

She chuckled as she disconnected with him.

"So you didn't mention anything to Zach about me meeting up with my WOL friends, did you?" Aimee asked.

Kiera looked up. "No. Why?"

"He won't like it," Aimee said. "But I've been thinking about doing it more and more. You think it's okay, don't you?"

Kiera frowned and moved her hands off her keyboard. "I understand that you feel close to them even with having never met them," she said. She and Pete and Dalton were close and worked well together in spite of living three thousand miles apart. "And I don't think meeting them is a bad idea. Why wouldn't Zach like it?"

"He doesn't get the online friendship thing."

Just then her phone rang with a text. From Zach. She rolled her eyes but opened it.

Is Pete your boss?

He wanted to know about Pete? She typed back. *Yes. And one of my best friends.*

So you're not in love with him?

She laughed. *No.*

Good.

She stared at the word for a moment.

Then she forced herself to concentrate on Aimee. "But this would be in person," she said about the meeting with her online friends. "Wouldn't Zach like that you were moving it into the real world?"

Aimee shrugged. "Yes and no. He'd like that I was being more social, getting out. But he wouldn't like to know how close I've gotten to them and that they've been helping me through everything."

Kiera frowned. "Why not?"

"Zach likes to be the one I need for everything," Aimee said. "He likes to be the one everyone needs for everything."

Kiera had no idea what to say to that. It didn't shock her. But she didn't want someone all mixed up in her stuff. Zach's wanting to be involved in everything all the time should be a mark in the con column. So why was it kind of attractive?

Another text came in. She was surprised to feel her heart flutter at the sound.

Have you had your heart broken before to the point that it made you hole up in your room for two months?

She shook her head. She wouldn't have personal conversations with him, but he thought she'd tell him personal things via text?

But as she thought about it, she realized this was a lot easier. She didn't have to see the other person or think about what they were seeing in her face. And she knew already that Zach would keep pushing.

Yes. Her breakup with Mitch had messed her up for longer than two months.

What happened?

First love. Mitch. Very controlling. Tried to change everything about me.

Kiera hit send before she thought about it or read it over. She couldn't believe she'd told him that. But maybe it was good for him to know where she was coming from. Their relationship was just a temporary, mostly fake thing. But it wouldn't hurt for her to put all her cards out there.

Change you?

She took a breath. *Hated all my hobbies, didn't want me to spend time with anyone but him. Wanted me to change my hair and the way I dressed. Wanted me to lose weight.*

You told the bastard to fuck off?

She smiled. Essentially that was exactly what she'd told him. *Yes.* She hesitated over her next words. But she ended up typing them anyway. *So he moved on to Juliet.*

Who's Juliet?

She was my best friend, Kiera told him, feeling the familiar stabbing pain in her chest.

What did she do?

Became his perfect woman.

And when he'd insisted that she needed to lose weight too, she'd developed an eating disorder that had landed her in the hospital. Kiera had gone to try to talk her into leaving him, to let Kiera take her home. But Juliet had chosen the emotionally abusive asshole over her best friend.

But you stopped it? Got her away from him?

His question made Kiera's heart squeeze. *Tried. And failed.*

He took a long time to answer. *I know how bad that hurts.*

She didn't know what to say to that. Juliet had met Mitch because of Kiera. If Kiera hadn't gotten involved with him, he would have never had Juliet on his radar. Kiera knew that, in part, Mitch had gone after Juliet because he'd wanted to get back at Kiera for rejecting him. So yes, she felt somewhat to blame. But Juliet had made her choices. Kiera had given her an option for getting out, and she'd turned Kiera down. It did hurt. But there was nothing she could do about it. Besides try to keep anything like that from happening again.

Something about Zach's answer nagged at her, though. Was Zach talking about his relationship with Aimee? He was trying and failing to help her? She never delved into other people's personal angst and drama, but suddenly Kiera needed to know.

"What have your friends been helping you through?" she asked Aimee hesitantly.

Aimee looked up from what she'd been doing on her computer. She blinked. "Getting over my sister."

Kiera felt a trickle of foreboding go through her. "What do you mean?"

Aimee sighed. "I don't know. I can't explain it. Even before Josie died, Leokin was this place where I could...get lost. And then after she was gone, it was the only place I felt like myself."

Kiera froze.

She didn't move or make a sound.

Holy crap.

She glanced up, but Aimee was concentrating on her own computer screen.

Kiera held her breath. Aimee had lost her sister? Zach had lost his sister? This was definitely messy family stuff. Was Aimee not handling it well? But Kiera knew...Aimee was immersing herself in the game to avoid everything.

Kiera got that. She so got that.

Aimee sniffed and shifted on her chair. "I feel bad sometimes, but I never had a sister in Leokin, so I didn't miss having a sister there. That made it the only place I wanted to be. I missed having a sister *everywhere* else."

Kiera felt her eyes stinging but kept her gaze firmly on her computer screen. What did she say now? Dammit, she was so bad at this stuff. She had to clear her throat before she asked, "Was your sister into gaming?"

"No, she was in a band. A rock band. She played guitar and sang. She was awesome."

Kiera could hear Aimee's smile, and she looked up to catch it.

"They were coming home from a gig really late one night, and Hunter, he was the bass player and the lead singer, was driving. He was so cool." Aimee's voice trailed off for a moment. Then she said, "He fell asleep at the wheel and crossed the center line into oncoming traffic."

Kiera blinked and forced herself to breathe as she stared

at her screen, where the stream bubbled happily by the tall trees and long grass of the meadow.

Kiera had to say something. And the thing was, she kind of had something to say. She didn't have any siblings, but she'd had someone she'd thought of as a sister. And she'd lost her. Not to death. Juliet had chosen to leave Kiera's life. Not the same thing exactly, but Kiera knew the pain of losing a loved one and knowing your life would never be the same.

But she was out of practice. Since Juliet's betrayal, Kiera had made a firm habit of staying out of people's business and keeping them out of hers. She believed that people needed to make their own decisions and their own mistakes.

Condolences weren't the same thing as advice, though. "I'm really sorry about your sister, Aimee."

"I miss her every day," the younger girl said softly.

"You'll miss her every day forever," Kiera said honestly. "But thinking about her won't always squeeze your heart so hard that you can't even take a deep breath."

There was a long pause, and then Aimee said softly, "That's exactly how it feels sometimes."

Kiera nodded. "I know."

Aimee swallowed hard. Then she gave a little nod and inserted her earbuds into her ears.

Each got absorbed in what was on her screen, and Kiera ignored all thoughts that went anything like, "Did I do okay?" "What's she thinking?" "Did I mess that up?"

She'd told her the truth. And Aimee wasn't her responsibility. Kiera knew the girl was hurting, but she had a big brother who was amazing and protective and sweet. He was taking care of her, Kiera was sure.

It took only about five minutes for her to get lost in her work, and they sat together quietly for nearly twenty minutes before she heard, "You girls are in so much trouble."

Kiera recognized the voice immediately, and her gaze flew to the clock in the corner of her computer screen. *Dammit.* He was early.

Kiera looked up to see Zach standing next to the table. He had his hands on his hips and was watching her with an eyebrow up and an expression that looked partly exasperated and partly amused.

He looked sexy.

She had an inkling that if she found him sexy when he was exasperated with her, she was going to be finding him sexy a lot.

"You said four o'clock," Aimee said, looking guilty.

Kiera wanted to kick her under the table. She needed to not look guilty.

"I said four o'clock because I intended to show up at three thirty to see what you were up to," Zach said. He kicked the empty chair out and sat. "I knew you'd be on your computers."

"We never said we *wouldn't* be on our computers," Kiera pointed out, surreptitiously closing the window she'd had open to work on new graphics.

She and Aimee were together. In person. In a public place. It was more social than either of them had been in several weeks without being coerced. So why did Aimee look guilty for their being caught on their computers? Why did Kiera *feel* guilty?

"I knew you would be. You've been away from it for a whole day. You were probably dying," Zach said drily.

Kiera couldn't deny that she'd been eager to get back

online. But she also couldn't honestly say she'd been completely away from it for a whole day. She'd checked in when she'd first gotten home. But her head had started hurting within two minutes. She didn't want to admit that either. So she just didn't say anything.

"When you said you were getting together, Maya, Sophie, and I assumed it was to, you know, talk to one another and do something together," Zach said.

Kiera snorted.

"You talked to Maya and Sophie?" Aimee asked.

Zach's eyes were on Kiera, but he answered his sister. "No. I'm guessing. But Maya and Sophie were led to believe you and Aimee would be doing something other than sitting across from one another, each on your own computer, for three hours straight, weren't they, Princess?"

She really liked when he called her Princess.

The truth was, Maya and Sophie had probably assumed that Kiera was going to see Zach today. They didn't know about Aimee. Kiera shrugged. "I didn't go into any details one way or another with them."

With his gaze on her, Kiera felt hot—probably still the guilt—and wiggly, as if she had an itch she couldn't scratch. Zach looked huge on the tiny wrought iron chair, and when he stretched his long legs out, he took up far too much space. Too much of *her* space. He was crowding into Kiera's area under the table, as if he was trying to be sure she took note of him. She could hardly help it. He linked his fingers together, resting them above his belt, and she also couldn't help that her gaze went to his big hands, and his flat stomach. Then below his flat stomach.

"Good to see something can pull your attention from your computer screen."

Her gaze snapped up to his. And the knowing smile below his gaze. *Dammit.*

As she met his eyes, *He's lost his sister* went through her head. The thought jolted her. He'd distracted her with his early arrival. And his grin. And how great he looked in uniform. But now that she'd remembered, she wanted to hug him.

And that was so uncharacteristic that she actually reached for her coffee cup to keep from reaching for him. Her empty coffee cup. She pretended to drink from it anyway, grateful there was a lid so he didn't know she was faking.

Kiera cleared her throat. "Aimee and I have had a nice time together," she told him. "Just because you happened to walk in at a moment when we were each checking in on the computer doesn't mean that you know for sure we haven't been chatting this entire time."

"Have you been chatting this entire time?" he asked.

"We—"

But he was asking his sister. Kiera had to squelch the urge to kick her again.

Aimee sighed. "Not the *entire* time. But we never said we wouldn't be on the computers."

"Exactly," Kiera agreed quickly. "We're not doing anything wrong."

Just then a beeping erupted from her computer. Her alarm. She scrambled to get it shut off. When she looked up, Zach was smirking. "If you weren't doing anything wrong, why did you set a timer?"

"That timer could be for anything," Kiera told him.

He nodded. "Interesting that it went off with just enough time to get your computers shut down and packed away before I was supposed to get here."

She was busted. "I had some work I had to do today. Whether or not that makes you and Maya unhappy," she informed him. "But Aimee and I have spent the time together and we did chat and I will readily admit that this was nicer than working alone in my room in many ways."

"In many ways?" Zach repeated. "Not in every way?" But he seemed more amused than judgmental.

"Well, I'm in real clothes instead of pajamas," Kiera said.

She probably should have expected the way his gaze tracked down her body with that comment, but she hadn't, and she felt the wave of heat that went from her scalp to the soles of her feet as his eyes roamed over her.

"And I've only had one bowl of cereal today," she added.

Zach nodded. "Poor girl."

She couldn't help the little grin she gave him. "The struggle is real."

Zach pushed back from the table and stretched to his feet. "And I haven't seen you in your pajamas yet, but I love the jeans. Let's go."

Yet. He'd said *yet* about seeing her in her pajamas.

"Are we going home?" Aimee asked, starting to gather her stuff.

"I've got a game."

"Basketball?" Aimee asked.

Zach nodded. "You two have been doing the computer thing all day. So now you have to put in some time of *actual* socialization."

"You play basketball?" Kiera asked Aimee.

The girl shook her head. "No. He does."

Yeah, Kiera remembered that. And that she knew almost nothing about the game.

Kiera watched Aimee tuck her computer into her bag and stand.

"Well, I guess I'll see you?" Aimee asked.

"Definitely."

Zach stood simply watching her.

"What?" Kiera asked.

"Let's go," he repeated.

"Go?"

"To my game."

Kiera felt her head start shaking. "No, that's okay. I don't really like basketball."

He gave her a slow smile. "Yet."

Kiera opened her mouth to protest, but then a crazy thought flitted through her mind. *Why not?* She'd gotten a lot done today, she was actually a little ahead on things for now, and...she was willing to watch a basketball game to spend some time with Zach.

Crap. She was in trouble.

Kiera got to her feet and pulled her bag up on her shoulder. His gaze ran over her again. "Yeah, this view of the jeans is even better."

Kiera felt herself blush. And was glad she'd worn the jeans instead of the yoga pants she'd had on first. *Damn.* She wasn't dressing for Zach. She was *not.*

Thirty minutes later they pulled into the parking lot of a YMCA. Kiera blinked at the front of the building. She realized she'd been expecting Zach to play in an expensive rec center or a members-only gym. Zach held the door for Aimee and Kiera. As she passed him, she looked up, noting the huge grin on his face. She felt a little flip in her stomach.

She liked seeing him so lit up. She tried to tell herself that it was because she'd just learned that he'd lost his sister in a car accident and that it was nice to see him happy about something. But she knew that wasn't the whole truth. She just liked seeing him happy, period. Even before she'd known about Josie.

But thinking about Josie made her want to hug him again. Well, that and the memory of how great it felt to be pressed up against him in general.

"Gym's down that way," he said, stopping at the doorway to the men's locker room and pointing. "Grab a seat. And be sure to whoop and yell loud."

She grinned up at him. "I won't know when to whoop and yell, Zach."

"Whenever the orange ball goes into the basket on my team's end of the court," he replied with a shrug.

"How about I just sit in quiet awe of your athletic prowess?" she offered.

He chuckled, and the sound made her smile grow.

"I can definitely handle having your eyes on me for the next hour or so, Princess."

Yeah, she was pretty sure she could handle that too.

Zach startled her by leaning in and giving her a quick kiss. She stared up at him as he straightened.

"Been dying to do that since I walked into the coffee shop," he said. Then he turned and headed into the locker room with his gym bag.

Kiera drew a deep breath. It was show for Aimee. She was supposed to think they were really dating. But the look in his eyes had seemed real to Kiera. She needed to be careful about not getting too caught up in their story herself.

She followed Aimee into the gym and up onto the bleachers.

"So you know a lot about basketball?" Kiera asked.

Aimee shrugged. "Yeah, I guess. I was a cheerleader for my high school team for three years."

Kiera looked over at her, surprised. "Really?"

"Oh yeah. Before…everything happened…I was a cheerleader, homecoming queen, really social and popular. The whole thing. That's why Zach's so freaked out."

Kiera turned her attention to the court and to the few guys already out there warming up. She could kind of see why Zach would be concerned with his sister's complete personality one-eighty, actually.

"Hey, speaking of being social," Aimee said.

Kiera looked over. "Yeah?"

"I've decided to meet my Leokin friends who live locally. I was wondering if you'd go to the coffee shop with me next Saturday. We're going to meet there and I thought it might be nice if you were there too, just to, you know, be sure it's all fine."

Kiera nodded immediately. "Of course. I think that's a great idea, actually." She was happy Aimee was getting together with her new friends, but was also glad she was being safe about it.

Aimee gave her a big smile. "Thanks."

"No problem." She glanced at the court again, then started to look back at Aimee. But something snagged her attention.

Zach. Who had just walked out of the locker room. Without a shirt on.

Her eyes widened as she took him in. Broad shoulders, sculpted arm muscles, wide chest and hard abs. She easily conjured the feel of all of those under and against her last night. The baggy gym shorts didn't keep her from appreciating his firm butt and muscled thighs and calves either.

This just might be the best hour of her life.

"Right, Kiera?"

She heard Aimee's voice but didn't turn her head. "Um, what?"

Aimee laughed. "How about I ask you again later?"

"Yeah." That would be great. She supposed.

The game started, and Kiera settled in with a happy sigh. Sweat-slicked, tanned skin moving over bunching shoulder, back, and ab muscles should not have been so mesmerizing. But damned if basketball wasn't suddenly her favorite spectator sport.

* * *

Zach walked Kiera to the train station after the game so she could catch the train back to Cambridge. Aimee was with them but was hanging back, clearly trying to give them some time alone. He smiled to himself. Man, this plan was brilliant. He got to spend time with Kiera and help his sister at the same time.

They stopped by the entrance to the station, and Kiera turned to him.

"Come back to my place for a little while," Zach said before she could speak. "It's early." He should be hoping she'd come over so he might have a chance at more time with Aimee, but truthfully, it was the peck on the lips he'd given Kiera before his game that made him ask. The quick taste hadn't been nearly enough.

"I should get home," she said. "I'll see you later this week, though."

"When?" he asked.

Aimee had stopped about a half block away, and Kiera

gave her a glance. She was leaning against the wall, her head bent over her phone.

"Wednesday?" Kiera suggested.

Wednesday was three days away. He needed to see her before that. "I work the next three nights."

"I thought your goal was for me to hang out with Aimee," Kiera said. "Keep her from being holed up in her room."

He nodded and moved in to brace his hand on the railing beside her hip. "But it's a win-win when we can both spend time with you."

"True," she agreed easily. "But Aimee could come over and hang out with me one of the nights you work."

Zach searched her face for a moment. "I can come pick her up after my shift ends at ten."

"Great," Kiera said quickly. Almost eagerly. Then she cleared her throat. "I mean, sure. That's fine."

He couldn't help but grin. He liked the idea of Kiera being eager for him.

"Thanks for coming to my game." He'd loved having her there. And every time he'd glanced up into the stands and seen her watching, he'd felt a kick in his chest.

She laughed at that. "Did I have a choice?"

"Don't tell me you minded," he said. "Your eyes were glued on the game."

The way she looked up at him from beneath her lashes was adorably hot. "I enjoyed it. But you and I both know that I wasn't watching the game."

"No?" He shifted closer to her.

She shook her head. "I was watching *you*. And enjoying the fact that you're a total geek about basketball."

He frowned slightly. "I'm not a geek about basketball."

Kiera nodded and grinned. "Oh yes, Zach Ashley, you definitely are."

He liked basketball. Loved it, even. But he'd never been called a geek in his life. "Maybe our definition of *geek* is different."

She lifted a shoulder. "I've seen how sports fans act when it comes time for a big game or event. They throw parties and they dress up in the team's colors and jerseys. Some even paint their faces. And they go out there and revel in being a part of something that makes them so happy. That's geekiness, Zach. Passion for something. Passion that you give time and energy to. The crazy way they yell at the refs and the way they go nuts because one team manages to put a ball where the other team doesn't want it…that's not acting, but it's also not *really* them. It's part of their personality. A part they only let out on certain occasions when they're around other people who share the same passion."

She paused, and Zach knew exactly what she was going to say next.

"That's how I feel and act about Leokin."

He sighed. He supposed she had a point. "I never thought of it that way," he said. "And I definitely didn't realize that all pretty much makes me a cosplayer."

He started to shift away, but she reached out and grabbed his forearm. "It was really hot watching how into it you got."

Zach lifted an eyebrow. "Yeah?"

"Yeah." She wet her lips and stepped closer to him. "You were so happy out there. It was sexy to watch you having such a great time. You were laughing and shouting and putting everything you had into it. It's clear you love it. You were intense, but relaxed at the same time."

He nodded slowly. "I feel different out there. All I have to do is concentrate on the game. All the other...stuff fades away."

She gave him a soft smile. "I'm glad."

"And now you like basketball," he said.

She shrugged. "I like watching you like basketball."

Something about her words made him stop and think. She'd lit up when she'd been talking about common interests with the injured while he bandaged them up. He'd seen the same thing in both Kiera and Aimee when he'd walked into the kitchen last night. There had been something in their faces and voices that had said they were in their element.

"Princess," he finally said, "I think it's possible that I'd like watching you like just about anything."

She smiled and then stepped forward and wrapped her arms around him.

Surprise quickly morphed into something he wouldn't have expected. Affection. He enfolded her in a hug that made him feel content and restless at the same time. Holding her felt good. But he wanted so much more.

She pulled back after a moment and looked up at him.

"What was that for?" he asked, not ready to let her go yet.

"Been dying to do that since you walked into the coffee shop," she said.

Then she stepped back, gave Aimee a little wave, and disappeared into the train station.

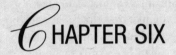

CHAPTER SIX

Kiera lay in bed staring at her ceiling Monday night.

Just as she'd done the night before.

During the day she'd been able to get into her work and not think about Zach. Then she'd made dinner with Maya and Sophie, and they'd spent time working on some new costumes and props for the martial arts exhibition at Maya's studio.

But now, in bed, in the dark, all alone... she couldn't stop thinking about him.

That was in part because she had a pretty good crush going. It was also in part because he'd texted her last night.

Sweet dreams, Princess. That was all he'd sent, but it had made her smile and had kept her awake thinking about him for nearly an hour.

She'd missed seeing him today. She'd met him two days ago, and she already missed seeing him. She'd also hugged him last night. She'd wanted to after learning about his sister Josie. But there had also been something in how he looked at her and how he made her feel that made it impossible to resist.

And now she missed him.

She'd been waiting for him to text her for the past hour. She knew he was working tonight and had no idea when he'd be home. But it was now after ten, and she really wanted him to text.

So she texted him instead.

I thought you should know that Aimee told me about Josie.

Kiera wasn't sure that was the best thing to lead off with, but she wasn't a small-talk kind of girl. She didn't think Zach was the type for trivialities either.

She waited a long time for a response. So long that she figured he was either still at work or asleep. Or, worse, that she'd brought something up that he didn't want to talk about.

She set her phone down on her bedside table and rolled to face away from it and closed her eyes, trying to think about anything but the hot EMT she was missing after only two days.

Her phone dinged nearly three minutes later. She sat up and scrambled to grab it, knocked it to the floor, and fumbled around in the dark before finally picking it up and swiping her thumb across the screen. Her heart was pounding simply being connected to Zach via their phones. She was in so much trouble.

I'm amazed. She hasn't talked about Josie to anyone, even her therapist. Thank you for being someone she can talk to.

That made Kiera's heart ache. Of course it was something hard to talk about, but she hadn't realized what a big deal it was for Aimee to have opened up.

I'm very sorry for your loss.

Me too.

She hesitated over the next words she wanted to type. But her thumbs moved in spite of her trepidation. *Want to tell me about it?*

Maybe he wouldn't. Maybe he would…

I thought I knew her. And I really thought she told me everything. I found out that she'd dropped out of school a year ago and had been with the band for two years. I never heard anything about it.

Kiera licked her lips. Oh boy. Texting was easier than talking. But this was still pretty involved stuff. *Why do you think she didn't tell you?* she asked anyway.

I wish I knew.

Because she thought you would have tried to stop her? Kiera wasn't sure how she knew that's what he would have done, but she did. He thought he knew best with Aimee. There was no reason to believe he hadn't been the same with his other sister.

Probably was his eventual reply.

Why? She held her breath waiting for his answer. She knew she was pushing. But he could end the conversation any time he wanted to. That was the beauty of texting. There was an off button. The thing was, she never pushed other people for information or details or emotions. And yet here she was, pushing Zach. And really wanting to know more about him.

She was going to be a teacher.

Ah. There were definitely some things about Zach that were very easy to understand. He had never hidden or downplayed the fact that he was a fixer. Maybe he thought the people he was closest to should be fixers too.

And that's a more important job than being a musician? she asked.

There was a long pause.

I thought it was, he finally said.

And she knew you thought so.

I'm sure. I was very proud of her.

Kiera was sure that everyone in Zach's life knew exactly how he felt about everything. She didn't know what else to say.

You still there? he asked after several long moments.

Her heart pounded. She could pretend that she'd fallen asleep. She could get out of the conversation without having to actually say anything meaningful. Or awful. Which was just as likely.

But she couldn't do that. So she said honestly, *I kind of want to hug you again right now.*

She waited.

And waited.

Zach?

Just calculating how long it would take me to get from your place to work tomorrow.

His answer was hot and sweet and funny at the same time.

Grinning, she typed, *You're coming over?*

I suddenly have an urge to be hugged. In real life. By you. Naked.

Her whole body responded to *Naked*.

I've been telling myself not to push, he added a moment later.

He hadn't been pushing? He'd completely taken over her thoughts and made her heart pound with a simple smile. What would happen if he did start pushing? Zach

Ashley was the type of guy to go all in. He was laid back and good humored and charming, but it didn't take long to realize he was also intense and focused, and he didn't hold back.

I don't know if I'm ready for you, she told him honestly.

Actually she did know. She wasn't. For a woman who had held herself back and avoided deep involvements, an all-in guy like Zach was the last person she should be messing with. There was no casual, superficial, just-for-fun option with Zach.

I know. That's why I'm not already there.

Instead of trying to talk her into it or reassure her that it would all be fine, he'd admitted that what he wanted was…more. And acknowledged that it might be too much for her.

The butterflies in her stomach woke up. She just wasn't sure if they were swooping around in excitement or panic. She was learning there was a very fine line between the two. *Come over anyway.* But after typing that, instead of the send key, she hit the delete key seventeen times. It wasn't just the sex with Zach she wasn't ready for. Actually she was feeling quite ready for that. It was the everything else.

You've had one-night stands before, right? she typed instead.

Yes.

And short-term, casual affairs? Not that she wanted to know all the details of his love life.

Can't say I have. One night or long term. The one-nights were only in the first three months after Josie died. It's been three months of nothing now.

One-night stands only since his sister died. That was

telling. He'd told her the first night that he couldn't make anyone else pancakes.

Finally she typed in, *Did you always want to be an EMT?*

Trying to distract me?

Trying to find a safer topic.

Because you're afraid I'm going to end up on your front porch?

She hesitated over her answer for a second. But she said honestly, *Because I'm about to beg you to show up on my front porch.*

Almost a minute went by. Then her phone dinged with, *I wanted to be an EMT since I was fourteen and in a car accident myself.*

He was moving on to the new topic. She felt relieved and disappointed at the same time. She frowned. *Car accident? Were you hurt?*

Badly. Would have died if not for the guy in the car we hit.

She sucked in a breath. Zach could have died?

What happened? You okay to talk about it?

Of course.

She smiled slightly and shook her head.

I was with my basketball coach. We were on back roads on our way to a basketball clinic I'd been invited to. My coach swerved to miss a deer and went into the other lane just as a truck came around the bend. We collided head-on.

Kiera covered her mouth with her hand.

The rest of his answer took some time in coming.

My coach was killed instantly. I had a piece of metal stuck through my abdomen. The guy in the other car was really banged up too. His leg was bleeding. I can still remember that his entire pant leg was soaked. But I didn't know how bad that was.

He came to the car and saw what was going on with me. Said he was an EMT. He examined my wound and said that we had to put pressure on it or I was going to bleed out.

We were two miles from the nearest house. But he couldn't leave me. He had already called 911 but they were ten minutes out.

He got in the car with me and held pressure on my wound and talked to me and kept me awake and calm.

By the time the ambulance reached us, he'd lost too much blood himself. He died on the way to the hospital.

Kiera felt the tears stinging her eyes as she reread the story a second time.

Someone had died saving Zach's life. Someone had sacrificed for him. And not just someone—an EMT. That all made perfect sense.

And now you're determined to do whatever you can to save anyone who needs you, she typed, feeling incredible affection for the man on the other end.

See, I'm not so hard to understand.

No, he wasn't. She was, however, pretty sure he was very hard to get over.

* * *

Zach loved this feeling. He barely recognized it—hadn't felt it in a long while—but he was pretty sure it was optimism.

He took the steps to Kiera's front porch two at a time and rang the bell, unable to help the huge grin on his face.

Aimee was out of the house, without any threatening or begging or bribing on his part. And she was hanging out with Kiera, the girl who had made Aimee smile, the girl who had kissed him as if her mouth had been made for his, the girl he'd been thinking about nearly nonstop over the past five days.

How was it possible he was this drawn to her?

Kiera pulled the door open a moment later.

Zach's heart missed a good three beats.

The soft, tan fabric of the dress she wore tonight clung to her breasts, stomach, and hips, bared one shoulder, and was cinched at the waist with a wide brown leather belt. The skirt hit at midthigh, leaving several inches of smooth skin between it and the top of the knee-high brown leather boots. Tonight all that skin was a sweet peach color instead of gold. Her face was devoid of any makeup, and her hair was pulled up on top of her head with curls spilling to her shoulder blades.

"Zach?"

She looked puzzled. Probably because he hadn't said anything, or blinked, in nearly a minute.

"You look..." He wasn't sure exactly how to describe how her outfit made him feel. He was surprised to find he was as attracted to her in this ensemble as he was to her in blue jeans. That didn't seem like him. "Amazing."

She glanced down at her outfit. When she looked up again, he saw she was blushing. "You're early again. We were trying on our costumes."

He grinned. "I'm going to keep being early. All kinds of interesting things go on before I show up."

She stepped back and gestured him inside. "Maya's studio is having an exhibition next week. Everyone dresses in costume for it. We were just putting finishing touches on ours tonight."

He stepped through the doorway, close enough to find that, no matter what she wore, she smelled the same. And the scent still made his cock ache.

"You meant to be out of this outfit before I showed up?" he asked.

She nodded.

"Then I'm especially glad I got here early." He stopped, nearly on top of her, loving that she didn't back up even an inch.

In fact, she bit her bottom lip, then leaned in and gave him a hug. Again. He wasn't sure why her hugging surprised him, but it did. He wrapped his arms around her as well, loving the feel of her against him.

"You don't seem like the hugging type," he said against the top of her head. Which seemed strange considering she'd climbed into his lap and kissed him the first day they'd met. But hugging was different somehow.

He felt her head move against his chest. "You're right. I'm not."

He squeezed her. "Well, I like it."

She sighed. "Me too."

"And I like hugging you in this outfit especially." He ran his hand over the silky bare skin of her shoulder and upper back.

She looked up at him, her arms still around his waist. "Well, if you like this, maybe I'll be able to talk you into picking up a sword after all."

"A sword, huh?" he asked, the idea not seeming as crazy as he would have expected. "I could probably get into some pillaging and plundering."

Was it a coincidence that those two words had never crossed his mind in his life before he'd met Kiera, and now they had occurred to him twice? He didn't think so.

She looked surprised. "Pillaging and plundering?"

"Isn't that what pirates do?"

She grinned. "You hear swords and go to pirates right away. That's interesting."

"Interesting? How so?"

"Knights also use swords traditionally. I would have thought you'd go for the nobler of the sword-wielding men. What with your hero complex and all."

Huh. He would have too. "Maybe I'm intrigued by the idea of being the bad boy."

"Since you've never been one?"

No. He never had. Not once. "Maybe."

And did warrior princesses go for the knight type or the bad-boy pirate deep down?

His attention went to her mouth. Her gaze dropped to his lips.

He really wanted her to go for the heroic EMT type who knew nothing about swords and hadn't dressed up like a pirate, or anything else, since he was nine.

Zach leaned in and kissed her, but he kept his hands on her back rather than letting them roam to all the places they wanted to. He also kept the kiss lips-only. Or tried to. That only lasted for a few seconds. Kiera was having none of the chaste-kiss stuff. She opened her mouth and stroked her tongue against his, making some of those amazing sounds that had haunted him over the past few nights.

They parted when voices from the other room infiltrated the lusty haze around him.

He let go of her and she stepped back, smiling at him. "You coming in, or should I go get Aimee?"

"Anyone else dressed in costume in there?" he asked lightly.

"Yep."

"Then I've gotta come in." He wanted to see the other costumes. And that was the craziest thing to occur to him in some time.

"Okay." That seemed to please her, and she started down a short hallway off to the left, her boots clomping on the hardwood. "This way."

The dress molded to her ass too, and as his eyes focused lower, he wanted to run his tongue along the creases at the backs of her knees. He couldn't remember ever having had that particular, and very specific, urge before.

"What's the exhibition for?" he asked as he followed her.

"At Maya's martial arts studio, new students come and sign up for classes. She does it every year right after school starts. Costumes are required. Even for the adults."

"You've been making costumes all afternoon?"

Zach tried to picture Aimee sitting around and stitching. As far as he knew, his sister believed clothes magically showed up in the mall, waiting for her and her credit card to rescue them.

"Just touching Sophie's and mine up," Kiera said. "And making Aimee's."

He stepped through the arched doorway into their dining room. Or what would have been the dining room in any other person's house. Zach looked around, momentarily speechless. One wall was a huge picture window. But that was the most normal thing about the room. The gigantic old-fashioned dining table in the center of the space was covered in fabrics in every color of the rainbow, and three sewing machines. Instead of dishes, the massive china hutch across the room held crowns and helmets, hats and tiaras. The wall to his left was covered in hooks that held leather loops attached to a variety of weapons, including knives, swords, hammers, lances, axes, and bows. But as the sight of garments hanging from the chandelier and the half-naked mannequins around the room sank in, her words also penetrated fully.

Making Aimee's. As in Aimee's costume.

No one else was in the room at the moment, and Zach wondered what these girls were getting Aimee into—literally. And where. "Aimee's got a costume for Maya's exhibition?"

"Of course," Kiera said.

She'd stepped to the other side of the table so that the wide surface, covered with lace, thread, scissors, pencils, and a few things Zach couldn't identify, was between them.

He sighed. "You're getting my sister into cosplay, Princess? Really?"

Kiera shrugged. "She was already into it, as in interested and knowledgeable. Now we're giving her the tools and opportunity."

"You," he said simply.

"Excuse me?"

"*You* are giving her the tools and opportunity. You said *we*." He followed her around the table, stepping over what looked to be green suede and a strip of red gauzy stuff.

Kiera stepped back as he got closer. "Sophie and Maya definitely helped. I can't make anything without them."

"But it was your idea," Zach said. "And it's you who knows that this isn't exactly what I expected—"

"Zach! Hi!"

His heart thumped hard in his chest at the sound of his sister's voice and, more specifically, the excitement in her voice. He didn't care what they'd been doing here tonight if it put *that* tone in her voice. He turned with a smile—that quickly died. If he had passed the girl in front of him on the street, he never would have recognized her as his sister.

Aimee's hair had been pulled back and covered with a wig of straight jet-black hair. She wore a long black dress under a dark-red cape, and an enormous pendant hanging from a silver chain around her neck. Silver earrings hung from her ears, and her hands were adorned with a multitude of rings. But most striking of all was the makeup.

Her face had been painted. Her skin was practically white, and her lips were a dark red that was nearly black. Her eyes looked huge, the lashes long and spiky. Purple, red, and blue makeup swirled from her eyelids out and up to her temples in dramatic swooshes.

"What do you think?" Her crimson smile was bright as she twirled for him. "Isn't it amazing?"

That was one word. "You look…incredible." That was one of those words that could mean "very good" or "very bad," wasn't it?

"They've invited me to Maya's exhibition. I'm going like this."

He nodded, not sure what to say really. More than the lashes that were three times longer than usual and the blood-red fake fingernails that he'd just now noticed, the most prominent feature in the whole ensemble was the glow of happiness. No makeup could disguise the fact that she was nearly giddy in the costume. She looked…great, actually.

Gone were the dark circles. The pale skin was now de-liberate. There was no frown, no pinched lips, no I-didn't-wash-my-hair-today messy bun, no faded T-shirt and sweatpants.

"Who are you supposed to be?" He finally managed to get past the tightness in his throat. "You know I don't know all of this stuff."

"Quinn. I'm a witch," she said with a grin.

He didn't need to ask where Quinn was from.

"Can I talk to you for a minute?" He felt Kiera grab his sleeve and pull.

He followed, only because he didn't know exactly what else to say or do.

She stepped through a swinging door, and Zach found himself in the kitchen. Kiera let go of him and turned to face him. "Just wanted to give you a breather before you said something you couldn't take back. She feels good, and she's having fun. Don't get upset about this, okay?"

Wow. Zach stared at her, feeling the rumblings of lust deep in his gut. The flash of emotion in her eyes was a turn-on and made him think of fiery warrior princesses again. He wanted her badly. Even though he didn't know what she was talking about.

"Excuse me?"

"You looked on the verge of saying something stupid out there," she said. "I know you're surprised to see her like that, but you need to think before you react."

She was feeling protective. But was she being protective of his sister, or of him? Either way, it made him want her even more.

She was right. He hadn't known how to react to Aimee. But he did know what to do with Kiera. He took her upper arms and walked her backward until her spine was against the wall next to the range. And then he kissed her.

It took only two seconds for her to arch against him, wrap her arms around his neck, and part her lips for him.

He kissed her with a strange combination of happiness, gratitude, and frustration. None of this was exactly what he wanted, and yet... it was. His sister was in head-to-toe costume, but she was happy. Kiera was a cosplaying gamer girl, but she made his heart pound.

After several long, delicious moments, he pulled back, still holding her against the wall, staring down at her.

"Thank you," he said roughly.

She looked up at him, and her surprised expression melted into a smile. "That's better."

He couldn't help but chuckle. "The kissing is better than putting my foot in my mouth with my sister?"

"Definitely." She gave a little shrug. "But the kissing is better than almost anything."

When it came to Kiera, he couldn't argue that. He'd liked kissing since he'd first done it in junior high, but there was something about kissing this woman that was different. Every kiss was an I-could-just-kiss-you-all-night kiss. He'd never had those before, but that was exactly how he felt. He wanted more, for sure, but even if there had been a soft horizontal surface and no other people around, he would have spent hours simply kissing her first. It was always just that good.

"Well, if you're going to kiss me every time I'm about to say something to piss Aimee off, you're going to be a busy woman."

Kiera didn't look shocked. "You do seem to have a tendency to be a little controlling," she said, with a note in her voice that told him she didn't think there was anything *little* about it.

"I often think I know best," he admitted.

Kiera lifted an eyebrow.

"Because I often do know best," he said.

She shook her head. "Wow."

"For instance, having Aimee spend time with you was one of the best decisions I've ever made." He meant that wholeheartedly. He had made some bad decisions where his family was concerned, for sure. But introducing Aimee and Kiera hadn't been one of them.

"So you're not upset about the costume and makeup?"

"It's a positive step—it got Aimee out of the house and interacting with other people and smiling. That is important to me, and I'm grateful to you."

Kiera worried her bottom lip between her teeth.

"But she can't walk around in that costume all the time," he went on. "She also has to start interacting in her regular world again."

"Relationships are about compromise," Kiera said. "If you want her to go to dinner with your parents and smile and participate in the conversation, then you need to let her do this stuff too. Sometimes in costume."

He sighed. He wasn't much of a compromiser, he could admit. People made poor choices all the time, and he cleaned up after them—drug use, drunk driving, thinking their fists were stronger than a brick wall. He saw it on every shift.

But there was something about Kiera—in addition to her eyes and lips and breasts and sweetness—that pulled at him. It was an urge to trust her, to turn it over, to not have to make every damned decision all the damned time.

"Fine. I have no problem with her going to the exhibition. As Quinn."

Kiera's eyes softened. "You remembered her name."

He moved closer and bent so his forehead rested against hers. "Yes, Princess Kirenda, I remembered her name."

"You know what would really go a long way with Aimee?" Kiera asked, running her hands up his chest to link her fingers behind his neck.

Zach moved to put his nose against her temple, drawing in her scent. "What's that?"

"If you came to the exhibition to watch. It would show that you're supportive."

Zach thought about how great it had been having Kiera at his basketball game, and her words came back to him: *I liked watching you like it.* And suddenly it wasn't just Aimee he wanted to see in her element.

"Will you be there?" he asked Kiera.

"Yes."

"In this outfit?"

She laughed lightly. "You like this one?"

"So much," he said with enthusiasm.

"I have others too."

"Maybe we can have a fashion show sometime." He bent farther to put his lips against her ear.

She shivered. "We could do that."

He ran his lips lightly down the side of her throat. "I'm in."

She arched into him and tipped her head, giving him more surface area to kiss. He licked along her collarbone.

"I know I really would love to see you with a sword," she said, slightly breathless.

Zach's first thought was that he wanted her *very* breathless. "I can rent something and be in your bedroom in thirty minutes." He almost couldn't believe he'd just agreed to that. But where was the bad? Dressed as a pirate to turn the cosplaying princess on? If he eventually got her naked, he could play along with a fantasy or two. If he got to bind her hands with a black silk tie, he might even throw in a yo-ho-ho.

She let her head fall back, and he kissed his way up the center of her throat to her lips.

"I was talking about the exhibition," she said, just before he pressed his lips to hers.

He was sinking into the kiss when her words fully registered. He lifted his head. "You want me to dress up at the exhibition? In public?"

"I do," she admitted. "Though in private too."

He looked at her flushed cheeks, her breasts rising and falling, and her parted lips. "You're trying to seduce me *into* a costume, and I'm trying to seduce you *out* of one."

She gave him a smile. "Really?"

"You didn't realize I was trying to seduce you?"

"I mean me. I've never seduced someone before."

He really liked that. "I knew the moment I saw you that you could make a Trekkie out of me."

Her smile was bright, but she wrinkled her nose. "*Star Trek*?"

"No? *Star Wars*?"

"*Galactic Renegades*."

Looked like he had something else to add to his to-watch list. "Well, whatever. If anyone could get me into a costume, it'd be you."

"Just for a night?" she asked, arching into him again.

He slid his hands to her ass, aware that the bare skin of

her thighs was only a few inches lower. "I have a feeling one night would never be enough."

Her eyes grew warmer. And Zach realized that if geek-iness was basically being passionate about something, he was going to be getting very geeky over this woman.

"It would mean a lot to Aimee," Kiera said again.

"What about you?"

She tipped her head. "What about me?"

"Would it mean a lot to you?" It would take a lot to impress a girl like Kiera. Wielding a sword might be worth a try.

"Seriously? You're considering it?"

"Maybe. I don't get the gaming, but this is hands-on stuff," he said, bunching the fabric of her skirt in one hand while sliding the other lower, to the curve where the back of her thigh met her ass. "That's how I like things."

"So you'd play pirate with me as long as you can be hands-on with the whole thing?"

There was a very sexy note in her tone now.

He had to admit that the idea of getting into a character who did whatever he wanted, took whatever he wanted, and said whatever he wanted without worrying about con-sequences sounded damned tempting. "You think you can handle my pirate side, Princess?"

"Oh, I think I'll be okay."

"Let's find out."

"You're on." She gave him a smile, her eyes sparkling.

"And as for your part of this compromise," he said, "you come to my game again Sunday and then out with me and my friends afterward."

Kiera straightened. "You're compromising with *Aimee*, not me."

"All relationships require compromise. Or so I've been told."

"Our relationship is fake."

"Is that right?" He pressed closer. "Doesn't feel fake to me. Feels like I have my arms full of a very real woman who is making me feel some very real feelings."

"Like lust?" she asked.

"Lust and fascination are both very real feelings." In fact, other than frustration, anger, and guilt, those two emotions were the strongest ones he'd felt since Josie had died. He liked these much more. And he intended to keep feeling them. Kiera was the key to that.

"Okay, I'll come," she agreed. "But your team needs to be the ones without their shirts again."

He grinned. "It might cost me a couple pitchers of beer, but I'll see what I can get the guys to do."

He was bringing a girl out with his friends. He never did that. And she was a gamer girl geek on top of it.

This would be interesting.

It was common to rehash calls when they all got together over beers. Many of his buddies were EMTs and firefighters, but he knew several docs and cops too. They loved to talk work and try to one-up each other. The tales in emergency management were a lot like fishing tales—they grew and grew the further from the pond they got. Most of that would probably horrify Kiera.

Maybe this wasn't a great idea. His friends weren't dicks, but he was certain that the scene at the convention center had been the closest any of them had ever gotten to cosplaying, and he wouldn't put it past them to make some disparaging remarks about some of the things they'd seen. A few of his friends probably played Call of Duty, but he doubted many would consider themselves gamers. Troy knew a lot about the movie franchises, though. Zach would have to be sure Troy spent time talking with Kiera so she didn't feel left out as they played pool and discussed their fantasy football picks.

"You don't have to stay long," he said. "We'll have some pizza and say hi to everyone, and we can head out."

"Will Aimee come with you, or should I pick her up?"

"No Aimee," he said. "Just you and me."

Kiera's eyes widened in surprise. And Zach had to admit it was a bit of a surprise to him too. But he wanted a date with Kiera.

Before she could say anything, the back door banged open, and Kiera jerked back. They both turned as Maya came in, her arms laden with grocery sacks.

Maya looked up. "Oh, hey! Sorry, the wind caught the door." She moved to the center island and dropped the bags.

"Uh, no problem," Kiera said, sliding her skirt down and smoothing it.

The other woman swung the door shut with her foot. "I might have gotten too much. But better safe than sorry when it comes to cupcakes, right?"

"Definitely." Kiera looked up at him. "Maya went out for snacks while Sophie and I worked on Aimee's costume."

Maya grinned at him. "I'm the weapons expert. When it comes to making dresses, I mostly just offer moral support. And junk food."

When Maya turned to put something in the fridge, Zach caught sight of a jagged scar that ran from just below her jaw down her neck to the sleeve of her leather vest. It was covered by her vest and top for several inches but it reappeared at the top of her arm and went to her elbow. Her short dark hair did nothing to hide it, and it was clear she wasn't worried about someone seeing it when she chose her clothing.

Just then Aimee and Sophie came into the kitchen, Aimee still dressed as Quinn and Sophie in a long blue sparkly dress with a tiara nestled in her blond curls. Zach got out of the way as they started going through the bags and Kiera moved to the cupboards to get dishes.

Five minutes later the kitchen island was covered with cheese and crackers, tortilla chips and salsa, fruit and mini cupcakes, and everyone was talking and laughing and eating.

Zach stayed to the side, a plate of crackers and cheese in hand, observing the women.

The three who lived here were clearly close and comfortable with one another, and Aimee seemed to fit right in. These women were older than Aimee by quite a bit, but it was still positive interaction with people in real life. He wasn't going to be picky. Especially when Aimee was grinning the way she was. He felt such relief at that, he almost couldn't describe it.

But as happy as he was to watch his sister laughing and talking, he couldn't keep his eyes off Kiera. For a number of reasons. The way the dress moved over her body. The way she ate the frosting off her cupcakes, dipping it off with her finger and then licking her finger clean—an action that made his jeans fit a little tighter—but didn't eat any of the cake. The way she looked at Aimee with clear affection.

He liked her. A lot. And he wanted her. A lot. And

more, he wanted to know everything about her. When she'd texted him Monday night, he'd been surprised. But, in spite of Josie being the topic of conversation, he was thrilled she'd initiated it. He'd been the one to text her first both Tuesday and Wednesday nights. After dialing and then disconnecting before the call went through. He fucking hated texting, and once he broke her of the habit, he wanted never to do it again. But if this was all she'd give him right now, he'd make it work.

Speaking of texting...

He pulled his phone out and typed in, *How did Maya get injured?*

Kiera jumped as her phone vibrated on the counter next to her elbow. She looked at the message, then up at him. She smiled. Then set her cupcake down and replied.

She was a cop. Got cut up and burned pretty badly doing a rescue at a car accident.

He wondered if he'd ever run into her at a scene before. *Was a cop?*

They put her behind a desk after she was through rehab. She couldn't take not being active and in the field so left the force and started her studio. Martial arts, weaponry work, fitness, and self-defense.

Zach looked over at Maya. She was kick-ass too.

She's not self-conscious about it at all. She talks about the injury with the kids in her classes all the time, Kiera told him.

What about Sophie? he asked.

She owns a little hole-in-the-wall theater. She's a playwright and actress.

Zach watched Sophie for a moment. She was much softer-spoken than Maya and seemed more of an observer.

It surprised him that she was an actress. Weren't they usually more outgoing and dramatic?

Immediately on the heels of that thought, however, was the realization that he had no idea what he was talking about. His sisters had been good students, obedient children, friendly, well liked, successful. His mother had been a dynamo in both her social and her volunteering circles. The women he was attracted to were outgoing, beautiful, social, sports fans, and very much regular girls.

Or at least that's how it had seemed.

The reality was that Josie had been playing in a band instead of going to college, and had been on the verge of moving to LA without a word to her family. His mother had a drinking problem and hadn't had a clue about her oldest daughter's activities, and had crawled into bed with a bottle rather than take care of her youngest daughter after Josie died.

Now he also had to wonder what secrets and lies had been behind the cute smiles and big breasts of the women he'd dated. He'd never gotten close enough for long enough to find out, but clearly his delusion that the only people in need were his patients had been exactly that…another lie. He was obviously not as good as he'd thought when it came to really knowing the people he was close to.

There were no lies with Kiera, though. The sweet introvert, who preferred time with her computer to real-life interactions and knew nothing about sports, was making him think twice about everything.

He felt like hugging her. Kissing her and doing a bunch of other stuff too, with her skirt hiked up around her waist and her boots digging into his ass, but definitely also hugging. He wanted to lose himself in this woman who was sure of herself and embraced who she was. And let him see all of it without apology.

She was a relief. Plain and simple. A relief he wanted to take to bed...for about a month straight.

CHAPTER SEVEN

She should not sleep with Zach Ashley.

Kiera lay in bed that night thinking about those seven words. One corner of her brain knew they were true. But it was the only part of her body that agreed. Everything else was all tingly and jumpy and let-me-at-him.

She rolled over and stared at the clock. Damn Zach for keeping her up late, all hot and bothered, mooning over the things he'd said. Damn him for wrecking her sleep with just a few hot looks and hot kisses and those hands. She could still feel his touch on the back of her thigh.

He was so...unexpected.

And she wanted to help him. Which was making her crazy. She didn't fix other people.

But tonight, watching him watch Aimee in the kitchen, Kiera had realized that Aimee wasn't the one who needed healing after her sister's death. Zach did. And that meant Kiera should avoid getting in any deeper with him.

Then another thought occurred, one even worse than the

ones about getting involved and helping Zach: *I wonder what he would do if I showed up on his doorstep right now.*

Of course, it would actually be in thirty minutes, after she got to the train, rode it downtown, and then got to his apartment down by the wharf. Which she wasn't doing at midnight. Not even for a booty call with Zach Ashley.

He might come to her, though...

She picked up her phone and pulled up his number. She lay staring at it for nearly two minutes. She just wanted to connect with him somehow. She wanted him to know she was thinking about him. And yeah, she wanted him to be thinking about her.

So she'd text him. That was enough. She wasn't *really* interested in having a phone conversation. It just kind of felt that way. For some reason.

Kiera considered her message. If he was already asleep, then she wouldn't be bothering him. He'd just see the message in the morning. Which meant it needed to be something innocuous.

You still awake?

There. That was definitely vague and harmless. She hit send before she could rethink it.

In the next few seconds, she realized she was *not* going to ask him to come over for a booty call. That would be ridiculous. And if he said no, she'd be crushed. And if he said yes, she'd like him even more.

Yeah, this was a bad idea.

You okay?

Her heart melted a little that his first response was concern for her.

You weren't sleeping?

Doesn't matter. I'm here anytime.

I was just thinking about you, she told him honestly.

Maybe I should come over and ensure you're not thinking about anyone else for the rest of the night. Or tomorrow. Or ever.

Oh boy.

Her thumbs hovered over the *Y*, the *E*, and the *S*. And the exclamation point.

Then a thought occurred to her. Zach was a hands-on guy. He probably didn't like texting, but he was doing it because she wanted to. She also knew it wouldn't last. He was going to want to get real-life with her...and she was going to let him. So maybe she needed to show him how fun texting really could be while she had a chance.

What I'm thinking about is you lying in bed, in the dark, thinking of me, she said.

Accurate, he sent back.

Naked.

She held her breath waiting for his response.

How did you know?

Her breath whooshed out.

Letting my imagination run, she told him.

I'm calling you right now to tell you all about what my imagination has been doing to me.

No calling. She wanted to draw this out. *Text only. Tell me what you've imagined.*

I want to hear your voice.

She decided to be honest with him...and to show him how this was going to go all at the same time. *I'll come too quickly if you talk me through it. Just type.*

There was a longer pause before he responded, and Kiera pictured his expression, a combination of surprise and heat.

In my imagination, the princess of Leokin is a dirty talker. Please tell me that's true.

Definitely true. How about you?

Are you asking if I will, at some point, say something like "I want to lick you from head to toe and make you come on my tongue?" Yes. Definitely.

Heat slid through her, settling low and deep. She moved her legs against the sheets restlessly as she typed, *Pretty good. What else do you have?*

Pretty good? You prefer "I want to lick you from head to toe and suck on your clit until you beg me to make you come?"

Holy...She was possibly in over her head. Already. *Yeah. That was better.*

Okay, big talker, how about you?

She took a breath. She had never typed the word *cock* or anything related into a text message in her life. But now that word and many others were clamoring in her mind. She channeled a little of her inner warrior princess who faced everything head-on with confidence and typed, *Wrap your hand around your cock.*

It felt deliciously dirty to even type the word *cock*, knowing that Zach was going to be reading it.

Done.

Kiera grinned. *Now imagine me on my knees next to you, my mouth open just above it.*

Done. And your gorgeous ass is toward my head, and you're leaning over just enough so I can see how wet you are.

Her eyes widened. And she'd thought *she* would be in control here?

She typed, *But you can't touch. You can only look or I won't get any closer.*

You don't want me to slide my fingers inside you, deep and slow?

Kiera's heart was thumping, and she became aware she was breathing hard. She squeezed her legs together. *I want to take you in my mouth first. Lick you and suck you. Take you almost to the edge.*

I'm on the fucking edge right now.

Ah, he was losing a little of his cool. She liked that. *So let me lick you. Just for a little bit. Move your hand and imagine my mouth. Hot and wet.*

You're pushing me, Princess.

I know. She hit send with what she was sure was a mischievous grin. *I want you to lose control.*

Not in your mouth. I won't come until I'm inside you.

She hesitated. Did he mean literally? He wouldn't come tonight while they were sexting? Oh, that wasn't an option.

I've got my vibrator right here but I'm not turning it on until you come.

It was in her bedside table. Close enough. Kiera sat up and stripped her pajama top and shorts off, tossing them to the side. She was all in here, and he'd better be too.

Run your finger over your clit.

She wanted to be the boss here. But if he insisted...

She ran the pad of her middle finger over the bundle of nerves. The touch shot a current of electric need through her. She circled and pressed a few times, the coil of craving winding tighter.

You're good at this, she texted back.

Damn right I am.

She really did love his cockiness. At times.

Stroke your

Her message was cut off by the next one he sent. *Your*

mouth is like heaven. Straddle me so I can get my tongue on you. Let's do this together.

Her mind instantly moved her into the sixty-nine position with Zach, and she reached for the drawer holding her vibrator. She pulled her pink friend out and pushed the button to start the low hum.

I'm with you, she sent back.

Are your nipples hard? I swear I can still feel them against my palms from the other night.

The other night. Her nipples remembered him too. They tingled and tightened from that simple reminder.

Yes. She couldn't really elaborate on that, could she?

I wish I could suck on them. Pinch one for me.

Okay, so *he* could elaborate.

She did as he asked, moaning at the sensation and suddenly wishing he were there doing it instead. Maybe he'd come over after all...

Her phone dinged with another message. *Are you doing it? Tell me how it makes you even wetter for me.*

On second thought, if he were here in person, she'd be a melted puddle of goo already.

I was already wet. But I'm doing it.

Now rub the vibrator on your clit. Imagine it's my finger.

She moved her hand to pick up the vibrator. She had to keep a hand free for the phone and was now regretting the texting-and-not-calling thing. Still, she could practically hear his voice as she read his words. This wasn't going to last long.

Are you still stroking yourself? she asked. *Imagining my mouth or my hand?*

Both. You can't take me fully with your mouth. You have to use your hand too.

She sucked in a breath and turned the vibrator up.

But I told you I'm not coming this way. Ready for your ride?

She so was. *You mean, am I ready for the rogue pirate captain to pillage me?*

There was another long pause. Then he sent back, *No pirate captain tonight. No princess warrior. Just you and me, Kiera. The real you and me.*

She realized that she'd thrown the pirate in there for some distance. And he knew it. This was intense. She had as much distance as she could have and still be connected to him. And yet she was feeling overwhelmed.

She pulled in a deep breath, her body begging her to finish what they'd started. *Okay, the real you and me*, she typed back.

Slide the vibrator into that sweet pussy where I wish I could be. Imagine it's me filling you up, making you moan and come.

She did what he said, sliding the vibrator lower and into where she was aching.

Her eyes closed, and she imagined Zach there with her, his big hands gripping her hips, saying all these naughty things in that rough, low voice, heat in his eyes as he watched her take him in. She started climbing, the need tightening low and deep.

She fumbled for her phone, needing to know that he was there with her, as consumed by all this as she was. It took her forever to type with one thumb, and thankfully the auto-correct gods were on her side. *I'm almost there. Tell me you are too.*

Oh, I am, Princess. In my mind, you're gripping me hot and tight.

She let her eyes slide closed again for a moment, moving the vibrator in and out, but after only a few strokes, her phone buzzed. She opened her eyes to see, *Come for me, Kiera.*

There was no stopping it. The image of Zach coming at the same time spiraled her to completion. She let out a soft cry as pleasure rolled over her.

For a moment she lay motionless, with no sound other than the thundering of her heartbeat and the low hum of her vibrator. The can't-be-beat contentment of a great orgasm followed shortly after, and she almost laughed.

She wasn't sure she'd had that great an orgasm ever before, and this one had been via text.

She clicked the vibrator off and tossed it onto the bed beside her, both thumbs now free to text Zach back. *See? Technology isn't all bad.*

You just wait until I get you alone in person. Hands-on is always better.

Kiera felt goose bumps erupt over her entire body. She covered her eyes with one hand. Putting her thoughts and wants in writing was an intimate act. She hadn't really thought about that before. And he could keep those thoughts and wants and reread them again and again.

She quickly texted, *You better delete this whole conversation.*

Not on your life. I might just start at the top again before I go to sleep.

Kiera felt her cheeks burning, but she couldn't deny her smile. *No, just go to sleep. Good night.*

Good night, Princess. Thanks for the new dreams I'll be having tonight.

How could a guy be so naughty and sweet at the same time?

But as she started to reach for her phone charger, a thought occurred to her.

She could reread the conversation from the top again before she went to sleep too.

* * *

Saturday morning was bright and sunny. Almost as bright as the smile Aimee gave Kiera as she met her in front of Zach's building. He was at work, and Kiera and Aimee were headed to the coffee shop where Aimee was meeting her clan in person for the first time.

"How are you going to know who they are?" Kiera asked Aimee as they entered the busy shop a few minutes later.

Aimee looked around, then held her hand up over her head, her index finger and thumb extended in the shape of an *L* for *Leokin*. Two girls at a table across the room held their hands up with *L*'s.

Aimee smiled at Kiera. "Like that."

Kiera laughed, but she had to admit that her throat got a little tight too. Seeing the Leokin *L* used like that was surreal. It was the classic "loser" *L* that everyone knew from middle school, but the Leokin fandom had given the sign a new, positive meaning.

"But we know what everyone looks like. We've live-chatted in Leokin too."

Of course they had. Kiera wasn't sure why she hadn't thought about them using the cameras in their computers to chat face-to-face. Maybe because she'd never used hers. She still preferred the text-type chatting. Like texting with Zach. Or sexting. She felt her whole body grow warmer.

She was still able to recall every word of the sexting from three nights ago. Probably because she'd reread them all half a dozen times since.

Aimee pointed to the counter, indicating she was going to get some coffee before joining her new friends. The girls nodded, and Aimee and Kiera moved into the line. It was long but seemed to be moving steadily.

"Are you nervous?" Kiera asked.

"About meeting them? Not at all. Excited."

"Really? Not even a little?"

Aimee laughed. "I know them. I've seen their faces, heard their voices. I'm more comfortable with them than I am with anyone."

"No kidding." Kiera hadn't realized how close Aimee really felt to her clan.

"They know things about me no one else does," Aimee told her.

"Like what?" It was nosy, especially for Kiera, but she couldn't help it.

Aimee shrugged. "They know everything about me, really. I can talk to them about Zach and how he drives me nuts. And my parents."

Kiera's heart stuttered a little. "Things about your parents that Zach doesn't know?"

Aimee chewed on the inside of her cheek as she met Kiera's eyes. Kiera could tell that she was worried Kiera would tell Zach whatever it was.

"Just between us," Kiera said.

Aimee took a breath. "My mom's an alcoholic."

Kiera frowned. "Zach doesn't know?"

"He knows, but he thinks she's going to AA."

Kiera chose her words carefully. "I can't imagine Zach

wouldn't know she was drinking." She had never met a person more involved in other people's lives than Zach Ashley.

Aimee seemed surprised by Kiera's words, but finally she gave a little nod. "I think you're right. That he knows, I mean. But we don't talk about it."

They moved up in line, and Kiera thought about dropping it. But she couldn't. "Why not?"

"Because I don't want to make him feel bad," Aimee said. "He already feels bad about so much. If he knew Mom quit AA, and his attempt to get her sober didn't work, he'd be pissed. At himself. If he knew how much her drinking bothers me, he'd try to fix it. But there's no way for him to do that. Mom has to do it."

They moved up in line again, and Aimee took a deep breath before she went on. "Just like he can't make me stop missing Josie. It's just how it is. Yes, it hurts. But he can't change it so that frustrates him and makes him feel bad. And I don't like him feeling bad so I don't talk about this stuff with him."

Kiera's heart squeezed. Aimee was trying to protect Zach. She was trying to make things better for him too, at least in her mind.

"He feels bad that you don't leave your room and seem depressed and withdrawn," Kiera said.

For a second Aimee looked sad. "Yeah," she agreed. "Me moving in helped him with some of that, but I thought it would help more than it has."

Kiera frowned again. "What do you mean that moving in helped *him*?"

"Zach didn't like how things were at home after Josie died. Mom was drinking more, Dad was never home, so I just stayed in my room all the time and tried to avoid everything. Zach insisted that I move in with him. I agreed, because I knew that would help him."

"Because that would make him feel like he was doing something to fix things?" Kiera guessed.

Aimee nodded. "I mean, it did make things easier for me in some ways. But ultimately it still couldn't fix the problem—Josie being gone."

The line moved again, and Aimee began perusing the bakery case.

"I'm sorry about your mom," Kiera said. "I'm sure losing Josie was horrible for her."

Aimee nodded. "But she always drank. Even before Josie died. Sometimes it's Irish cream in her coffee or vodka in her orange juice. It's not like she passes out on the couch every night or anything. But she's tipsy a lot."

Kiera's heart ached. Aimee was right that it would have hurt Zach to think that his attempt to help had failed. She knew how hard it was to know someone you loved was doing things that would hurt them and that your influence wasn't enough to help them.

They moved up again. There were now only two people in front of them in line.

Aimee turned to her. "You can't tell Zach that my friends have been the reason I'm out and feeling better, okay?" she asked. "Or about Mom. I just want him to be happy too."

"I won't tell him," Kiera said. She felt a similar temptation to protect him. She wanted to wrap him up and keep him from the news of his mom's drinking. She wanted to see him smiling and happy and relieved that Aimee was doing better.

Kiera had kept herself out of other people's business so she wouldn't be hurt by their decisions. She now kind of wished Zach felt the same self-preservation instinct and that he wouldn't worry so much about everyone else.

"Zach thinks that I'm the reason you're getting out more," Kiera told Aimee. "So that's not really him helping you either, is it?"

Aimee gave her a smile that was far more mature than her seventeen years. "But he brought you to me, and he's the reason you're staying around. So indirectly he still feels responsible."

Kiera thought about that. "He's not the only reason I'm staying around."

Aimee smiled and leaned in to give her a quick hug. "Thanks. I'm glad to hear that."

Kiera hugged her back, but her stomach was in a knot as she finally placed her coffee order. She wasn't going to be around after their parents' party. That was the agreement. She and Zach were going to break up, and then it would seem that she really had been in all of this because of him.

By the time Aimee had picked up her cup of coffee and muffin from the end of the counter, a boy had joined the two girls at the table.

"He's cute," Kiera commented.

Aimee blushed. "That's Cody. And yeah, he is." She grinned at Kiera. "He's also a fifth-level wizard and is one of only six people to make it through the Dilirion Desert."

Kiera was impressed. "Well, I hope this meeting is everything you want it to be."

Aimee gave her another quick hug and then headed for her friends.

Kiera claimed a table by the window where she could

keep an eye on Aimee. She opened her laptop and prepared to work. But she couldn't focus. She couldn't keep her thoughts from Zach.

Not that it was a new problem. But since learning about his mom, she'd had the very unfamiliar urge to call him. To ask him how he was and what she could do to help. Kiera frowned. That was so outside her comfort zone she wasn't sure what to do with it. When Sophie and Maya wanted to talk about something, she listened. But they came to her. Now her fingers were itching with the desire to dial Zach's number. Not text him. But call him.

She shook her head and opened up her latest files, looking over graphics she'd done a couple of days ago. They weren't final and wouldn't be until she saw what Pete and Dalton were working on, but she had some details she could fill in no matter what they ended up doing.

Kiera finished one character, proud of her focus. She saved it and started to open the next, but the sound of someone's laughter pulled her attention from the screen. She looked up, recognizing Aimee's laugh.

Kiera's heart swelled. Aimee's face was bright, her smile huge, and she was leaning in closer to Cody, who had his arm over the back of her chair. The other girls seemed completely engaged in the conversation too, and Kiera found herself grateful to these three. She didn't know them, knew only that they were into Leokin, but they were making Aimee happy. And Kiera loved Aimee.

The thought was startling at first, but after only a second, Kiera realized it was true. She was proud of the woman Aimee was and the potential Kiera saw in her. She enjoyed time with Aimee, and, yes, she cared about her. She wanted her to be happy.

The fact that those three people could make her that obviously happy made Kiera care about them too.

That's how Zach feels about you.

That thought didn't startle her, however. She knew Zach was grateful to her for making Aimee happier. But Kiera wasn't concerned about Aimee. She was, however, concerned about Zach.

With a big breath, she picked up her phone. It would mean a lot to him if she called rather than texted. So with her fingers tingling with nervousness, she dialed his number.

Then hung up.

But it had rung once. *Dammit.* She'd panicked.

Her phone rang a moment later. It was Zach. Of course it was. He wouldn't not call back. She could let it go to voice mail, but then he'd worry. And probably leave work to come see what was wrong.

She answered quickly. "Hello?"

"Kiera?"

"Hi."

"Everything okay?"

She loved that he always asked that first. "Everything is great."

"Oh." He paused. "You called and hung up?"

"Yeah." She couldn't explain it, so she didn't even try.

"But everything is okay?"

She could picture him, poised for action, ready to take care of whatever she said was going on with her or Aimee. "Aimee and I are having a great time at the coffee shop, and I was just thinking about you and…thought I'd call."

She didn't know how this type of small talk went.

"I'm glad you did."

She could hear that he was relieved, and she smiled. "Sorry to worry you."

"Don't get me wrong, I love hearing your voice in the middle of my day, Princess. Just a first for us, you know?"

Kiera felt her smile grow. "Yeah, I know. I should have texted you a warning."

He chuckled, the sound low and rough in her ear, sending tingles down her body.

Suddenly she wanted to tell him something more. Something significant. Something that would show him that he was not only someone she could talk to, but someone she wanted to talk to. "So, um, Aimee and I were talking a little bit ago," she started. She now knew something about his parents, and she wanted to tell him something about hers. "She was saying—"

Suddenly she heard an alarm and then a muttered "Dammit" in her ear. "Princess, I have to go."

Right, he was at work. "Yeah, okay."

"I'm sorry... Shit. I'm sorry. I'll talk to you later?"

"Sure, yes, of course."

And then the phone line went dead.

Kiera sucked in a breath, staring at the phone screen. Wow, that had been close.

* * *

"We're gonna shoot around for a while," Troy said to Zach as their shift ended. "You sticking around?"

They'd put up a portable basketball hoop in the back parking lot, and it wasn't uncommon to find the EMTs there during lulls in the action or hitting the makeshift court for twenty minutes before heading home. They were often joined by other ER staff as well. It was a great way to unwind after a hard day or to keep the blood pumping in between calls. EMT work was unpredictable, and it seemed that either they had busy shifts with one call after another or they sat around on their asses wishing for something to happen.

Zach glanced up from tying his shoe. "I don't think so."

Troy stopped halfway out the door and looked Zach over. "You already showered?"

"Yep."

"You're not staying?"

Zach grinned. He knew Troy's "You sticking around?" hadn't been a sincere question. He'd fully expected Zach to join them. Zach always joined them. Hell, it was usually his idea.

But he had something better to do tonight.

"I've got a date," he told Troy. And he knew he was wearing a stupid, lovesick smile.

Troy definitely noticed. "A girl? Over basketball?"

Zach nodded.

"What time?" Troy asked.

There was no set time. Kiera didn't even know he was coming over. They were supposed to go out after his game tomorrow night. But he wanted to surprise her tonight. "As soon as I get there."

"So you could stick around another fifteen minutes," Troy said.

"I could. I'm not going to." Zach stood and slung his bag over his shoulder.

"Okay." Then Troy turned and yelled down the hallway. "Get your mittens, boys, hell's freezing over." He shot Zach a grin. "Have fun."

He fully intended to. In fact, he couldn't remember looking forward to something this much in a very long time.

Forty minutes later he was on Kiera's porch waiting for someone to answer the door. He shifted back and forth and considered, for the first time, that calling ahead might have been a good idea. He'd been excited to see her and hadn't thought about the possibility that she wouldn't be home. She loved to be on her computer, and her social calendar had revolved around Aimee this past week. But Aimee was out tonight, so he'd thought...Zach shook his head. What an ass. He'd been caught up in the idea of seeing Kiera, and the elation over the fact that Aimee was out with her friends. He'd also been caught up in the fact that Kiera had called him today. Called. Not texted.

Finally he heard movement inside, and the door swung open. Sophie stood in the doorway.

"Zach! Hi!" She was clearly surprised to see him, but she gave him a big smile.

"Hey, Sophie. Is Kiera home?"

"Yeah, we were just... Yeah, she's here."

Sophie moved back, and Zach stepped into the foyer. "Am I interrupting?"

She laughed. "Not really. She didn't say you were coming over."

"She didn't know. Thought I'd surprise her."

"Well, that would explain it."

"Does she like surprises?" Zach asked. He hadn't thought of that either.

Sophie looked up at him. "I think it's safe to say that Kiera isn't surprised very often. But I think you've been surprising her from the very beginning. And she definitely likes you. So I think you're okay." She paused, then added, "Thank you, Zach."

"What for?"

"Falling for one of my best friends and making her so happy," Sophie said. Then she turned and headed down the hallway. "Come on, we're in here."

Zach couldn't take that first step for a few seconds. He was making Kiera happy? He wanted that to be true with an intensity that startled him. But the other part... "Falling for one of my best friends." Was he falling for Kiera? He took a deep breath as Sophie disappeared into the dining room. He was standing in the foyer of the house of a woman who he hoped was in a sexy pirate slave costume in that dining room.

Yeah, he was falling for her.

He followed Sophie. He could hear Maya's voice and Kiera's laughter from the hallway, and when he stepped through the door, he saw they were sitting at the dining room table. Kiera was in a chair, her back to him, facing Maya. Maya was leaning in, doing something to Kiera's face.

Maya looked up at him, and her eyes widened. Kiera turned to see what had caught her friend's attention, and her eyes also went wide for a moment, just before she jumped to her feet, bumping into Maya and banging her knee on Maya's chair as she turned.

"Zach!"

And he would have greeted her, but his tongue seemed stuck to the roof of his mouth. Because she was, indeed, dressed up. And it was as something far sexier than a pirate slave. She was dressed as a sports fan.

Of course, with a Kiera flair. She wore a short black

skirt and a red tee that had been embellished with a black sparkly basketball. And rather than team face paint like the beer-guzzling guys tailgating on the weekends, she had another basketball shape made out of black and silver sparkly gems on one cheek.

But she was wearing his Sunday night basketball team's colors.

"Hey, Princess," he finally managed, his voice gruff. "You look great."

She looked down, then quickly up at him, her cheeks nearly as red as her shirt. She stepped around her chair as she started rambling. "We were just...I told them I was going to your game..." Her hand flew to her cheek and, much to Zach's dismay, she began peeling the tiny gems from her skin.

He crossed to her quickly and took her wrist, stopping her. "I've never seen anything hotter than you cosplaying for basketball as my own personal fanatic."

Kiera looked up at him, her lips parted as she took a deep breath. "We were just messing around."

"You weren't going to wear this tomorrow?"

"Maybe the shirt," she said quietly.

He looked down, taking in the whole ensemble up close. The sparkly basketball covered the center of the shirt, drawing even more of his attention to her chest. The red cotton top hugged her breasts, and the hem barely touched the top of the skirt. And he knew if she put her arms up to cheer, or to wrap them around his neck, it would show several inches of smooth skin. "I love this shirt."

"Yeah?"

"I'll give you anything you want if you wear this tomorrow."

"Anything, huh?"

There was a mischievous twinkle in her eyes now, and he knew she was relaxing.

"But we need to add a few sparkles," he said. He put the tip of his finger over her heart. "We need the number eleven right here."

"Why eleven?"

"That's my number." And did he want her marked as his? Fuck yeah. Especially if she was sitting in the stands where all his friends would see her. He didn't want any of them mistaking her for some general fan. She was his.

"Oh, I wouldn't know that, since you didn't wear shirts," she said, the mischief in her eyes now also in her smile.

"It's on the bottom of the left leg of our shorts too," he said, grinning back at her.

"Bottom, huh?" she asked. "Guess that would explain it. I don't think my eyes made it past the top half of the shorts."

He really loved flirtatious Kiera. He pulled her closer and realized that Maya and Sophie had slipped out of the room, leaving them alone. He also loved Kiera's friends.

"I really like this outfit."

"I thought you might," she said.

They stood just looking at one another for a long moment.

"What are you doing here?" she finally asked.

"I couldn't wait until tomorrow to see you," he told her honestly.

Her eyes widened at that. "Really?"

"And I wanted to check on you. After the phone call and all."

She looked down and fiddled with the front of her skirt. "That was just..."

"Nice. It was really nice," he told her when she didn't finish the sentence. She smiled up at him. "And," he added, "I'm in an amazingly good mood."

"Oh?"

"Aimee's out with friends tonight." He knew he was grinning like an idiot.

Kiera's smile grew, and she nodded. "I know. You're happy about it?"

"I'm freaking thrilled about it," he told her. "She sent me a photo—she has her hair done, makeup on, she's dressed in something other than sweatpants. It's a miracle."

"She didn't wear sweatpants when we met at the coffee shop last week or today," Kiera pointed out.

"Only because I made her change clothes that first day. But you're right," he admitted, "today she dressed appropriately to see you. You're having a great influence on her."

Kiera ducked her head, smoothing the front of her skirt. "She was in a great mood today when I saw her. I think she was really looking forward to tonight."

"I do too. So I was thinking that you and I should go do something. Celebrate Aimee feeling better. Celebrate—" Damn, he'd almost said *us*. What was that? *Celebrate us?* That sounded so cheesy.

"Go do something like what?" Kiera asked.

"I have an idea. But it's a surprise."

She seemed to be considering that, but eventually she nodded. "Okay. Let me go change."

He hated to see her take this stuff off. "But you'll wear it tomorrow? The whole thing?"

She smiled. "I don't know about the cheek gems."

"Yes, the cheek gems too," he said firmly.

She gave him a funny look. "Really?"

"Princess, I love you all sparkly."

"You do?"

"You were sparkling the first time I laid eyes on you."

He must have said something really right. Her eyes went soft, and she moved in and hugged him. Zach wrapped his arms around her, marveling at how good something so simple could feel.

After a moment Kiera slipped out of his arms. "I'll be right back." She was out the door and out of sight before he could respond.

Alone in the dining room, Zach looked around. He had no idea what half the stuff in here was called—the various tools and types of fabrics and accessories—but it all made him smile. Even if he didn't get it completely, he liked it.

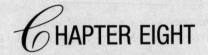

CHAPTER EIGHT

Zach met Kiera by the front door a few minutes later. She'd changed into blue jeans and a much less sparkly top. She'd removed the little gems from her face, but as she turned to open the door, the light caught a glimmer of something near the outside corner of her eye. He looked closer. She'd missed one. But he didn't tell her. He loved it. All night long he'd look at it and think about how she'd put those on for him.

As Zach maneuvered out of her neighborhood and onto the main street, he felt what could only be called anticipation. He was excited about his surprise for her. He hadn't felt that way in a long time.

"You know, when I called you earlier, it was for a reason," Kiera said after a few minutes.

He looked over. "Yeah?"

She nodded. "I know I don't open up or get close to people easily, and I know that bothers you, so I was going to tell you part of the reason why."

Zach squeezed the steering wheel. She was about to tell him something personal. On her own. In fact, she'd *called* him earlier to do that. It was ridiculous how happy he was about this. And how pissed he was that he hadn't been able to talk earlier.

"Okay," he said easily, not letting on how much he wanted this.

"My mom and dad were both writers. My mom's a songwriter, Dad's a novelist. They both worked at home and needed to be alone and have peace and quiet. So when I was little, I spent a lot of time playing quietly in my room, with my books and my toys and my imagination." She gave a soft laugh. "It's also why I like cereal so much. I could get that for myself so I ate a lot of it."

Zach scowled at the road. "They just left you alone?"

She shrugged. "I didn't feel alone. I could always hear Dad's typewriter and Mom's guitar. I liked my imaginary world. I didn't know any different."

"But you had to feed yourself? Entertain yourself? Stay in your room?" he asked, a streak of anger moving through him.

"They didn't force me to stay in my room. I liked it there. I had a TV in there. I've watched a million movies and I've seen every Looney Tunes cartoon a hundred times. There's nothing better than Looney Tunes, I don't care what you say."

Jesus, she was trying to make him feel better, Zach realized.

"You didn't have any real friends?" he asked. "Neighborhood kids or something?" The anger was now building.

"We lived on twenty acres. Far from anyone else. It kept things quiet."

Kiera glanced over. Zach was sure she could see that he was gritting his teeth. Her parents had neglected her, and she was trying to convince him she'd liked it. She hadn't had friends growing up, hadn't hung out with anyone but animated characters, but it was okay? No, it wasn't fucking okay.

"What about when you went to school?" he asked.

She was quiet for a moment, and Zach looked over, wondering if she was going to answer. Kiera was staring out the side window. But she pulled in a deep breath and said, "I still spent a lot of time alone. I liked the kids in the books I read more than most of the kids I met at school. I would sit on the playground and read my book every day, and I was fine. No one bullied me; no one made fun of me. They just left me alone. Until one day in third grade, this little blond girl sat down next to me at lunch with the same book I was reading and told me I was going to be her best friend."

Zach let the quiet moment pass but then said, "And?"

Kiera glanced over with a sad smile. "And then we were. She just sat there next to me at recess every day reading. It was a low-maintenance relationship for several months."

"That's all you did with your best friend?" he asked, unable to even fathom being quiet and alone that much.

"At first. But no, we eventually starting doing more. Talking. Spending time together. We were inseparable from third grade until about three years ago."

Zach cared about this. A lot. He cared that Kiera hadn't had doting parents, he cared that she'd sat alone at recess, he cared that something had happened with her best friend three years ago. And it struck him that Kiera might need a little fixing too.

"What happened three years ago?" he asked gently.

"She chose a controlling asshole over her best friend," Kiera said flatly.

Zach looked over quickly. "This was the friend who hooked up with your ex?"

She nodded.

Zach blew out a breath. If nothing else, she needed to see that people wanted to be around her—hell, *craved* being around her. That she was important to people, and that at least one person was finding himself completely consumed by her. Damn, he was glad he'd chosen to surprise her tonight.

"I'm just trying to help you see that it's not you," Kiera went on. "I'm not used to having people around all the time and paying attention to everything I do. You're not failing me or anything, Zach. This is just me. I wanted you to know that."

And now she was trying to comfort him about all of this. He almost laughed. Well, he wasn't going to let her keep thinking she was insignificant.

He relaxed his grip on the wheel. "Tell you what, Princess. I appreciate you looking out for me, but you don't have to do that."

Kiera shifted on the seat so she was facing him. "Really? Who looks out for you?"

He glanced over. "What? No one. I mean, my family and friends."

She shook her head. "I don't think anyone does. I think that the last time someone took care of you, he ended up dying, and now you feel like you can't let anyone do it. And you're determined to make his sacrifice worth it, so you throw yourself into taking care of everyone around you. And you see so many people hurt and sick and in bad situations that you never let yourself think that your problems and feelings are worth any attention."

Zach felt his heart pounding through his whole body. He worked on breathing and driving, the two most essential things at the moment. He pulled into the parking lot of their destination five minutes later, choosing a spot away from the doors to the building and the rest of the cars. He shifted into park, took a big breath, and then turned to face her.

"That was a lot of insight from someone who doesn't get involved in other people's stuff."

Kiera nodded. "I know. I can't...help it with you. I tell myself I don't want to be involved, but I find myself thinking about you all the time. And then when I learn more about you, I find more and more that I want to..."

He leaned in as she trailed off. He pinned her with a look. "You want to what? Run? Or get closer?"

She hesitated for a moment. Then nodded. "Yes."

Zach felt relief and frustration wash over him at once. At least the desire to get closer was one of the things she was feeling. He nodded. "Fair enough. But you don't have to worry about me, Kiera."

She smiled. "Well, too bad, I guess."

There was something about that, about her, that made him feel completely...humble. She worried about him. She thought about him. She cared about him. And she seemed resigned to continue to do all those things even though they scared her. The fact that she was doing them anyway got to him.

"We're here," he finally said, because he didn't know what else to say.

She frowned, then looked out the window. He also liked

that she'd been wrapped up in their conversation to the point that she hadn't realized where they were.

"An arcade?" she asked, looking back at him.

He grinned. "Yep."

"This is our surprise date?" she asked.

"Yep. Thought I should see what all the hype was about video games."

In truth, he just wanted to take her someplace that would make her smile.

Kiera nodded slowly. "Okay. We're going to game."

"Yeah." Zach got out of the truck and rounded the front bumper to pull her door open. She slid to the ground, and they walked into the arcade together, holding hands.

And as with the hugging, he wondered if he'd ever truly appreciated how great just holding hands could be. Once inside the door, they both looked around.

"Where do we start?" he asked.

"Over there, I think," Kiera said, pointing to a long counter that had several large stuffed animals hanging on the wall behind it and additional toys and prizes in the glass case in front. They exchanged money for tokens and then headed for the games.

"What's your favorite?" Zach asked.

"Uh…" She glanced from side to side. "Do they have Pac-Man?"

Zach looked down at her. Something seemed off, but he couldn't put his finger on it. "I'll bet they do."

"Let's find it." She headed deeper into the arcade.

They did, indeed, have Pac-Man. And Ms. Pac-Man. And it took only two games of each for Zach to figure out what was going on.

He, predictably, sucked at the games. But Kiera sucked even more.

"Princess?" he asked, as they both watched her final Ms. Pac-Man be eaten by a ghost.

"Yeah?"

"Have you ever played Pac-Man in your life?"

Kiera looked up at him and sighed. "No."

"Then why did you want to start with it?"

She chewed on her bottom lip for a moment. Then admitted, "It was the only one that came to mind."

Zach leaned against the Ms. Pac-Man console so he could see her face fully. "Why is that?"

"Because I've never played *any* of these games in my life."

Zach just watched her for a moment. The humor of the situation finally made him chuckle. "You don't play these games?"

"No, I didn't game until Leokin, and I started because of my friends. And Leokin is live-action role playing, not an arcade game."

Why in the hell did she think he would understand that distinction? "Why didn't you say anything?"

She finally chuckled too. "Because you were being so sweet trying to find something to do that I would like. You seemed so excited to bring me here. I had to play along."

He shook his head. "I was excited to bring you here because I wanted you to be excited."

She stepped close and took his hand. "It was really sweet."

"Yeah?"

"Definitely. Big points for trying."

He tugged her closer. "I just wanted us to do something together that we could both get into."

"We don't have to be into the same things, Zach. I don't have to totally get why you love basketball. And you don't have to fully understand Leokin. We just have to know and care that it matters to the other person."

He nodded. "Okay."

"But," she said, turning away from him and pulling him with her, "I do want you to teach me to shoot a basket."

They stopped in front of a basketball toss game. It was made up of full-size basketballs, a full-size basket, and a timer that kept track of how many baskets they made. That was it. For the first time since stepping foot inside, Zach felt as if he might know something. "Deal."

He positioned her in front of the hoop and put a ball in her hands. He showed her how to hold the ball, tuck her elbow, and follow through. She missed the first five tries. But finally one went in.

"Yay!" She turned to him, throwing her arms around his neck.

His hands naturally settled on her waist, and he grinned down at her. "And that's how it's done."

"Easy." She smiled. "But I'd still rather watch you do it."

He rubbed his thumbs over the bare skin between her jeans and her shirt. "I get it. I wouldn't mind a bit if you were shirtless right now."

She laughed. "This is a family place."

"Yeah. Too bad." He stroked his thumbs over her stomach again, loving the goose bumps he felt erupt. "Maybe I'll get one of those mini hoops on the back of my bedroom door and we can play strip basketball."

She laughed. "So every time I miss, I have to take something off?"

"Yep." He grinned unapologetically.

"Then I'd better get one too so I can practice. I'm going to need you taking some things off too."

He ran his thumbs along the top of her jeans, his voice dropping. "If you're taking things off, I promise I'll be taking things off too."

She arched into his touch, and Zach felt something hard under his thumb. But it wasn't the button on her jeans. He stroked over it again, then pulled back and looked down. In the dark arcade, he couldn't see anything, but he knew what he was feeling. "Are these the little gems like you had on your cheek earlier?" he asked.

She grimaced. "I changed so fast I forgot about those." She swallowed. "Maya's idea."

"I love Maya," Zach said. He ran the pad of his thumb over the circular shape just to the left of Kiera's belly button. "Is this a basketball too?"

"Yeah. That one's red and black. We were going to make it orange, but Sophie thought that clashed with the shirt and..." She trailed off as if she realized she was rambling.

He pulled in a long breath. "Damn, that's hot."

She smiled. "It's silly."

"No." He shook his head. "Definitely not silly."

He lowered his head and kissed her. He wanted to devour her, ravish her, drink her in. But he kept the kiss soft, brushing his mouth over hers. When he lifted his head, he took a deep breath and asked, "Want some popcorn?"

"I—" Her brow creased. "Popcorn?"

"Kettle corn, actually."

"Um..."

He smiled. "I wanted to take you on a date. To spend time with you, to show you that I'm interested in the things you are, even if I don't get them, and that our time together doesn't always have to be about Aimee."

She smiled. "That's really nice. I love it."

"But now I want to back you up against the side of that Pac-Man machine and run my tongue all over the basketball on your stomach."

Her eyes widened. But so did her smile. "I'd really like that too."

"But I don't want to just make out with you."

"I hope that means that you want to do *more* than make out with me," Kiera said.

He had to clear his throat as heat shot through him. "I most definitely do."

"Then let's—"

"Have kettle corn."

She sighed. "You really want to be sweet, huh?"

He really wanted to cover her in sugar and butter and have *her* for a snack.

* * *

Kiera didn't care about kettle corn. But she did care about Zach. And this was how Zach did things—the right way. Or the way he thought was right, anyway. He'd told her that, for him, women were either around for one night or they were long-term. There wasn't anything in between. She and Zach were already past the one-night-stand stage. No, they hadn't slept together yet, but they were definitely in deeper than that.

"I really want this to be about more than how much I want to take you to bed," he finally said.

Kiera started to reply that she wanted to talk more about the taking-her-to-bed thing, but...he'd brought her to an arcade. To try to do something with her that he thought she was into. She couldn't say no to anything after realizing that.

She nodded. "Okay. Let's have kettle corn."

They chose a high round table with stools in the snack bar area. Zach bought kettle corn and two sodas, and they sat looking at each other and munching popcorn for nearly a minute before either of them said anything.

"I asked Aimee about Leokin today," Zach said.

That surprised her. "You did?"

"Yep, we texted for a few minutes this afternoon."

"You asked her about Leokin in a text?" Kiera asked. "Did you get hit in the head today?"

He laughed. "Yes, I asked her in a text, and no, I didn't get hit in the head."

Kiera grinned and ate some more of the surprisingly delicious popcorn. "What did she tell you?"

"The basics. It's a magical world with creatures and powers and battles and spells."

Kiera laughed at the simple summary.

"I asked her if she's filled you in on basketball," he added. "Apparently you haven't talked about basketball at all."

She decided to be honest. "I'm a huge fan of basketball now and don't need to know one single rule."

He leaned even closer, his eyes growing warmer. "I know what you mean."

"You do?"

"I don't need to know that there's a pond in Leokin where the water can make someone invisible for three hours after they bathe in it. I don't need to know that there are medallions hidden all over that cause confusion and anger and envy until the person finds them and gets rid of them. I don't need to know that there are dragons that shed a glittery dust that regenerates anything it settles on—grass or plants, a dead dog, a severed hand. All I need to know to be interested is that someone I care about is interested in it."

She stared at him. Wow, that was...nice. Of course, she couldn't help but wonder whether the person he cared about who was interested in Leokin was Aimee or her.

"So now you're fine with Leokin?" she asked.

"Anything that you love this much and that gets my sister talking to me for twenty minutes straight—even if it's via text—is definitely tolerable."

Relief swept through Kiera. Was it possible that she'd already accomplished what she'd wanted to? Had she already helped bridge the gap between Zach and Aimee?

"Did you meet Aimee's friends tonight?" Kiera asked.

"No, she met them wherever they were going."

"Oh." Kiera picked up another kernel and chewed. So Zach didn't know who Aimee was out with. Crap.

"But I've met them before," he said. "Of course."

"You have?"

"She's had the same friends since seventh grade," he said with a nod. "And I'm so grateful they were patient with her and let her work through her issues. Six months is a long time to not talk to anyone and to avoid going out or seeing them."

Kiera nodded and took a sip of her soda. "It is."

"I'm relieved she's out tonight. And maybe they won't talk about everything tonight. It would be okay if they just concentrated on having fun."

"I agree," Kiera said. How could she bring up that Aimee was with *new* friends? Friends that Zach didn't know?

It would hurt him, she knew, to find out that Aimee was spending time with people she hadn't introduced to Zach. People she'd met online. Even though Aimee was spending time with these people in real life now, she knew that Zach wouldn't like that Aimee had met them through Leokin. It would bother him that Leokin and the people there had pulled Aimee through something that Zach couldn't.

Kiera had to be careful here. She didn't want to lie to him, but she also didn't want him hurt. Did it matter how Aimee had met these people? She was happy. That was what was most important. Kiera knew Zach would agree with that.

"I don't think it's true that she hasn't talked to *anyone* about Josie and everything," Kiera said.

Zach shook his head. "Her friends all learned about the accident from their parents or at school. She wouldn't talk to any of her teachers, or her cheerleading coach. She broke up with her boyfriend, and she stopped seeing her friends. All she wanted to do is sit in that room, by herself, and play that fuc—that game. Thankfully, that's over."

Kiera winced. Partially from the sharp tone, but also because that fucking game was one of the most important things in Kiera's life. "The game was her way of coping, Zach," Kiera said gently. "Everyone copes differently."

Zach looked at her with weariness. "Please don't."

She frowned. "Don't what?"

"Don't tell me that all of this is okay. I know you're into all of that. But she was a cheerleader, she was social, she went out, and she was happy and smiled and laughed. For six months, she's been none of those things. She's threatened to move out on her own once she turns eighteen. She's said she doesn't want to go to college."

Kiera pressed her lips together. He was concerned. But maybe, if he could just understand about Aimee and her online friends, he'd feel better. Kiera had to at least try to reassure him. "She has been talking to people, Zach. She's got friends."

"Who?"

"Her clan." Kiera didn't outwardly flinch, but she did inside a little.

"Her *what*?"

"Her clan. Her family. Her...tribe."

"In the game?" he asked. "You think she's telling the elves and dwarves all her problems?"

Probably more the other witches and some wizards. Witches didn't often have elves in their clans. But Kiera didn't think Zach would appreciate a lesson on the social dynamics in Leokin at the moment.

"Yes," she said truthfully.

He blinked at her as if surprised by her answer. "She's talking to elves?"

Wizards. "Well, the people *behind* the characters."

He frowned. "What?"

"The people behind the characters talk. They become friends. They get to know each other really well. Sometimes the anonymity makes people incredibly open and honest."

"She's in online chat rooms or what?"

Relieved, Kiera nodded. "Yes."

"Oh, that's great!" he exclaimed. "She's in online chat rooms talking about who knows what with who knows who."

Kiera's felt her mouth drop open. "I'm saying that she's talking to her *friends* about her feelings and problems."

"Online."

"It happens to be online, yes."

Zach shoved a hand through his hair.

Okay, this was clearly not making him feel better. "Aren't you glad she has somewhere to go to talk it all through?" she asked.

He looked up at her. "Are you kidding? Am I *glad* she's turning to a bunch of strangers *online* instead of to her friends and family? Fuck no."

"These *are* her friends. They're almost like family in a lot of ways."

"*I'm* her family."

"Of course. But these people are very close. They care about her."

He scoffed. "Come on, Kiera."

"I'm serious." She wanted him to understand so *he* would feel better. Aimee was being taken care of. Yes, online, by people she hadn't met in person until recently, but that didn't make them any less real. "It's the connections and emotions that matter, not the mode of delivery," she said.

"You have deep, serious online relationships?" he asked.

"I do."

"Really?"

"Really." In fact... "I feel like I've gotten closer to you in the times we've texted each other."

Zach gave a heavy sigh, but he didn't argue.

"She's okay." Kiera reached out and took his hand.

"Everything has changed so much," he said, shaking his head.

"Of course it has," she told him. "After you all lost Josie, of course things changed. But we all change. Life changes. That's normal."

"I don't want her to be changed by or trying new things because of Josie's death or my mom's drinking," he said bluntly.

"Zach—"

"When Aimee changes, I want it to be because of good things, positive and happy things. If she tries new things, I want them to be good, positive, happy things. College classes or a trip to Europe or white-water rafting or falling in love. And I want her to know she has a supportive brother who would do anything to bring her out of the dark stuff."

Kiera didn't know what to say. She understood what he was saying. But life didn't work that way. And if he kept insisting on fixing everything for everyone else, he was the one who was going to get hurt. Finally she just slid off her stool.

"I need to go to the ladies' room."

What she really needed was to breathe.

* * *

Zach propped a shoulder against the pole just outside the restrooms at the arcade.

Kiera had walked away. When things got emotional and intense, she'd headed in the opposite direction from the situation as fast as she could. He hated that her way of dealing with intense emotions was to leave.

He didn't walk away. Ever. Not when he knew there was something he needed to do anyway. And Kiera was something he needed to do. Not in the show-me-your-hidden-sparkles kind of way but in a she-needs-to-be-fixed kind of way.

Okay, also the hidden-sparkles kind of way.

The women's restroom door finally swung open and Kiera emerged.

She didn't look shocked to see him. She looked resigned. "Thought I was going out the bathroom window?"

"Is it big enough?" he asked.

"It is."

"So you did think about it."

"Absolutely."

He moved in closer to her. "I don't walk away, Kiera."

"So I see," she said drily.

"But you do."

She lifted her chin. "I leave people alone and let them figure their own shit out. It makes them stronger, and it hurts me less in the meantime when they're ignoring everything I say and doing damage that I can't prevent."

He nodded. "And it occurs to me that all of this makes us even less compatible than the cosplaying and basketball stuff."

She crossed her arms. "You're right."

"But you need to learn that not everyone will walk away."

She looked at him for a long moment. "There's a difference between being there for someone, being a constant support in their lives, and not allowing them to change and try new things."

A constant support in their lives. Yeah, Zach wished he could claim that he'd been that. "Since Josie died, I've found out things about my family that I didn't know before, things they've hidden or that I've been happy to ignore because I loved the idea that my family was fine and normal and healthy and strong. And not at all like all the messes I see and help clean up every day." He pulled in a breath. "I just want a few things, a few simple things, to be the same, to be what I've always known. Everything else feels foreign and…broken."

Kiera was staring at him, gripping her crossed arms hard enough that he could see the indentations from her fingers. "You realize that you are different too, right? Josie's death changed you. Aimee could be the same exact girl she's always been and your life would still be different."

He stared at her. "You've been thinking about this. About me."

"Of course I have."

That mattered. A lot. "I've been functioning for so long with the belief that I came from a stable, happy home where people made good decisions and took responsibility for their actions and took care of each other. That all helped me go out every day as an EMT and believe that I could help other people. I gave people advice. I told them how my dad was always there for me. I told them I had two younger sisters who I wanted to be a role model for. I said that I wanted to make my mother proud. I said things like, 'Think of your family' and 'Do it for your kids' and 'Your brother needs you.' And now I look at my family and think, 'How can I help strangers if I can't even help the people I love the most?' and 'What the hell do I know about family when mine's been lying to me and hiding things all this time?'"

Kiera pressed her lips together. He could practically feel

her urge to run. She wanted to leave; she didn't want to hear all of this. He was pulling her in, and he could feel her fighting it.

But finally she said, "You can still help other people. What's going on in your family isn't your fault. You've tried. But if they don't want your help, you can't do anything about that. The more you insist on being involved, the more hurt you're going to get. You have to let them make their own choices. And mistakes."

"I don't know if I believe that," he said, shaking his head slowly. "Loving them means when they're hurt, I'm hurt. We don't live in separate little bubbles, Kiera."

"Bubbles are less painful," she said. "I was in a bubble until Juliet came along. Instead of breaking it and letting the world in, she climbed in with me. We didn't care about the rest of the world. We were happy. It worked. But then…"

"It broke."

"Worse," she said. "I popped it. I let the world in. It was my choice. And after that, the safe bubble was gone forever, and I couldn't get back in."

"You really wanted back in?"

"Definitely. After everything with Juliet and Mitch, I reconstructed as much of it as I could."

"Bubbles are lonely."

"They're peaceful. No angst, no drama, no…failure."

Zach felt his chest tighten. "Bubbles might keep that stuff out, but they also keep out joy and excitement and passion," he finally said.

"Those are all pretty intense emotions," she said. "Maybe peace and comfort is more my thing. Don't you want some of that, Zach?"

"I don't think so," he said, honestly. "There are some really great intense emotions that aren't painful."

The sparkly gem by her eye caught the light and twinkled, and he knew exactly what he needed to do. He grabbed her hand and started for the door.

"Where are we going?"

To prove to her that inside a bubble wasn't where she wanted to be. "Where we can have a private conversation."

"I thought we were having a private conversation."

"This is going to get a little more private than is appropriate for here."

He got Kiera to his truck and put her in the passenger side. Literally. He had to open the door and nudge her inside. He wasn't exactly forcing her, but he could feel her resistance—physically and emotionally.

He could talk to her right here and now. And put her up against the side of his car and kiss her from head to toe. But he didn't want to risk interruption. Or a citation for public indecency.

He understood that closeness was difficult for her. He also knew that, while he could have had sex with her that first night, now that she knew him better and had been pulled into his life, she would shy away from true intimacy because it was less risky. She might go for a quickie in the backseat of his car, but that wasn't how this was going to go between them. When he finally took her to bed, it would definitely be intimate. All in. Completely absorbing.

Tonight he needed to give her a taste of all of that. He needed to show her that everything between them was emotional now. He was climbing into her bubble.

They drove through the city streets without speaking. Zach wasn't surprised. He simply turned the radio on and headed for Cambridge. Twenty-six minutes later he pulled up in front of her duplex.

"Thanks for the ride," she said, reaching for the handle.

"This is the perfect place to continue our conversation," he said.

She lived on a quiet street. The big, old houses were mostly duplexes or had been converted into three- and four-family homes. Several had cars in narrow drives between the houses or on the street. But there was little traffic now, and the houses all glowed with interior lights where people were settling in for the night.

"You want to come in." It wasn't a question or an invitation. She said it almost resignedly.

He smiled. "Nope. The porch is fine."

She sighed. "Fine."

When they were both out of the truck, he grabbed her hand and tugged her up the front steps. He pressed her against the house, beside the door, where the shadows would hide them but where he could still see her expression in the faint glow from the streetlights.

"Zach." Her voice was breathless, but she didn't say anything more.

He inched the hem of her shirt up slightly. The gems under the edge twinkled. The gems she'd put on because of him. For him. He moved the shirt up farther, slowly, so she could stop him if she wanted to.

She didn't stop him.

He looked down at the sparkly basketball he'd uncovered. The gems were black and silver, like the ones on her cheek had been, and they made him groan with desire. Zach met her gaze again, and with his eyes on hers, he went down on one knee.

She gasped softly as he traced over the design with the pad of his finger. Then he dragged his tongue around the perimeter of the basketball shape. "So hot," he breathed against her stomach.

Her hand went to his head, her fingers sliding into his hair.

He kissed the center of the shape.

"I know how much you love dressing up," he said, his voice gruff as he stretched to his full height again. "That it brings out something inside you that means a lot to you. The fact that you dressed up for basketball makes me feel...important." He ran his thumb over the basketball shape again. "This basketball is proof that I've gotten close to you and gotten you outside of your bubble a little bit. That makes me feel like a giant and makes me want you so much I ache with it. But," he added, "these sparkles are hidden."

"What do you mean?" she asked, her breathing a little faster now.

"I want to cover you from head to toe in these gems," he said. "I want you showing the world everything about you that sparkles and makes me want you." He pulled tiny stickers from the basketball shape and placed one at the outside corner of each of her eyes. "Like your eyes and every emotion I see in them." He also put one at each corner of her mouth. "And your mouth. It makes me crazy. Not just how your lips feel under mine, but the things you say and the way you smile." He paused to peel another gem from her stomach. "Your wit." He applied the sticker to the center of her forehead. "And your intelligence." He placed another gem next to it. "And the way you have been there for my sister even though you don't like to get involved."

He put another gem between her eyebrows. "Even the

way you frown at me when you think I'm full of shit." He stuck another one to the center of her chin. "The way you lift your chin when you're feeling determined about something."

She took a deep breath, and he peeled another gem loose. He tugged the V-neck of her T-shirt lower and applied another sticker right over her heart. "And the way you care about people even though you don't want to and you know you might get hurt."

She opened her mouth, but before she could say anything, he inched her shirt higher.

She snapped her mouth closed.

Once her shirt was above her breasts, he dropped his gaze. His mouth watered at the sight of her breasts cupped in purple satin.

He peeled off a sticker and placed it on the curve of her left breast just above the bra cup.

"And here I thought all of the things you were marking were so sweet," she said. Her voice was breathless.

He grinned, unabashed. "Hey, there were a lot of those. And at least I named them off first."

She chuckled softly. "I guess you get points for that."

He leaned in until his lips were nearly touching hers. "But honestly, Princess, you don't have enough stickers here for me to really mark everything that makes me want to be close to you."

"So you say when I'm half-naked."

He reached behind her and unhooked her bra—with one hand, he might add—and pulled the cups up, exposing the breasts he'd been dreaming about for days. "There. That's half-naked."

He leaned back to get a good look. Before he got a good taste.

"Gorgeous," he muttered, fumbling to peel another sticker free.

She took his hand. "I got it. You like my breasts."

He looked up to find her smiling teasingly.

"How about we keep your hands busy doing other things now?" she asked.

"See? We can be on the same page once in a while." He lifted both hands, cupping the firm, sweet breasts that he'd been dying for.

She moaned as he ran his thumbs over the hard tips before lowering his head and taking one in his mouth.

"Zach."

His name had never sounded sweeter. Her head fell back, and he turned his attention to the other side, imprinting the feel of her nipples on his hands and tongue.

He touched and licked, tugged and sucked, until she was panting and arching against him. After dragging his lips over the soft skin of her chest, her throat, licking the tiny jewel he'd put on her chin, he finally settled his mouth on hers, kissing her deeply.

"God, your mouth," he said gruffly when he came up for air.

"When do I get to stick jewels all over you?" she asked.

"You like a few things about me, Kiera?" He heard how rough his voice was and hoped she knew how much it was taking for him not to spread her out right here on the porch.

"I do like a lot of things about you," she said softly.

"Tell me three." He had only about enough time to hear three before he needed to start touching and kissing her again.

"Ironically it's all stuff that also drives me nuts," she

said. "How protective you are of your sister, and that you want to save the world, and I'm completely hot for your arms and shoulders."

He lifted his head. "My arms and shoulders?"

She gave a little sigh as her gaze went over his upper body. "Yeah."

He palmed a breast with one hand and put the other on her ass, pulling her up against him.

She sighed again. "How can I be this attracted to someone so different from me?"

"Because you like adventure, Princess." He pinned her with his gaze. "And I'm the biggest adventure you've ever been on." And she was his biggest adventure. She was making him adjust his thoughts, his attitude, everything, at almost every turn. And he didn't hate it—that was probably the most surprising thing of all.

He kissed her again, taking her mouth fully with a touch of aggression, no holding back as he stroked over her lips and tongue and gripped her ass. Within seconds her fists were knotted in his shirt, and she was making those noises that made him hot and hard.

He moved his hand from her breast to the front of her jeans. He got them open, cursing the denim as he moved his hand down the front. He'd have more room to move if she'd worn...anything else. Dammit. *No more jeans*, he told himself.

Then his fingers encountered hot, wet silk, and he forgot about everything else.

"Zach." Kiera ripped her mouth from his as he slid his finger over her clit.

He felt her grip his shoulders, and he moved again and again, winding her tighter and tighter.

He watched her face as he rubbed her through the increasingly damp fabric of her panties. Her cheeks were flushed, and she was breathing faster, but when he circled over her clit again, her eyes slid shut.

He somehow moved his hand within the confines of the fitted denim—probably by sheer will and the power of lust—and slid his middle finger past the edge where her panties snugged up against her leg.

She moaned, and her head fell forward onto his chest. The feel of her hot breath through the cotton of his shirt fired his blood. He slid his finger into her, relishing the tight grip of her inner muscles as they contracted to draw him farther in.

"I've been thinking about this hot, tight, wet sweetness since the other night. And now I get to actually feel what it's like to make you come, Princess."

She whimpered, gripping his shirt in her fists.

"Oh yeah. Just like you did with your vibrator the other night thinking of me," he said gruffly, the zipper of his own jeans pressing painfully against his cock.

"Zach," she whispered. Then she did the most amazing thing—she lifted one leg and wrapped it around his, opening her legs and pressing against his finger.

He slid his finger all the way into her slick heat, and he was the one to moan this time. "Damn, Princess."

"Move your hand," she begged.

"I can't wait 'til I have a chance to get my tongue here," he told her, pumping his finger deep while swirling over her clit with his thumb. "I can't wait to make you beg for me to take you, spread out on my bed, looking up at me with those big chocolate-brown eyes."

She looked up at him then. Her bottom lip was wet—

obviously she'd been biting it—and he leaned in to kiss her, increasing his rhythm, needing to feel her orgasm.

He could feel her getting close, her inner muscles flexing and pulling on his finger, as she pressed against his hand.

"I have to see you," he said, lifting his head, wanting to look into her face as he felt her climax building. "I want to picture you coming when I'm in bed tonight, imagining my hand is your sweet, tight body milking me until I'm coming with you."

That was apparently what she'd needed. She cried out softly and gripped his shirt tighter as her body clenched hard on his finger and she went over the edge.

She clung to him for several long moments afterward. Finally the leg she'd wrapped around his dropped to the ground, and she took a long, deep breath.

Zach pulled his hands from her pants and sucked in a breath of his own as she straightened her clothes, rezipped her jeans, and covered her breasts.

When she was put back together, he pulled her close and kissed her. It was a softer, less ravenous kiss than the ones before it, but his desire had only grown.

He cupped her face, looking into her eyes. He stroked his thumbs over her jaw. "Good night, Princess."

Her eyes widened. "You're not coming in?"

He kissed her quickly and dropped his hands, stepping back. Everything in him wanted to go inside. To be inside her. Except for the one tiny corner of his mind that insisted it wasn't right yet. Or maybe it was a tiny corner of his heart. "Not yet."

"Not... yet? So later?"

"Another night." He couldn't help but love—and be tempted by—her wanting him to come in.

She tipped her head back, staring up at the stars. "You're going to make me work for it?"

He kissed the tip of her nose. "No, I'm making me work for it."

She frowned. "Work for what?"

"Making you want to be outside your bubble some of the time."

That clearly surprised her. "Only some of the time?"

He looked at her as he backed toward the porch steps. "Well, it's possible that my way isn't always the only way to do things."

She looked amused. "Do you really believe that?" she asked.

He did. Or was starting to. Zach laughed. "Not entirely."

She shook her head, but she was smiling.

"But let's just say I'm willing to give it a try," he said.

Her smile turned from amused to pleased.

He was at the bottom of the steps when she said, "I'm really glad you were still awake last night."

"I'll always be there when you need me, Kiera," he said honestly.

She bit her damned bottom lip, and he had to force himself to move in the opposite direction rather than storming the porch, throwing her over his shoulder, and heading straight to her bedroom.

"What if it's not sexting?" she asked when he got to his car.

"Even then, Princess."

CHAPTER NINE

*K*iera went to Leokin for about an hour, but her heart wasn't in it. Which hadn't happened in...ever.

But the truth was, not even the multiclan quest for the hidden dagger that Pete and Dalton had added last week could distract her from real life with Zach.

She argued with herself for almost an hour after shutting the game off.

Text him.

You can't text him. It's one a.m.

He said you could.

But you shouldn't. Just end the day with that nice moment outside...

She took a deep, shivery breath. *Nice* was such an understatement. The memory of his hands on her, his deep voice saying such naughty things, the way he'd looked at her...

And then he'd left.

She was still shaking her head about that. What was that about?

She supposed she could text him and ask.

I can't believe you left tonight.

She hit send and bit her lip.

He answered a minute later. *I can't believe how much I wanted to stay.*

She smiled. He was there. She actually couldn't believe how much she'd wanted him to stay tonight either. She'd never wanted a man the way she wanted Zach, and that want was only growing. Even as she got to know him better and realized how different they really were, she was still more and more drawn to him.

She was learning that there were alpha guys who felt the need to dominate and control because it was about *them*, and there were alpha guys who dominated and controlled because they felt it was good for the people they cared about.

Zach liked to be in charge, but his intentions and motivations were so different from Mitch's. Kiera could acknowledge that some of it seemed similar on the surface, but she was learning that Zach could back down. He would listen, and he was willing to compromise.

Were you asleep? she typed. She wanted to talk to him, and she didn't want to sext. Well, she *did*, but she also, as scary as it was, wanted to just talk to him more.

Nope. Wide awake. Thinking of you.

The guy was smooth, no doubt about it. She grinned as she sent back, *You don't have to sweet-talk me to get into my pants. Obviously.*

His response was immediate. *First, I think I was pretty sweet prior to that, and second, we probably shouldn't talk about that.*

She giggled and started to type, *Why not?* But his next text beat hers.

My hand is gonna get sore.

Heat flooded through her. For a moment she closed her eyes and imagined him lying in bed, naked, his hand...

Yeah, they shouldn't talk about that. She should not go over there at this time of night, and that was really the only way this would end satisfactorily.

She sat up against her headboard. *Should I let you get to sleep then?*

I'd rather text with you.

Good answer. *What do you want to talk about?*

Tell me something I don't know about you.

She thought about that. Her first thought was that there was a lot, but she was shocked to realize that wasn't true. Zach knew a lot about her. All of the big, important things that mattered to her and that had shaped her.

But there was one thing he didn't know about. Her job. Her work with Leokin. Damn. It was probably time to spill.

She wet her lips and took a breath. *Okay. But you have to tell me some stuff too.*

I'll tell you anything you want to know, came his reply.

Of course he would. Zach was an open book.

But again, that thought didn't seem quite right. Kiera frowned. Zach probably thought he'd tell her anything, but she knew, somehow, that Aimee wasn't the Ashley who hadn't dealt with their sister's death. Zach was so busy fixing everyone else that he hadn't dealt with his own loss.

She started to ask her first question: *Tell me how you really feel about Josie's death*—because why not just jump in with both feet if she was going to go in at all?—when another text came through from him.

Tell me about the work project you start next month.

Okay, well, talk about a great opening.

I'm working on a huge expansion for WOL.

There was a long pause before he replied, *Is there another WOL?*

Nope. Sorry.

You work for WOL?

I'm the lead graphic designer. I've been with Leokin from the beginning. From before the beginning. The creators—Pete and Dalton—are two of my best friends.

Again there was a long pause. *And two of your deep, serious online relationships?*

Ah, he'd remembered that. *Yes.*

Does Aimee know?

Oh boy. Zach didn't like secrets. *Yes. She recognized me the first night I was at your house.*

And neither of you told me?

After finding out that there was nothing on earth you hated more than WOL? Kiera asked. *No.*

Yeah, okay.

Kiera frowned. What did that mean? She typed, *It's okay?*

I wish you'd told me sooner, but I get it. And, well, maybe now's a better time to tell me anyway.

Kiera pulled her bottom lip between her teeth. *Why is now a better time?*

Well, a few days ago I thought video games were a silly waste of time. Turns out there might be some good things about them after all.

Whoa. That was…*Did you really just say you were wrong?* she asked.

I just read that back and I never said the word "wrong."

She laughed. *Sorry. Thought it was implied.*

Yeah. It was.

She blinked. Then she decided to tell him something else he didn't know about her. *My mind has changed about a few things too, now that you mention it.*

Do tell.

Turns out not all hot guys are assholes. The response was flippant, and suddenly she had the urge to make it more meaningful, so she added, *And turns out that not everything exciting and worthwhile happens on a computer screen.*

* * *

I probably should have told you more about the exhibition.

Zach read Kiera's text with a bit of trepidation, if he was totally honest. It had been a week since the arcade, and the exhibition at Maya's studio was now only two days away. And Zach was very aware that he was going to be completely out of his element there.

Okay, hit me, he typed back.

The exhibition is kind of more like a play.

He frowned. *A play?*

It's a live performance. We've done it three years in a row. Sophie writes and directs it.

I'm not following. Thought it was a demonstration of the things they teach in the classes.

Yeah, it's that too. We all show up at the studio like it's just an open house. A time for parents to sign their kids up for classes and for the kids to see the place and meet the instructors and talk about what they'll do in class. Everyone comes in costume. There's punch and cookies. The whole bit.

But? he asked.

Well, at some point in the midst of all of that, the show starts. One year it was an alien invasion. Another time it was mobsters coming in to hide out from the cops. Last year two girls from the past time-traveled to the studio and needed the kids to teach them about modern times.

He chuckled. *Okay.*

It's really cute. The actors use the martial arts and self-defense moves and even some of the weapons stuff that Maya's studio teaches. It gets the kids excited and entertains everyone more than just standing up there and explaining it.

Sounds good to me.

You're okay with it?

He paused. *Do I have to be one of the actors?* And would he do it if she said yes?

LOL. No. But I am.

You're wearing the short skirt and the leather boots, right?

Right.

And you'll be doing some sword fighting?

Yes.

I'm in. 100%.

You sure talk big, came her response.

What's that mean? he asked.

It means that you pretend you're all turned on by me, but you're acting like a monk.

He laughed out loud. *You've felt plenty of proof of how much I want you, and monks don't put their hands and mouths the places I've had my hands and mouth.*

He loved that she wanted it as much as he did. Over the past week, they'd had multiple opportunities, but he hadn't let it go beyond heavy making out. He really wasn't teasing her. He wanted more from her than sex. He'd even told her that. But she hadn't asked, "Like what?" He knew she wasn't ready for more yet. But he was willing to wait.

What he wanted was for her to open up to him, face-to-face, in real life, and not get spooked by all the feelings. He wanted her to dig in, in spite of her fears, and *be there*.

It seemed simple, but he knew it wasn't.

But he'd wait. He was proving to her that people did stick around and that he could be counted on. It would take time, but eventually she'd trust him. He needed her to trust him.

Every shift he worked, he had people entrusting him with their well-being. He knew the patient whose heart he'd restarted yesterday had trusted him. He knew the woman whose little girl had stopped breathing at the park had trusted him. He knew the grandmother who had fallen down her back staircase had trusted him.

But he wore a uniform and drove a truck with a siren on it and was dealing with physical issues that had answers. What he really needed was someone he cared about, who knew him and knew he had flaws and shortcomings, who knew that he didn't actually have all the answers, to trust him anyway. His parents and sisters hadn't. He needed Kiera to.

You're driving me crazy, Kiera finally typed.

Okay, that was sort of emotional. *Are you angry?*

Frustrated. And scared.

You never have to be scared with me, Princess. I'd never hurt you.

There was a very long two minutes before she replied, *The scariest part is I'm starting not to care about getting hurt. I want you anyway.*

Zach felt as if she'd wrapped her hand around his heart and squeezed. *I never want you to be scared, Kiera. Not of me. Not of what we've got here.*

He held his breath waiting for the response. They could talk this out—or text it out, at least. He'd reassure her. He'd even admit that he was falling in love with her. He just needed an opening for more...

It's getting late.

Fuck. Zach let out a sigh.

I should get to sleep. Can't wait to see you at the exhibition.

His jaw tightened. *I won't see you before then?* That was still two days away.

I need to catch up on some work. Pete and Dalton are coming to town in a few days, and we're meeting about some new things. I need to have graphics done.

The project was going to keep Kiera holed up in her room in her pajamas and eating cereal. And not seeing him.

He wanted to be supportive. But he didn't have to like it.

Okay, I'll see you at Maya's.

Great.

Kiera?

Yeah.

Text me. Anytime.

Okay.

"Okay." That was it. He hated texting so damned much. Zach gripped his phone and forced himself to set it on the coffee table instead of hurling it against the fireplace. He picked up the laptop from the cushion beside him and went back to the search he'd been doing when Kiera had started texting him.

"What are you doing?"

He looked up to find Aimee padding through the living room on her way to the kitchen.

Trying to convince myself not to go over to Kiera's house and hold a boom box over my head on her front lawn until she comes out and talks to me.

There. He did see movies.

"Buying an eye patch."

Aimee stopped in the doorway to the kitchen and turned back. "Did you say eye patch?"

"Yeah. Maya's thing." He looked down at the screen in front of him. "I guess I'm supposed to wear something?"

"And you're going to wear an eye patch?"

He looked up again. "And a sword."

Aimee came back across the room and climbed up to sit on the arm of the couch next to him. She grinned. "Seriously?"

"You don't think so?"

She studied his face. "I don't see pirate in you."

He sighed and looked back at the screen. Pulling off the bad boy thing should be easier than this. "That's the point, right? An escape from reality?"

"I guess sometimes for some people," Aimee said.

Something in her voice made him look up. "But?"

She shrugged. "I think the best costumes are the ones that make you feel like who you most want to be."

He sat up straighter and set the computer to the side. He turned to face Aimee more fully, draping his arm along the back of the couch. "Is that how you feel about being Quinn?" he asked.

She smiled and he knew he'd gotten points yet again for remembering her Leokin character's name. Why did everyone assume he'd forget that?

"Definitely," she said. "I'm completely comfortable when I'm her and in Leokin." She gave him a small smile. "My gamer friends make me feel normal and my regular friends make me feel weird. Ironic, right?"

He couldn't help but give a little laugh at that. "I don't know—there's a girl from Leokin who has managed to get me a lot closer to normal than I've been in a long time."

Aimee's grin widened. "But she's got you looking at pirate costumes."

"Not costumes." Not unless he was in Kiera's bedroom and they had a good several hours to make the most of the role-playing. Alone. "But eye patches, yeah." He nodded. "Talk about weird."

"Maybe you just didn't know what your real normal was before Kiera."

Zach looked at his sister and, maybe for the first time, saw her as the almost-eighteen-year-old woman she was. She'd grown up. In the past six months more than ever. And she knew him. And loved him. "I think you're right."

There was a pause. Then Aimee said, "After Josie died, I didn't think anything would ever be normal again. That's why Leokin and Quinn were so important to me."

She didn't hesitate even slightly over Josie's name or the word *died*. While Zach almost couldn't breathe. He and Aimee hadn't spoken about Josie at all to one another.

He didn't feel as if things were normal. There was almost nothing familiar about his life now. Work. That was about it. And even that was filled with a new pressure to do everything he could and then some. He'd always felt that, but since Josie's accident, he'd felt an even stronger drive to make it all work out, to be the savior.

Zach cleared his throat. "But now you feel back to normal?"

"Not back to normal," Aimee said. "At least, not like it was before. A new normal, I guess."

Part of him wanted to argue against that. Her old normal had been so good.

But had it? He was so used to believing what he had about her life—what he'd wanted to believe—that it took him a moment, even now, to remember that her mother was a closet alcoholic and her father was never around and her sister's good influence had all been a lie.

"So online with Leokin you can forget about everything?"

"Not forget." She lifted a shoulder. "Online I can... manage stuff, I guess. In real life it felt like everything was coming at me at once—Josie not being here and Mom going off the deep end and you freaking out and hauling me over here. There was no escaping all of that. I felt like everything was happening *to* me, and I couldn't change any of it."

He grimaced but didn't interrupt.

"In Leokin I was Quinn, a fourth-level witch. Nothing more or less. Everything anyone knew about me was on that screen. And I was kick-ass. When everything in the real world was confusing and completely sucked, all I wanted to do was to be in Leokin." She paused. "Online, I was in control. Or I could just shut it off when I didn't want to deal at all. Unlike off-line, where everyone knew everything and it was all constant and impossible to shut off."

He looked at her. The calm in her eyes. And the peace. God, he loved seeing that. But when had she gotten so insightful?

Then a thought occurred to him. "Did you know about Josie's band?"

Aimee nodded. "Yeah. And she begged me not to say anything."

Zach scrubbed a hand over his face. This wasn't as much of a blow as he might have expected. As he and Kiera had discussed, he would have tried to stop her, and that would have been totally based on his own opinions and biases and narrow view. "I understand," he finally said.

Aimee looked so relieved that Zach felt like a complete ass.

"Am I that hard to talk to?" he asked.

"You're hard to...disappoint," she said. "I mean you're *easy* to disappoint. I mean...*that's* hard on us. On me," she finished, with a touch of sadness at the reminder that she was now his only sister.

Zach knew that he couldn't promise to let up entirely and leave her completely alone. He'd never be able to pull that off. "I'll always love you, no matter what."

She nodded. "I know. And I know you'll always be there."

"Always," he said firmly.

"But I want to trust *myself* more," Aimee said. "When I put that costume on for Quinn the other night, I realized that there's a strong, sure part of me. I just need to bring it out." She ducked her head. "That sounds kind of dumb, doesn't it? That a dress and a cape and some makeup can get me in touch with something that technically should be there all the time?"

Zach shook his head. "Three weeks ago I would have said yes, that sounds strange. Now not so much."

Aimee looked up with a grin. "Kiera."

He sighed and nodded. "Kiera."

"She's the best."

That was one word. "She is. She's also shown me that, if you're doing something you love and have a passion for, you shouldn't hide it. If Josie believed in what she was doing, she should have been proud enough of it to tell me and not care what I thought." The words came out before Zach could really analyze them.

Aimee sat up straighter on the arm of the couch. "Really? You would have been okay with the band going on the road?"

He shook his head. "Probably not," he said honestly. "But I would have respected her standing up for herself. And maybe my opinion shouldn't have mattered so much."

Aimee's look of surprise probably mirrored his own. He'd spent most of his life believing his opinion should matter. To everyone.

"But when you love someone and respect them, their opinion does matter. It just does," Aimee said. "Even if you hate it sometimes, their voice is in your head."

Zach shifted on the couch. "Okay, in that case, let me put *this* in your head, in my voice—I love you and I'm proud of you and I want you to be happy above everything else. And if you find something that makes you happy, I want you to go for it, even if I don't understand."

Aimee blinked at him, and he thought maybe she was holding back tears.

"I should have said that to Josie," he added. "I wish I had."

Aimee launched herself at him, wrapping her arms around his neck and squeezing hard. "I love you too, Zach."

His chest felt tight.

"So maybe you should do pirate for one night," she said, finally pushing back and wiping her cheek.

He didn't comment on the tears. He reached for his laptop and turned to prop his feet on the coffee table and set the computer on his thighs. "You think so?"

"It's got to be exhausting being the good guy all the time. You should have a night off once in a while," she said with a nod. "Let someone else do the worrying for a change."

Damn. That sounded great.

* * *

"Okay, everyone, it's time!" Sophie called. She was dressed as a lady-in-waiting, a member of Kiera's royal court in Leokin.

Tonight's show was about a princess being kidnapped by a knight from another land and then saved by her own people. Kiera didn't know how many of the younger kids knew much about Leokin. Their primary demographic was ages fourteen to thirty-six. But she knew even the younger kids would understand and love the princess and knight characters and the sword fighting.

She glanced around, but Zach and Aimee weren't there yet. She smoothed her dress and straightened her spine. Fine. This wasn't Zach's kind of thing. Or maybe he'd gotten held up at work. In any case, the show had to go on.

Maya's staff and friends gathered just inside the door to welcome everyone and direct them into the main studio where everything was set up. Kiera pasted on her smile as the doors swung open and a horde of tiny superheroes, fairy princesses, soldiers, witches, wizards, and monsters tumbled into the building.

She smiled and greeted them as they all came past, checking out her outfit and her sword and all talking at once. When they were all gathered in the main studio room, Kiera took her place along the wall farthest from the door, meaning that her would-be captors would have to come across the room and so would her rescuer, both meeting in the middle for the big sword fight.

The exhibition was kicked off by Maya and her staff. Maya did a welcome and a quick rundown of how the classes worked, then she and some of the other instructors went through some martial arts routines as well as some hand-to-hand combat patterns, and finally Maya and her favorite sparring partner, Ben, demonstrated a bo staff routine.

Kiera watched the kids and their parents. They were, predictably, impressed with the presentation. Kiera felt the anticipation building, though. Some of the past students knew something was coming, and Kiera herself was excited to get Sophie's cue to start their part of the show.

The signal came five minutes later. Sophie pulled on her earlobe, which, to the secret actors and actresses in the room, meant *action*.

Rob strode into the room, dressed as a knight in shining armor, his sword raised. "I am here for Kirenda, Princess of Leokin," he announced, interrupting Maya's explanation about the bo staff. "Turn her over to me and I shall spare you all."

Kiera grinned and scanned the room, taking in the wide eyes and big smiles on the kids' faces. They were eating it up. Then her eyes landed on one of the dads. Or who she'd assumed in her peripheral vision was one of the dads.

A tall, handsome man stood with his shoulder propped against the main doorway. He wore jeans and a button-down shirt—and an eye patch and a scabbard with a sword.

And that was the moment she officially fell in love with Zach Ashley.

Suddenly Rob was in front of her, blocking her view of Zach. He grabbed Kiera's arm and jerked her around to face the room. "My land now holds your princess captive. If you want her back alive, I suggest you begin gathering the things you value most. We will meet in the east meadow at dawn in five days' time. If you are not there or try to hold anything back from us, you will never see your princess again."

They started for the door as scripted, but just then Aimee jumped in front of them, her cape billowing behind her.

"Not so fast, Sir Robert."

"Ah, Quinn, the great enchantress," Rob sneered. "I have heard the tales of your powers."

"Then you know that you should surrender now. You'll never make it to the border of our land," Aimee told him.

Aimee was here. Good. That was good. But Kiera's thoughts were completely scattered. Because Zach was here. With an eye patch.

"I'm not really Kirenda," Kiera suddenly said loudly, pulling out of Rob's grasp. Because he hadn't been expecting her to actually try to get free, he hadn't been holding her tightly. Kiera spun toward the room. "There! She's over there! That's the princess."

She was pointing right at Sophie.

Sophie gave her a what-the-hell-are-you-doing look. Rob looked from Kiera to Sophie.

"Go," she whispered to him.

Rob shrugged. "Don't think you can fool me!" he declared, and started across the room to Sophie.

Kiera, on the other hand, made a beeline for her pirate as her friends made their way through the rest of the performance. Thankfully Sophie knew every line by heart.

"Princess," Zach greeted her with a roguish smile as she got close.

"You're..." *Gorgeous, amazing, the last guy I should be falling for, the guy I'm definitely falling for anyway.* "A pirate," she finally said.

"Yeah. Kind of. At least for tonight." He stroked his thumb over her cheek. "You look beautiful." His voice was husky, and his eyes were hot as he looked at her.

"You're killing me, Pirate Zach."

"Yeah." He looked grim for a moment. "I know what you mean."

She started to say more but Maya was suddenly at her side. "Are you okay? What's going on?" She noticed Zach a second later. "Oh, hey. I was kind of hoping you'd show up as a handsome prince."

He grinned at her. "You need a prince tonight?"

"Every night, Zach," Maya said in a teasingly wistful tone. "But I'll have to settle for a knight tonight in my play and a prince in my dreams."

He chuckled. "It's just as well. I'm a bit of a novice at the prince thing."

Kiera smiled at him. "I'm not so sure about that."

The guy who came to everyone's rescue? The guy who was concerned with everyone else's happiness and well-being?

"Well, maybe the pirate could rescue the—" Maya started.

"No," Kiera broke in. "He's busy." Kiera grabbed Zach's sleeve and started down the hallway in the opposite direction, tugging him with her.

"Where are we going?" Zach asked.

"Maya's office."

"Oh. Why?"

She pushed him ahead of her through the door, then shut it behind her. "Because it locks." She turned the lock with a loud click.

CHAPTER TEN

He didn't look nervous, exactly, but he did look a little suspicious.

"So that's Rob."

She nodded. "That's Rob."

"Your good friend."

"My very good friend." She moved to Maya's desk.

She unbuckled her belt and removed her scabbard and sword, then placed them on the edge of the desk.

Zach swallowed hard as he followed her motions with his eyes.

Kiera unbuttoned her leather vest and shrugged out of it, leaving herself in the short tan dress and boots from the other night. Tonight, though, she had vines and leaves painted on her face.

"I don't really like Rob." Zach hadn't moved a step from where she'd left him by the door.

"Why is that?"

"Because he knows you better than I do."

Her heart warmed. "You don't need to be jealous of Rob."

Zach pulled his eye patch off. "I am anyway."

She couldn't catch her breath for a second. Zach Ashley had dressed up as a pirate for her.

Rather than try to put words to whatever she was feeling, she crossed to him and removed his belt and sword. Then she started on the buttons of his shirt.

"Kiera—"

She looked up at him. "You don't have to be jealous of anyone else. You don't have to win me over with arcades and eye patches. I'm yours. Completely."

Hot possessiveness flared in his gaze. "Tell me something about you that no one else knows."

She hesitated for only a second. "I would do *anything* for a guy who would dress up as a pirate for me."

He gave her a smile as he let his shirt fall to the floor. "I actually already knew that."

She grinned and spread her palms over his chest, then ran them back and forth over his hot skin. "I promise you there are definitely some things you know about me that Rob doesn't."

He swiftly turned her, crowding her up against the door. "Like what?"

Her whole body tingled. "You don't know?"

"I want to hear you say it."

"You know exactly how to touch me to make me moan, Zach." She lifted her arms as he stripped her dress up and over her head. Her hair fell back to her shoulders, and she said, "You know how my breasts feel in your hands."

He quickly divested her of her bra and filled his hands with her breasts, running his thumbs over her nipples.

"What else?" he asked huskily.

"You know exactly how to kiss me to make me melt."

He lowered his head and claimed her mouth, running his tongue over her bottom lip as he circled her pebbled nipple with the pad of one thumb.

But he didn't stay long. He lifted his head. "More."

"You know how...I feel...around your finger..." She blushed hotly.

He simply grinned. "How you feel? Do you mean this?" He lifted his hand and traced the tip of his finger over the vines that swirled over her cheeks and forehead.

His touch anywhere on her body was amazing, but she shook her head. "You know what I mean."

"I want to hear you say it."

"You want to hear me say that you make me hotter and wetter than anyone else ever has?"

Again that flare of heat showed in his eyes. "Yes. And more."

"You want to hear that no one has touched me like you do?"

He pressed closer and lowered his voice. "Touched you where?"

"All over."

"Say it."

"Zach," she protested quietly, tipping her head back against the door behind her.

"You won't say *pussy* for me, Kiera? You won't tell me that I can touch you and stroke you and make you come like no one else?"

She shook her head back and forth but smiled. "Yes. All of that."

He chuckled and lowered his head, then kissed the side of her neck and slid his hands over the silk panties she still wore. "Rob doesn't know how you sound when you come? He's never heard you say, 'Oh God' as he presses on your clit just right, he's never felt your sweet pussy clenching hungrily around his fingers?"

"No." She gasped as his hands slid lower, the tips of his fingers pressing against her clit exactly as he'd said.

"Good girl." He took her mouth again, slipping a finger underneath her panties and into her heat. He thrust deep, then circled her clit while circling her tongue with his.

She fumbled for his pants, her fingers forgetting every few seconds what they were supposed to be doing. But eventually she got his fly open and her hand inside his underwear, wrapping her fingers around his hard length.

He ripped his mouth away, then rested his forehead on hers and breathed hard. "God, Princess, your hand is like heaven."

She ran it up and down his length. "I need you, Zach. Please. This time, please."

Whatever the reason, whatever had changed, he suddenly bent his knees and gripped her butt, lifting her.

She wrapped her legs around him. Her panties and his boxers all that separated them.

He turned and took the three long steps to the couch that sat under Maya's window. The shades were drawn, and they were encased in a temporary cocoon, just the two of them.

Their own little bubble.

"I can't wait any longer," he said gruffly as he lowered her onto the couch and followed her down. "I want you too much."

"Yes. Finally," she said.

He grinned. "I promise there's been a reason I've been waiting."

"What is it?"

He looked down at her bare breasts. "I completely forget."

"Well, *this* better not be about Rob."

"It is," he said. "But only in the sense that he was a part of the show and the friendship you have here. The inner circle I want to be a part of because it's part of your life."

Her heart flipped, and she felt like yelling, "Yes, yes, yes!" Instead she cautioned him, "My life involves dressing up on a semiregular basis."

"I know."

She looked up at him, her grin growing slowly as understanding dawned. "You like the eye patch."

He didn't admit it. But he didn't deny it either. "I like knowing that, whatever the rest of the world sees you dressed as, *I* get to see you *un*dressed."

And she wanted him to.

She realized that he'd wanted her no matter what she wore or how she looked. She might get to choose what she showed to most of the world, but not Zach. He saw all of her. Of course, most of the world wasn't looking as hard as he was.

The people who mattered looked closer. Maya, Sophie, Rob. Pete and Dalton. Aimee. But they also left her alone, for the most part, when she insisted. Zach didn't do that. Zach didn't let her retreat into her bubble.

She took his face between her hands. "We're going to do this."

"Damn right we are."

"But you have to give me a minute."

He started to lean in to kiss her but then realized what she'd said. "You need a minute?"

She pushed him back, and he rose up to kneel between her knees.

"Just one."

She slid off the couch and padded to the desk where her purse was stashed in a bottom drawer. She rummaged inside and pulled out a condom and a pack of makeup remover cloths. She turned to face him and tossed him the condom. He caught it in one hand, his eyes glued on her. She opened the cloths as he watched her. Then she swiped one over her face. It wasn't enough to remove everything. The gold paint in particular was tough to get off. But it would take off the light green. And most importantly, it would make her point.

She wiped it over her forehead as she walked back to the couch.

"I've always had a fantasy about making love to a dashing rogue pirate." She stopped and put a knee on the couch cushion where he was still kneeling, his large, hard erection pressing against the front of his regular-guy cotton boxers. "So keep the eye patch. But lately my fantasies have been filled with a handsome, charming EMT that I want to make love to more than I've ever wanted anything. Even more than I want the *Buffy* replica scythe that Maya is giving me in exchange for doing the show tonight."

His eyes softened as she wiped the cloth over her cheek and chin. "*Buffy*?"

"*Buffy the Vampire Slayer.*"

"That's kind of an old show, isn't it?"

"It's a kick-ass scythe."

The corner of his mouth curled up. "And you won't get it now?"

"I left the show to have sex with my boyfriend in her office. No way am I getting that scythe."

He grasped her wrist, stopping the makeup removal. She met his eyes. She knew the "boyfriend" thing meant a lot to him.

"I'm more important than the scythe?"

"Yep."

"Wow. That's a big deal," he teased.

She chuckled. "I'm glad you know that."

He pulled her in, kissing her roughly. He took the makeup cloth from her fingers and tossed it away. "Just you and me, Princess."

"Kiera. Zach and Kiera."

"Okay." He gave a single nod. "Hey, Kiera?"

"Yeah?"

"Take your panties off."

She laughed and slid them off before she wiggled around him to lie back on the couch. He stood and swiftly pushed his jeans to the floor, then shed his boxers.

Kiera caught her breath. She'd felt him over the past two weeks but hadn't had the pleasure of *seeing* him. And certainly not fully, every inch of skin and muscle exposed to her gaze. And her hands. And her tongue.

He started to kneel over her again, but she stopped him. "Hang on there, hot guy."

He quirked an eyebrow. "What?"

"Just give me a second to look." She propped up on her

elbows and dragged her gaze over him from head to toe. She watched raptly as he rolled the condom on.

"Kiera," he growled. "Killing me."

"Well, okay," she said with a sigh, lying back. "If you insist on ravishing me, I guess, go ahead."

He leaned over her and scooped a big hand under her to roll them. "Oh no, you're ravishing me, Princess. I'm at your mercy."

She braced her hands on his chest and looked down into his handsome face. "It's been a long couple of weeks."

His fingers curled into her hips. "Totally worth it."

She laughed. "We haven't even done it yet."

"Not that. I was talking about the look on your face."

She shook her head. "What's the look on my face?"

"Totally happy, trusting, open. Because of me. For me."

For a second it felt as if the butterflies in her stomach had picked her heart up and were swooping around with it in her chest. She leaned in and put her lips against his. "I don't have a lot of practice *saying* amazing things like that, so I think I'll just *do* a few amazing things, if that's okay."

He squeezed her hips again, this time more playfully. "You could start practicing the word thing now."

She lifted her head. She licked her lips. Her mind spun. "All I've got is *You're amazing, Zach.*"

He laughed and pulled her head down to his. "I'll take it."

Then he started kissing her, and from there they resorted to phrases like *yes* and *like that* and *right there* and *more* as their hands traveled over each other and their mouths freely tasted and their bodies pressed and rubbed. She licked her way down his chest and stomach, tracing the ridges of his muscles with her tongue, but didn't quite get as far south as she'd planned before he hauled her up and fastened his lips around one of her nipples.

She arched her back, her fingers tangling in his hair as he moved a hand between her legs and stroked her nearly to the peak before backing off.

When he finally slid her down, guiding her hips until his erection nudged against her, Kiera caught her breath. "Thought I was ravishing you, hot guy."

"Oh, you are, Princess. You totally are."

She pushed herself up off his chest, changing the angle slightly, and moved her hips, taking him in.

They groaned together.

"Damn, girl," he muttered, his breathing ragged, his big hands bracketing her rib cage, holding her still.

But she wanted to *move*. She ached with the need for more friction. "Zach," she protested, wiggling against him.

"Just a sec," he said, his eyes squeezed shut.

She waited a second. And then another. But eventually she blew out a breath. "Zach. *Please.*"

"Putting this off for two weeks might have been an error in judgment," he said, through gritted teeth.

She couldn't help it. She laughed. And apparently that caused a motion that created either intense pleasure or intense pain because she felt his hands tighten on her and a muttered "*Fuck*" under his breath.

"That'll serve you right," she said, probably with too much glee in her tone. She took his hands from her waist, threaded their fingers together, and then swiveled her hips, taking charge of the ravishing after all.

She moved on him for several delicious minutes, reveling in everything about the moment. The way he looked, sounded, and felt. Every inch of her felt affected, and she wanted it to last all night. But the tense look on Zach's face told her that he was barely hanging on. However, he was hanging on. And suddenly she wanted to make him lose control. He loved to be in charge, loved to make the decisions and call the shots. She'd love to be the cause of him coming undone.

She lowered her chest to his, and his arms wrapped around her. She felt safe and cherished even as she was feeling more pleasure than she'd ever imagined. "Zach," she said against his ear.

His hands moved down her back to her ass. "Yeah, Princess?"

"It's my turn to know how *you* sound and feel when you come."

He froze. For a second. Or maybe only half a second. But almost immediately his hands tightened, his rhythm increased, and he thrust into her full and hard.

Words. That was the key with him. No matter what they were doing.

She gripped his shoulders and hung on as he drove upward, over and over, taking them both closer and closer to climax. His big hand covered the base of her spine, and he somehow moved her on him, against him, in a way that sent bolts of electric pleasure streaking through her as she watched his green eyes grow darker and hotter.

"Need you to come first, Kiera," he ground out, his jaw tight.

She nodded, so close, but unable to tell him.

"Want to hear my name," he told her.

And somehow he pressed her pelvis against his in a way that made her eyes cross and her orgasm crash over her all at once. "Zach!"

"Yes, fuck, yes, Kiera," he muttered, slamming his hips into hers three more times before his whole body tightened and he went over the edge too.

The postcoital look on Zach's face was simply one more thing she loved seeing on him. She leaned in and kissed him, then rested her cheek against his chest, taking deep breaths and letting her heart slow.

Her pulse had just evened out when it was kicked up again by the sudden piercing beep that erupted from somewhere in the vicinity of Zach's pants.

"Dammit." He shifted immediately, rolling her off him and sitting up.

"Your pager?"

"Yeah." He snagged one leg of the pants and pulled them toward him, quickly silencing the beeping but then frowning at the screen on the pager.

"You're on call tonight?" she asked.

He stretched to his feet. "No. Everyone's being called in. Something big."

He dealt with the condom and wrapper in Maya's trash can, and Kiera knew she'd be hearing about that the next time Maya used her office. Like later tonight. She didn't care.

"Something big like what?" she asked, grabbing for her dress.

"Something they need multiple units for," he said, pulling his pants back on. "Like a convention center ceiling falling in during Comic Con."

She wrinkled her nose at him as she stepped into her panties. "Such a random example. As if something crazy like that would ever happen."

He shrugged into his shirt and then grabbed her wrist and pulled her close. He kissed her softly, then ran a hand over her cheek. "Once-in-a-lifetime kind of thing."

And just like that she was this close to telling him how she *felt* about him. Real feelings too. Serious ones. Good thing he had to go to work.

"Be careful," she said, kissing him.

He was clearly reluctant to pull back as he buttoned the bottom three buttons on the shirt and grabbed his jacket. "Always careful."

"You're going to wear the eye patch?" she teased as he scooped it up from the floor.

He grinned. "Damn right. I plan to tell the guys that this patch got me laid by a hot princess."

She nudged him toward the door. "You can tell them that. But it's not true."

"I'm not saying my two weeks of amazing foreplay didn't help…"

He turned back as he stepped through the door, and she kissed him once more. "Trust me, hot guy, I much prefer you *out* of costume."

He grabbed her before she could step back and pulled her onto her tiptoes for a real kiss. "I'll text you later," he said when he finally let her go.

Kiera bit her lip on the invitation to just come over. But she did give him something. "Or call me."

He paused, then nodded. "You got it, Princess."

Then he was gone.

Off to be someone else's hero for a little while.

* * *

Her phone almost never rang.

Given that she conducted most of her business through e-mail and most of her personal relationships via text, it took her a second to recognize it.

Plus it was three in the morning, and Kiera had been fast asleep dreaming of princes swooping in to kidnap and ravish her...on a pirate ship.

She frowned and shook the dream off, reaching for her phone. "Hello?"

"It's me."

Zach's deep voice rolled over her, making her inner muscles clench. All her inner muscles.

She rolled to her back, pressing the phone hard against her ear. "Where are you?" *Please say my front porch. Please say my front porch.*

"Just got home a little bit ago. I wasn't going to call. It's late. But..."

He trailed off, and she sat up.

"I'm glad you did," she assured him. There was something in his voice that made her ask, "Are you alright?"

There was a long pause. "It was a rough call."

She frowned. "I'm sorry." She swallowed hard. "Do you want to talk about it?"

Holy crap. She'd offered to talk. About something that was obviously making him emotional. More, she'd *meant* it.

"It was...a car accident."

She was trying to picture his expression, trying to put herself there in the moment, but she'd never heard Zach sound like this. And that bugged her. "You were out for a long time."

"It was multiple cars on the freeway. High speed."

He sighed, and she thought she heard his breath shake.

"A lot of victims."

"Oh, Zach, I'm sorry."

"There was a girl..."

Kiera's heart clenched before she even heard the whole story. Even the whole sentence.

"She was twenty-four. She was in the back, right-hand side. The other car crossed the median. They think the driver fell asleep."

Oh God. Exactly like Josie.

"Zach—"

"She died."

Kiera's eyes slid shut. Zach didn't do well with losing patients. He'd told her as much himself, though it had been no surprise. But to lose a girl who reminded him of Josie...She could feel his pain as if it were grabbing her by the throat. "I'm so sorry."

What else was there to say? What could she do?

Zach cleared his throat on the other end. "I, um, just wanted you to know why I hadn't texted."

"Zach, I—"

"I need some sleep, Princess. I'll see you tomorrow."

"I, um...okay. Yes, sleep. I—" She had no idea what she'd been about to say.

Or maybe she knew exactly what she'd been about to say and got scared.

"I'll see you tomorrow," she finally said.

"Night."

They disconnected, and Kiera flopped back onto her pillow, her phone clutched against her heart. Her pulse was racing, and her mind spinning.

She got up and went into the bathroom for water. She drank a glass. Then another. Then she had to pee.

She finally got back in bed, pulled her blankets up, and closed her eyes.

It took only thirty seconds for her to realize that she wasn't sleeping tonight. At least not here.

She flopped onto her back. It was the middle of the night. But Zach...needed her.

And she wanted to be there.

She got back up, aware that every step she took was a step closer to being as involved as she'd ever been. And she couldn't have stayed away for anything.

Twenty minutes later she was in front of Zach's door. There was an amazing lack of traffic this time of day, and the doorman on duty recognized her, so getting to him had been easy.

She lifted her hand to knock, but then realized it was 3:40 in the morning. She didn't want to wake up Aimee or startle anyone. Instead she pulled her phone out and texted, *Are you there?*

And that was when she realized that, if he was asleep, she might be in trouble.

But a moment later he replied. *Yeah.*

She bit her lip, suddenly nervous. Zach would know what it meant that she was standing outside his apartment at this time of night. But she couldn't go back.

Then she remembered how he'd sounded on the phone, and she knew she wouldn't go back anyway.

Are you okay?

She let her breath out, her heart squeezing. He was having a horrible night, and yet he was asking about her. She needed to get her arms around him.

Will be in a second. I'm outside your door.

The next thing she heard was the sound of footsteps coming closer and closer.

The door swung open, and he stood staring at her, his expression a mix of emotions in the glow of the light from the hallway.

"Jesus, you're really here." He reached for her, pulled her inside, wrapped his arms around her, and buried his face in her hair.

"I had to come," she whispered against his chest.

"I'm so glad."

Her heart swelled as he ran his hands over her head and down the length of her hair. "You could have asked me to come," she told him.

He pulled back and looked down at her. "No. I couldn't."

No. He couldn't. Even in the midst of his own pain, he would have thought about the fact that she didn't do this stuff.

She took his face in her hands and pulled him down. "I'm here, Zach. I'm not going anywhere." She kissed him, and he held on to her as if she were a piece of driftwood in a stormy sea.

He finally lifted his head. "I didn't come to you because I don't know if I can be...anything...for you tonight. I'm a mess."

She knew it was hard for him to admit that. Zach was always the one who was together. Who pulled other people together.

"You don't have to be anything for me, Zach. Being here, holding you, is all I need. I'll be whatever *you* need."

Three heartbeats ticked off, then he took her mouth

again, kicked the door shut, and started walking her backward.

He tugged the zipper on her hoodie down and shoved it down her arms. She pulled her hands free, and he tossed it to the side.

"You're in your pajamas?" he asked.

She looked down. "I didn't do anything but grab Maya's hoodie and Sophie's flip-flops."

"You didn't tell them you were leaving? Did you drive? They'll be worried."

He slid his hands under her tank top and pulled it up and over her head, tossing it too.

She gasped as his hands cupped her bare breasts as he nudged her backward toward the stairs.

"I'll text them," she said.

He lifted her, and she put her arms around his neck as his hands cupped her ass.

"Later," she added.

He carried her upstairs and down the hall to his bedroom. He put her on her feet again and tugged on the end of the tie at the front of her loose pajama pants. They fell to her feet. She didn't wear panties at night, and he growled his approval. She stepped out of the pants as she continued backward toward the bed.

He never took his eyes off her as he also untied his loose pants and shoved them off. He opened the bedside table drawer and dumped a box of condoms onto the top next to his alarm clock. He took one and rolled it on without looking.

Then he leaned over her. "Need you, Kiera."

She wrapped her arms around his neck. "Yes."

He put a hand between them, stroking a finger through

her folds. She was already hot and wet for him. It wasn't arousal like she was used to feeling for him. This was more a desire to be close to him, to give him something that she could best give with her body.

He slid his finger deep, and she whimpered.

"I'm so fucking glad you're here," he muttered.

He surged into her a moment later. She wrapped her legs around his waist and opened up to him in every way.

But he didn't move. Instead he put his arms under her and crushed her against his chest and kissed her.

They were completely joined, every part of her around every part of him, holding tight, and they stayed like that for several long minutes.

When he did finally move, it was in long, slow strokes that felt more like caresses.

Just having him inside her was heavenly, and she simply let him lead, taking whatever he needed.

They moved together like that for long, blissful minutes. It was sex, but it was so much more too. It was about easing the pain, celebrating the good, being close to and connected with someone.

Finally the heat and friction began to build. Zach increased the rhythm, driving harder and harder.

Kiera didn't think she was going to get an orgasm out of the deal this time but didn't mind a bit. Emotionally she was spent, and all she cared about was making Zach feel good. But then he reached between them for her clit while saying, "I could lose myself in you, Princess. Get lost with me."

She shot straight over the edge, amazed to learn that there were different types of orgasms—the ones that gave that bone-deep, amazing sense of completion and satisfaction, and the ones that made her want even more—

things like holding hands and talking and pancakes in the morning.

She remembered him saying he couldn't make anyone else in his life pancakes.

She really wanted those pancakes now.

She wanted to be close to him, important to him. Involved.

He rolled to his side, and she followed, cuddling up against him for several long, delicious minutes.

"I'm sorry about your night," she finally said softly, her hand over his heart.

"I just kept thinking about her family," Zach said, his voice a little rough. "They were at home, probably watching TV, and had no idea their world was about to change forever. They'll think about the last time they saw her. They're going to replay that last conversation a million times. And I was just praying that it was all a good memory."

She lay still, not saying anything for a moment. But finally she asked, "What was your last conversation with Josie?"

He took a deep breath. "It was just a normal conversation. She needed me to come over and unplug her shower drain. She called me for that almost every other month. I asked her if she was plugging it up on purpose."

Kiera smiled. If that was a surefire way to get to see Zach, she'd plug her shower drain up on purpose for sure.

His finger was tracing up and down her arm, but he seemed lost in thought.

"We just…talked," he said. "It was nothing unusual. But thinking back—her guitar was lying on her bed. Seeing her guitar in her room was nothing new—she'd always had a guitar—but I remember specifically that it was out and lying on her bed that day. I've wondered since then..." He took another deep breath. "I've wondered if she wanted me to ask about it. Or somehow give her an opening to tell me about the band. Or something. Because after...the funeral and everything...we went through her things and there was band stuff everywhere. All over her room. Demo CDs and notebook pages with song lyrics and photos and even a poster." He gave a hard laugh. "Can you believe that? There was a poster for her band on her bedroom wall. I never noticed." He sighed. "It's strange how you see what you want to see."

They lay quietly for a few minutes. Kiera didn't know what to say to comfort him.

"Thank you for coming. I needed you, Princess."

Her heart filled. She thought about her response for a second, but finally couldn't *not* say, "I'll be here whenever you need me."

She felt her heart pounding, aware that what she'd just said was huge. She hoped Zach realized that. And then promptly hoped he didn't.

"Yeah?" he asked, his arm tightening around her.

She had to be honest. "Yeah."

He shifted them until he could pull the comforter up over them both but didn't let her go. His breathing slowed, his muscles relaxed, and he fell asleep.

Kiera lay with her hand still on his heart and finally admitted that her life had just become very complicated. She was in love. With Zach Ashley.

She sighed, prepared to be awake for hours thinking over everything, replaying every word and touch and conversation that had led her to this point.

But the next thing she knew, the sun was streaming in his bedroom window, and she'd had nine hours of the deepest sleep she'd had in as long as she could remember.

* * *

Zach woke and stretched, immediately reaching for Kiera.

The bed was empty. Without opening his eyes, he rolled and put his face in the pillow she'd used. It smelled like her, so he knew her being there hadn't been a dream. He also knew it had been a big step on her part. And he knew he was in love with her.

She'd come to him when he'd needed her. She'd been there. And she'd stayed through the night even after he'd unloaded about the accident and his memories of Josie.

But he'd hoped she'd still be there this morning.

He growled and flopped onto his back. *Son of a bitch.* He was going to be patient with her. He was. But that didn't mean he wasn't pissed. And hurt.

Fuck. People didn't just get a good night's sleep and get over everything. She knew that. Jesus, she was still nursing wounds from three years ago. He wasn't judging her for that. But she needed to move on, and he'd thought that he was going to be a part of that for her. He'd thought last night was a sign it was happening.

He sat up swiftly. He was going to *her* now. She wasn't going back inside that bubble. It was time she understood that he was a patient guy, but that she'd just reached the end of his wait-and-see. He was going to tell her how he felt about her and make her face how she felt as well.

Zach pulled on blue jeans and was still yanking his

T-shirt over his head when he swung the bedroom door open and was hit in the face with the smell of bacon.

His stomach rumbled at the same time his heart turned over and said, "Kiera" even as his brain said, "It might be Aimee." It might be. Stranger things had been happening with her than cooking. Like her being curled up on the couch in front of a movie last night when he'd come home instead of on her computer. And her taking one look at his face and getting up to get him cookies.

He padded down the stairs, almost as if afraid of spooking whoever it was. When he came around the corner, his heart swelled. It was Aimee. And Kiera.

They were laughing and talking as Kiera cooked.

She was, indeed, making bacon. And eggs. And blueberry muffins.

He stared. She was making him breakfast. Them. She had stayed, and she was making breakfast for him and Aimee.

"Good morn—" Kiera's greeting was cut off as he strode forward and swung her up into his arms.

"Be back in a little bit," he said to Aimee.

Kiera looked from him to Aimee and back. Then she wordlessly handed the spatula to Aimee.

Zach carried her up the stairs and down the hall to his room. He set her down, shut the door and locked it, and pulled his shirt back over his head.

"I'm in love with you," he said without preamble.

Her wide eyes went from his chest to his face. "Wha—what?"

"I'm in love with you, and you would make me incredibly happy if you'd take off your clothes and get back in my bed."

"It's the bacon talking," she said. She gave a little squeak as he moved to stand almost on top of her.

"Take your clothes off, Kiera. Or should I say my clothes?"

She was in one of his T-shirts and her baggy pajama pants and bare feet. Her hair was tied up, she had muffin batter on one cheek, and she looked rumpled and...happy. She looked happy.

"Need you naked, Princess." He reached for the bottom of his shirt and their fingers bumped as they both worked to get the shirt off over her head. "Pants," he said simply as he shed his jeans.

Her pajama bottoms hit the floor and he lifted her up and tossed her onto the bed.

She lay back, obviously anticipating him climbing up with her, but instead he knelt by the edge of the bed and pulled her toward him.

"Zach." Her eyes were wide again, and she was shaking her head.

"Oh yes." With his gaze on her face, he spread her knees. He ran a finger over her mound to her clit and watched as her eyes darkened and her lips parted. He did it again, then slid his finger into her slick heat. A breath hissed out between her teeth.

He leaned in and kissed the inside of her thigh. "You smell like blueberry muffins."

She gave a soft laugh. "I do not—" She broke off on a sharp gasp as he put his tongue a little higher.

"But you taste even better," he told her. Then he licked again. A few times. Before he sucked her clit between his lips.

"Zach!"

"That's it. That's exactly what I want." He returned his mouth to her clit and lower, tasting every inch of the pink sweetness before him and relishing every moan, gasp, and *Zach* and *yes* that she gave him.

She climbed fast, and he wanted to push her over the edge, but more, he wanted to be as deep in her as he could get so he could feel every ripple from her head to her toes. He rose, dragging his body up hers until he could kiss her. His mouth on hers, he reached for the little pile of condoms he'd made on the bedside table last night. Even he was impressed with how he got it open and on with only the slightest amount of shifting and rolling. Then he pulled one of her knees up and eased into her.

She was tight and hot and...everything. The woman in his arms was, quite simply, *everything*. She frustrated him, made him laugh, made him think, and made him a better man than he'd been a month ago.

Kiera wiggled underneath him, tipping her hips so he could sink even deeper. Oh yeah, she also made him crazy, hot, and hard.

"Princess, you're rushing me."

She smiled up at him. "You're the one who makes me like this."

"Like what?"

"Hot. Horny. Insatiable." She stroked her hands down his back and grabbed his ass.

"Some of my favorite words." He flexed the muscles under her hands and thrust into her. "But *insatiable* might be the best of the bunch."

"Yeah?" she asked, arching to meet his next stroke.

"It means you'll be staying." He thrust. "In bed." He thrust again. "With me." Another thrust. "All day."

Kiera arched her neck, her head tipping back on the mattress. "Throw in all night too and you've got a deal," she panted.

"Well, if you insist." He thrust again and reached between them for her clit.

She moaned and her fingers dug into his butt.

"I could have you in my bed with me all day any day," he said, circling her sweet spot.

"Zach," she groaned.

"Say it, Kiera. Tell me there's nowhere you'd rather be than spread out on my bed with me buried deep, making you moan and come again and again."

Her head rolled back and forth. "Zach." He let up on the pressure slightly. Her eyes flew open. "Hey."

"Tell me."

"Will you wear the eye patch later?" she asked.

He felt his smile spread, but he narrowed his eyes. "If you'll be the stowaway I tie to my bed as punishment."

She grinned, and Zach wondered when the last time a woman had *grinned* in bed with him. Then again, he wasn't sure he would have noticed. He'd never been as fascinated with a woman's facial expressions, particularly her eyes, as he was with Kiera's. He'd nearly run out of chocolate-brown things to compare them to.

"Thought you decided you weren't the pirate type." Her Hershey's Kisses–brown eyes twinkled at that.

"Turns out I have a little bit of bad boy in me after all," he said. "At least when it comes to the list I'm compiling."

"The list?"

"Of sounds you make and how to reproduce them consistently."

She smiled. "How long's the list so far?"

"Fourteen different sounds, nine of which are caused by more than one thing."

She laughed. "What about the other five?"

"Produced by more specific things I do or say." He circled her clit again, and she made the one that sounded like a hum and a groan put together.

"Fourteen?" she asked, breathless again.

He grinned. He'd totally made that up. She did have a number of sounds, and he was all about getting her to make them over and over again, though. "Going to need more study," he said, stroking deep as he used his thumb to circle the sensitive hum-groan spot.

"I'm thinking you might get new noises if you play pirate," she told him.

"You do have a thing for bad boys?" He pulled almost all the way out and then plunged forward.

She gasped, then shook her head. "No, but I have a thing for a regular guy with a big-enough heart and sense of humor to go along with something silly for fun."

He stroked in and out again, getting a sound that was a cross between a gasp and a sigh. "There's nothing silly about the idea of you dressed as a tavern wench waiting for my ship to come into port."

"Whoa, you've got a couple scenarios all worked out, I see. I can't be a pirate queen, with my own ship? And we meet on some deserted island for our rendezvous?"

He moved his hips again, relishing the feel of her under and around him, hot and wet, even as they teased and joked. For a girl like Kiera, talk of costumes and pretend play might just be the best aphrodisiac of all. "Being princess of all of Leokin is enough being in charge. You'll be at my mercy in this story, wench." He thrust again, and she moaned.

He thought it was as much the wench thing as the thrust.

She stretched and wrapped her arms around his neck. "Well, I have a *very* big thing for you, Zach Ashley. The guy. No costumes of any kind needed."

"I know exactly what you mean, Kiera Connolly."

He picked up the tempo then, sliding in and pulling out in long, deep strokes that quickly took them from the low burn that had been simmering between them to a full, rolling boil of need.

Her soft noises mixed with the occasional *Zach* made it impossible for him to hold back, and Kiera met him thrust for thrust until they were both flying. Zach's body pulsed hard and hot into hers until he felt as if he'd been completely wrung out.

When the waves of pleasure finally subsided, he rolled to his side, dragging her with him. He was still breathing hard, and he was gratified to see her chest heaving as well.

"*Now* it's time for breakfast," he said.

"I wanted to make you pancakes. But I don't know how."

He grinned at her. "Are *these* pancakes literal or metaphorical?"

She returned his smile. "Both."

CHAPTER ELEVEN

This is not exactly what I had in mind when you said your parents were having a dinner party," Kiera said a week later as Zach escorted her into the Imperial Ballroom at the Boston Park Plaza Hotel.

She took in the room. The ceiling was probably twenty feet high, with three huge crystal chandeliers hanging from it. The floor was covered with a gray-and-burgundy-swirled carpet, and the high windows along the far side of the room were draped in deep burgundy velvet. The walls were a pristine white, as were the tablecloths on the forty tables with ten chairs circling each. In addition, there were five balconies on each side of the room where more tables and chairs were set up for special guests.

And being named a special guest in this group was something. The room was full of Boston's rich and famous, from local politicians and officials to a few musicians, artists, and actors.

"It's dinner. It's a party. And my parents are hosting,"

Zach said, a hand on her lower back as he led her through the room to the stairs that would take them to the balcony on the right side of the room, which was closest to the stage. Yes, there was also a stage.

"You knew that I would freak out if I knew that you were bringing me to meet your parents at a banquet with the entire upper crust of Boston society," Kiera said.

"Let's say I've figured a few things out about you." Zach looked inordinately pleased.

"Are you sure I'm dressed okay?" she asked. He'd told her the occasion was "very dressy" and had mentioned a "white-tablecloth kind of place." He hadn't mentioned there would be fifty such tables. He had texted her a few days ago and said simply, *Wear white.* But she'd been picturing a nice restaurant with wine she couldn't afford. Not the Imperial Ballroom at the Park Plaza. With an entire menu she couldn't afford. With five hundred of the Ashleys' closest friends.

Zach stopped her at the top of the steps to the balcony and pulled her around to face him. "You look gorgeous." He ran his hand up and down her arm. "And you don't have to impress anyone."

She pressed her lips together and nodded. "Okay, thank you."

"Thank *you*." He lifted her hand to his lips.

She took a deep breath. The tuxedo he wore did more to make her insides mushy than the pirate eye patch had. Because it was real. She hadn't seen the grew-up-rich side of him much, but it was clear that he was completely comfortable in the tux and in the social setting. She wouldn't have thought that would be so attractive. Her own parents had spent their share of time at upscale dinners and parties, and she'd been dragged along early on, but she'd never enjoyed them. But maybe that was because she'd never been with Zach before. The guy could probably make her like a root canal.

Zach laced his fingers with hers. "You ready?"

"Ready as I'm going to be."

She was, in truth, wishing for a little sparkly eye shadow, but she'd be okay. She loved her new dress. It was a long white A-line that fit against her hips but flared slightly below her knees. The bodice was held up with a crystal-studded loop around her neck, and behind it was open to her lower back. It was the kind of silky material that clung, so she'd had to leave the bra at home and needed to go for the thong. She'd put her hair up in a simple twist and used a sparkly clip. But she'd left the sparkly eye shadow and body gems in her makeup bag. Her earrings sparkled a little, but they were also modest—tiny crystal balls that swung from small silver hoops through her ears.

Zach led her to the table in the balcony that overlooked the incredibly beautiful ballroom. A gorgeous woman who looked just like Aimee and a handsome man who gave her an exact picture of Zach in twenty-five years were already at the table.

"Where's Aimee?" Zach asked her softly.

"She said she'd meet us here," Kiera said. "I thought she'd be here already, though."

Zach frowned and glanced down at the roomful of guests. But there was no way he was going to spot her. Finding a beautiful young woman in that crowd was like looking for a snowflake in an avalanche. Sure, up close they might all be unique, but mixed with the others and from a distance they just became a part of the big, stunning picture.

Especially when all the "snowflakes" were actually dressed in white.

"Everyone is in black and white," she commented, though there was no possible way that was a coincidence.

"My mother likes the glamor of it."

"Zach." His mother rose from her seat and leaned over to kiss his cheek.

"Mother, this is Kiera. Kiera, my mother, Susan."

"It's very nice to meet you, Mrs. Ashley." Kiera extended her hand.

Susan Ashley shook it, studying Kiera closely. "You're the girl who's been playing that game with Aimee?"

Kiera nodded. She felt that was a simplistic summary of her relationship with Aimee, but she also didn't feel like going into it in any more depth. "Yes, that's right."

"Mother," Zach chided, "Kiera and Aimee do more than that. They're friends."

"We are," Kiera agreed. "But we do play Leokin together. Almost every day."

"And Kiera's teaching Aimee to cook," Zach added.

His mother looked surprised and impressed. "You cook?"

Kiera laughed. "Just enough, really. I've shown her very basic things. My roommate Sophie does most of the cooking."

"Kiera's a wonderful cook," Zach said.

She glanced up at him, puzzled. She'd made him muffins, bacon, an omelet, and chili to date. And one night he'd had leftover baked ziti when he got home from his shift.

"Yes, Aimee said you have two roommates?" Susan asked, almost as if Zach hadn't spoken.

Kiera smiled. She was glad to hear that Aimee and Susan had been talking. "Yes. Maya and Sophie both own their own businesses—a martial arts studio and a small playhouse."

"Oh, Jack, this is Kiera," Susan said as her husband turned away from his conversation with two other men.

He smiled at Kiera and held out his hand. "Nice to meet you, Kiera."

"You too, Mr. Ashley."

"Kiera is an amazing graphic designer," Zach said.

"Oh, how nice," Susan said. "I'm not artistic at all."

"I've always loved to draw and paint," Kiera said.

"I took a pottery class last year," Susan said. "I wasn't very good, but it really was fun to create something. You start with this simple ball of clay and then, by the end of class, it's a vase. Or it's supposed to be, anyway," she said with a little laugh. "Still, it looked completely different by the end."

Kiera nodded and started to respond. But Zach talked right over her.

"Kiera does the graphics for the fastest-growing video game franchise in the country," he told his father. "They're a multimillion-dollar company, and they've only been around for a couple of years."

Kiera gave him a little frown. Why did he think he needed to present his parents with her résumé?

Jack nodded. "Impressive."

Susan saw someone over Kiera's shoulder. "I'm sorry. We should go say hello to a few people. Please make yourselves comfortable at the table. They're going to serve dinner in a little bit. Then we'll have the program around eight."

Susan and Jack moved off to mingle, and Kiera turned to Zach. "You're trying to make sure your parents approve of me?"

He sighed. "No. My parents have a bias against World of Leokin. I wanted to be sure they knew there was more going on."

Kiera tipped her head. "Wonder where their bias came from?"

"A bit of ranting and raving from one of their children," he admitted.

"Uh-huh. And what if Leokin was all Aimee and I were doing?"

He sighed again. "I know. It's not what it seems, and it's been helping her, and I probably should have said that."

There was something in his tone and body language that made her hesitate. He was smiling, and he seemed truly glad to have her there with him. But there was something else underlying all of that. He was tense. He had been for two days.

Zach pulled a chair at the table out for her. Kiera sat, but she immediately turned to him when he took the seat next to her. "Your mom mentioned a program?"

He shrugged. "There's a presentation after dinner. This is a fundraising dinner."

"Fundraising?" Okay that was nice. Maybe it was some amazing charity. "For what?"

"A foundation they're starting in my sister's name."

Ah. Yes, amazing, then. And very personal. Kiera took his hand. His tension made sense now. This could be an emotional night. "What's the foundation do?"

"They provide musical instruments and lessons for kids who can't afford them on their own."

"Guitar and drums and stuff?"

He shook his head. "Violin and flute and stuff."

"Oh ... I assumed with the band and all that she'd taken guitar lessons."

"She did, eventually. But she started out with more classical instruments. She paid for her own guitar and drum lessons. She did, however, use the piano lessons my parents insisted on when she played keyboard in the band. Much to their chagrin."

Kiera grinned. "They weren't fans of her rock music either?"

Zach frowned. "I never said I wasn't a fan. I'd heard her play a few times. She was really good."

"But you didn't want her to be in the band."

"Instead of finishing college and getting her teaching degree? No. But that didn't mean she couldn't have kept playing at the small bars on the weekends, or doing wedding receptions, or whatever."

"Okay. Got it. Teaching was better than the band, but the band wasn't the epitome of all evil."

Zach reached for one of the water goblets and took a chug. "So, yeah, we're here supporting the establishment of a music program for classical music in the name of my sister who hated the violin *and* the flute."

Kiera thought about that for a moment. And watched Zach's throat work as he swallowed. And resisted the urge to put her lips against the cord of muscle that ran up to his jaw. "That's okay," she finally said.

He looked at her. "It is?"

Kiera looked around. The room was full. It was glamorous. It was like a fairy-tale ball. And nothing like a club where a live rock band would dress the way Josie and her band had in a photo Aimee had showed Kiera.

"This isn't about Josie," she finally said. "This is about your mom and dad. This is their way of dealing. Just like Aimee turned to Leokin, and you made your little sister live with you so you could feel like you were doing something—"

He gave her a fake exasperated look. Exasperated because this kept coming up. Fake because he knew she was right.

"This is their way of healing," she continued. "It doesn't matter if Josie would have liked it or not. It's for them."

Zach turned in his seat and put one elbow on the table in front of her and one on the back of her chair, caging her in. His knees bracketed hers. His gaze caught hers and held it.

"You are amazing," he said quietly.

"Yeah?" she asked.

"Definitely."

"Then quit trying to build me up to your parents."

"I wasn't trying to hide who you are," Zach said. He looked down at the floor and took a breath, then looked back up at her. "I'm sorry. This makes me crazy."

"What does?"

"All of this. Making sure everyone is happy, and no one says anything to hurt anyone else, and no one makes unfair assumptions, and everyone gets along and has what they need."

Kiera leaned in and put her hand on the back of his neck. "You don't have to do all of that, Zach. We're all grown-ups."

"I know. But grown-ups have problems sometimes too."

"And you want to save them all."

"Well, I definitely prefer grown-ups who are having an actual heart attack versus suffering heartbreak," he said wryly. "I know what to do about the heart attack."

She rubbed his neck. "Relax. Everyone else's actions and feelings and decisions are not your responsibility all the time."

He looked frustrated. "You have no idea how much I want to believe that."

"Maybe knowing that you'll always deal with everything and fix everything has made your family less able to handle their own stuff."

He studied her face. "And the people in your life know they have to handle their own stuff because you won't do it."

It was true. Basically. But it sounded bad. Not because of the way he said it but because he cared so much about everyone. He didn't take care of things because he liked to be in control. He did it because he loved them.

"People have an amazing capacity to learn and grow and heal," she said carefully. "If we let them. Or, yes, sometimes make them."

"No one should ever need anyone else?"

She thought back to the night a week ago after the car accident. He'd needed her, and she'd loved being there for him. "Not never," she said. "Turns out I'm not right about everything I've always believed. Either."

She gave him a little smile that he returned.

"Zach! Nice to see you."

Zach pushed his chair back and rose to greet the man who had approached their table. Kiera took the chance to slide out of her chair and step to the railing of the balcony. Where was Aimee?

She knew looking for her in the room of women in

white was futile, but…then she saw her. Turned out look-ing for Aimee in a room of women in white was not futile at all—because Aimee was wearing bright red.

It was only her shoes and jewelry that were red—along with her date's bright-red bow tie and vest—but in the roomful of white, she stood out.

Oh crap. What was going on? Kiera glanced over her shoulder to where Zach was still in conversation with the other man. She caught his eye and gave him a smile, then gestured down the steps and mouthed, "Restroom."

He gave her a nod of understanding.

Kiera got to her before Aimee could start up the steps to the family's balcony.

"What are you doing?"

Aimee put her shoulders back. "What do you mean?"

She was dressed in a short white dress that hit at midthigh and had long, winglike sleeves. Her hair was done up in an elegant twist. Her makeup was bold, but not over the top. Though her lipstick matched her acces-sories perfectly. And the shoes and jewelry weren't gaudy or tasteless. They were just red. Really red. Just as Cody's tie and vest were. The tuxedo was nice. Top of the line, in fact. But the red was vivid.

Kiera looked around, then took Aimee's elbow and steered her through the ballroom doors and out into the hallway. "What's going on?"

"This party is supposed to be about my sister," Aimee said. "Josie would have hated all of this black and white. So I decided that at least one person here should actually honor *her* tonight. Not what my parents wanted her to be, not what they wished for, but who she really was. She made a statement. She stood out."

Kiera felt her heart squeeze. "Oh, honey—" She broke off and looked around. The hallway right outside the ballroom where the Ashleys' friends and business associates were coming and going was probably not the best place for this conversation. "Come on."

"Aimee—" Cody started.

"I'm okay," she told him. "I'll be right back."

Kiera led Aimee down the hallway to the ladies' room and nudged her inside.

Aimee swung around to face her immediately. "I thought *you* would understand."

Kiera quickly checked under the stall doors, relieved to find they were alone. She took a deep breath and faced Aimee. "I do understand. I know that you want to remember Josie and..." She stepped closer and put her hands on Aimee's shoulders. "I know that you're trying to channel your inner Quinn because that's the only way you can face this night."

Three heartbeats passed before Aimee sniffed. "Cody and my clan encouraged me. They said I should do what would make me feel good. This whole night is about Josie being gone."

"Your parents are remembering her tonight," Kiera said.

"No. They're not. She hated her classical lessons and the violin."

"And how's the red jewelry help you remember her?"

Aimee looked down at her shoes. "These are hers. And she would love that I'm here, doing what Mom wants, dressed the way Mom wants me to, but with my own flair."

Kiera didn't know what to say. She didn't know Aimee's mother well, but she had the definite gut feeling that this would annoy her. And Zach. Because he was trying to keep the peace tonight, trying to keep everyone happy and positive.

Kiera wanted the night to go well for him. She wanted *him* to be happy and positive.

"It's funny," Aimee said. "Before she died, I would have happily put the white dress on and not thought anything of it. I've always worked on doing what Zach did. Following the rules and doing what was expected of me. He was my role model. Never Josie. I loved her, and I thought she was cool, but I never wanted to be like her. She rocked the boat, and it seemed like she made things so hard. Everything was a fight. She was always standing up for something." Aimee took a big breath. "But now that she's gone, I realize that she was the one who had fun, who made memories and had great stories and really lived life. She only had twenty-four years, but she had more fun and more friendships and more adventure in those years than a lot of people do in twice as much time."

Kiera swallowed hard. "You realized all of that on your own?"

Aimee shook her head. "I realized it by telling stories about her to my friends."

"Zach doesn't have fun?" Kiera had to ask.

"Not often. He doesn't let himself. Basketball is about it. Until now, with you."

Kiera honestly didn't know how to respond.

"Zach, obviously, embraced the black and white," Aimee said, gesturing at Kiera's dress. "But there's no way Josie would have come in here in a white dress. She would have dressed in head-to-toe red, probably. And now as I think about her, I realize that she was happier than Zach has ever been."

That made Kiera's heart hurt. She wanted Zach to be happy. More than anything.

Aimee went on. "I think if she'd showed up in bright red, it would have made my mom roll her eyes, but she would have smiled too. Josie always brought color with her." Aimee was quiet for a moment, then added, "I want to be more like her. Not completely. Sometimes she fought just to fight. But I want to be more like her—more sure of myself, of who I am. I want to worry less about what everyone else expects. I want to be less...like Zach."

Just then the door bumped shut as someone came in, and they both turned.

But it wasn't just someone. It was Zach.

And he'd clearly heard what Aimee had said about wanting to be less like him.

"What's going on?" he demanded.

"Zach! This is the ladies' room!" Aimee exclaimed.

"Are you alright?" he asked, coming forward. He took in her jewelry. "I assume the guy in the hallway with the bright-red vest is with you?"

Aimee nodded. "That's Cody."

"Who the hell is Cody?"

"The guy I'm dating."

"You're dating someone, and you didn't tell me?" Zach asked.

"Yes."

"Where did you meet him?"

Aimee's chin went up. "Leokin."

Kiera stepped forward and took his arm. "Zach, just listen. This is a hard night for her."

"You met him online?" Zach asked, not even looking at Kiera.

"Yes."

Zach drew in a long breath. "Do you have any idea how dangerous that is, Aimee? For fuck's sake! At least try to be like me enough to stay safe!"

Aimee winced. "I've known him online for almost a year. And when I first met him in person, I met him in public, and Kiera was there so I was totally safe."

Kiera felt as if someone had suddenly doused her with cold water. Oh crap. She looked up at Zach to find him watching her with disbelief.

"You knew?" he asked.

She nodded.

"And tonight is the first night we've been alone, and I still met him here," Aimee said. "Usually our whole group goes out."

"Your whole group…" Zach trailed off and shoved a hand through his hair. "Your clan, right?"

Aimee nodded, clearly noting the disdain in his tone. "Zach, you have to give him a break. He's the reason I'm here tonight. They all are. My friends talked me into coming and feeling better about all of this."

"They're the reason you're here," Zach repeated. "Not me, not Kiera. Not Mom and Dad. Or Josie. Your online friends that have known you for only a few months."

"I've known them longer than I've known Kiera!" Aimee threw her hands up. "If I was here because of her, you'd be fine. But not my friends. The people who have been there for me through everything."

Zach's jaw tensed, and Kiera could see he was trying to calm down. "Fine. We'll talk about this later. You need to go home and change." He looked at his watch. "It's already late. Mom and Dad have been waiting for you."

"Then let's go out there," Aimee said. "I'm not going home."

"You can't go out there like that," he said.

"Do you really think people are going to give less money to the project because I'm wearing red shoes?" Aimee asked him.

"This is about respecting Mom and Dad. Mom wanted this to be black and white."

"And that's ridiculous. People are thinking this is just another fundraising dinner. They're not really thinking about why they're here. When I walk in there like this, they'll think of Josie—how bold and bright she was, how she did things her way. That's what I want from tonight," Aimee told him.

"Well, tonight isn't about what you want," Zach told her. "You need to go home and change."

Kiera opened her mouth to intervene, but Aimee spoke first. "The other day you said that you would have respected Josie for standing up for herself and that you know you're not always right. What happened to your opinion not always being the most important one?"

Kiera looked into Aimee's eyes and saw the betrayal she was feeling. She looked up at Zach and saw the pain in his eyes.

"And what happened to the part where you said that, when you love and respect someone, their opinion always mattered?" he asked his sister.

Aimee lifted her chin. "I do love and respect you. And I trust you. I trusted you when you said that, if something makes me happy, I should go for it, even if you don't understand it."

* * *

Zach felt as if Aimee had kicked him right in the chest. He swallowed. "I just wanted tonight to be nice for everyone."

"But it's not your job to make things nice for everyone all the time, Zach," Aimee said.

His mind was spinning in a million directions, and he didn't know who to focus on or how to even feel for sure. Was he angry? Worried? Both? Neither? And if it was neither, then what did he feel? Beyond confused, of course.

"Mom's drinking isn't about you, Zach," Aimee said. "Dad's attitude isn't either. Neither are my shoes. Half the things that you feel bad about aren't really about you. Not everything is your responsibility."

Kiera had said the same damned thing. And as much as he'd like to believe that, he wasn't sure Kiera was the best one to give advice about responsibilities, frankly. Her way of dealing with things was to walk away. And what did Aimee know about responsibilities? She was seventeen years old, and he'd been taking care of things for her all her life.

"Well, they have to be someone's responsibility," Zach snapped. "If it's not me caring about all of this shit, who's it going to be, Aimee?"

He expected Aimee to yell. Or cry. Or run away.

But she did none of those.

Instead she looked concerned as she moved closer and looked up at him. She shook her head. "You're wrong."

She was concerned about *him*?

He scowled. "What do I have wrong?"

She swallowed hard. "Mom's back in AA. And she and Dad are going to counseling. And I signed up for classes the other day. And you didn't do any of that for us. We all got there, because of our friends and each other and ourselves. And we're okay."

Dammit. Why didn't *anyone* in his family tell him how they were really feeling and what they were going through and what the fuck was happening in their lives?

"Why haven't they said anything?" he asked, proud of how calm his voice sounded.

Aimee's eyes widened. "You really don't know?"

"No. Why?"

"They've been protecting you."

Zach stared at her. "Excuse me?"

"They didn't tell you because they knew you'd want to walk me to class every day and go to the AA meetings and sit on the couch next to them in the counselor's office. You take everything on."

"I would have tried to help, yes," he said. "How is that a bad thing?"

"Because they're not your problems to solve!"

Her words hit him directly in the gut.

"Things don't really get better if we're not the ones making it better," Aimee said.

He didn't know what to say. Or even what to feel. He thought through everything she'd said. "They don't tell me anything so I don't try to get involved where I'm not wanted?"

"They do it so you don't try to fix something you can't fix and then beat yourself up over failing."

His parents knew him that well? And they'd been putting forth all that effort for him?

He didn't remember the last time someone had tried to save *him* from something.

Except for Kiera. She'd been trying to save him from screwing things up with Aimee.

"And by the way, when you constantly think you need to fix me, it makes me feel more broken than I really am,"

Aimee said. Then she pushed past him and stormed to the bathroom door, yanked it open, and disappeared through it without a look back.

Zach dragged a big breath into his lungs. He should go after her. He should...

But no. He didn't need to go after her. She didn't need him. Cody was there. And the rest of her friends.

"Zach?"

Kiera's soft voice pulled him out of his head. He focused on her and just looked at her for a long moment.

"Should we go after her?" Kiera asked.

He slowly shook his head. "No."

"No?" She was clearly surprised.

Because he always went after people. Always.

"She doesn't need me. I'm not going to—" He broke off and shook his head again. "I even tried to change you. The last person on the planet that needed fixing."

She gave a short laugh. "Seriously? I'm screwed up too. We all are a little."

He stared at her beautiful face. She was amazing. And she left people alone to figure their own shit out. She'd been happy and pain-free for years.

He wanted some of that. Right now.

He turned and started for the door.

"Where are you going?"

"I'm done."

"Done? What does that mean?"

"I'm done trying so fucking hard."

"Zach—"

"Everything I wanted is a reality. Aimee is happy and has friends again. My mom's getting sober. My dad's at least trying."

"It's all great," Kiera agreed.

He gave a humorless laugh. "And I had nothing to do with it. They didn't confide in me when things were bad. When I found out and tried to help, it didn't work—Aimee holed up, my dad shut down, and my mom drank anyway. And then eventually they all figured it out themselves."

"And it's still a wonderful thing, Zach," Kiera said. "They're getting better. Happy. I know you love being a hero, but like Aimee said, not every problem is yours. Other people love the people you love too. They can help them. And sometimes people can help themselves."

He nodded. "Yep, guess so." And just what the hell was he supposed to do with that? "I guess that means you're free to go."

Kiera blinked at him. "What?"

"Tonight was our last night. You can go home to your computer and cereal bowl."

He saw the hurt flash in her eyes, but he ignored it. Kiera Connolly definitely didn't need to be fixed. He needed to leave her alone.

"You're going back in there by yourself?" she asked softly.

"No. I'm not going back in there period." He turned and headed for the door. If he didn't need to worry about how other people felt anymore, he was going to start right now.

* * *

Kiera let herself into the house through the back kitchen door. She felt numb. No, she *wanted* to feel numb. Instead she felt…confused. Stunned. Pissed off.

Zach had walked away.

That was all she was sure of.

Kiera dropped her purse on the table by the back door and barely noticed when it slid to the floor.

"Hey." Maya straightened from where she'd had her shoulder propped against the cabinets, apparently watching Rob replace the lightbulb in the fixture above the center island.

"Hey."

"How was the party?" Rob asked.

"Um..." How did she even begin? "The hotel was gorgeous, the dresses were gorgeous, met the mom and dad, disappointed the sister, and watched the boyfriend walk out before dinner even started."

Rob lowered his arms, and Maya came forward.

"What happened?" Maya asked.

Kiera shook her head. "I'm not really sure."

Maya pushed her gently into one of the chairs at the table in the nook by the window. "You don't look so good."

"I don't feel so good."

"Zach walked out?" Maya asked. "That doesn't sound like him."

"I know."

"So what happened?"

Kiera felt her chest tighten as she looked up at one of her best friends. A woman she loved and trusted and knew would always be there for her. And yet Kiera didn't confide in her. She didn't share. She didn't let Maya all the way in.

But Maya was still there for her. So was Sophie. So was Rob.

Not letting them close, not letting them really be fully a part of her life, had been a huge mistake.

So Kiera recounted the whole story. Then she raised

her gaze to where Maya was leaning against the table, watching her with a funny look. Kiera took a shaky breath. "He walked away from Aimee, his mom, his dad, everyone. People weren't doing things his way, and he just...quit." She shook her head, dropping her gaze to her hands.

"Kind of sucks, doesn't it?" Maya asked.

Kiera lifted her head quickly. "What?"

"Sucks when you really care about someone and want to help, but they just block you out."

Sophie was the softer, sweeter one. Kiera knew that. But in spite of the pang of hurt near her heart, she knew Maya had every right to say that. Kiera had been doing exactly what Zach had done tonight. For the past three years.

"Yes. It does," she admitted.

Images flashed through her mind. Of Sophie making Kiera soup when she'd been sick, even though she'd missed Sophie's big opening night at the theater because she'd been working. Sophie making Kiera's costume for this Comic Con even though Kiera had skipped out on helping with the set for Sophie's last play. Maya leaving a new pair of mittens on the counter in the kitchen after Kiera had left ones she'd borrowed from Maya on the train. Maya buying Kiera's favorite coffee, even though Kiera only knew that Maya preferred tea and had no idea if she had a favorite. Rob coming over and changing lightbulbs for them even though they should be perfectly capable of doing it themselves and never came over to his place to do anything but drink beer.

The list was endless. They were always there for her. Even when she didn't hold up her end, even when she was selfish and absorbed in her own little bubble and withholding her affection, these people were there for her. Those things seemed small, simple. But added up over time, they made... a relationship.

"So, what are you going to do?" Rob asked.

Kiera took a deep breath. This hurt. Getting involved with Zach and Aimee had been wonderful, but painful in the end. And it was over. She'd done what she said she would do. She'd put the month in. She needed to start working on the Leokin stuff tomorrow. She could walk away and not feel guilty. That would be the easiest, most predictable thing for her to do.

"I don't know," she told her friends. Because she didn't want to walk away. "I don't really know how to go after someone."

"Well," Maya said, "what would Zach do?"

Kiera started to smile, then realized that Maya had a point. Zach always went after the people he cared about. He didn't leave. He dug in and *stayed*.

More images went through her mind. Zach knocking on Aimee's door every night to see if she was okay and if she needed anything, even when she said terrible things to him or said nothing to him at all. Zach showing up at his mom and dad's house for dinner even though he knew his mom might be tipsy and his father doing nothing for anyone. Zach showing up at work day after day with the hope that he would save someone's life, even though he knew there was always the chance the opposite would be true. Zach leaning against the post at the arcade, waiting for her to come out of the restroom and face what they'd been talking about.

Zach showed up even when he knew things would be bad, even when he was being pushed away, even when he was facing things that would hurt. Because, for him, the love he felt was stronger than the possible pain.

"Zach would come after me," she finally said. "He'd be there no matter what I did or said. Or didn't do or say."

Maya nodded. "Then you know exactly what to do."

Kiera felt her heart flip over. She did. Because of Zach. "I'm...sor—"

"Stop it," Maya said, holding up her hand. "Sophie will kill me if I finally get a mushy, emotional, spill-our-guts moment with you and she misses it."

Kiera smiled, in spite of everything. She got to her feet. "Well, then this part will be just between us." And she pulled Maya into a hug.

She was becoming a fan of hugging.

"I found him."

Kiera looked up to see Aimee coming into the kitchen. She knew exactly who Aimee was talking about, of course. She stood swiftly. "He was lost?"

"After you left the party, Mom called. She was crazy with worry because we'd all left. I couldn't believe that Zach just walked out," Aimee said. "So I started calling his friends. No one knew where he was. They went and checked the gym and the bars, but he wasn't anywhere. He wasn't answering his phone. Nothing."

Worry tried to take over, but she focused on Aimee's initial words. "But you found him?" Her heart was pounding so hard that everything sounded muffled.

"He's at home. He's been there the whole time, I guess. But he's holed up in his room. He never hangs out in his room, so I didn't even look in there."

Kiera grabbed her purse. He was at home. That was all she needed to know. "I'm going over there."

"He's, um…" Aimee was clearly hesitant to tell her the rest.

"He's what?" Kiera asked. She grabbed Sophie's car keys and started for the door.

"He's in there…"

Kiera glanced back. God, did he have a woman in there with him? But she rejected that thought right away. Was he drunk? High? "*Aimee.*"

"He's gaming."

Kiera stopped, frozen. Then she turned to face Aimee. "Excuse me?"

Aimee nodded. "He's gaming. He's in Leokin."

Kiera shook her head. "What do you mean?"

"I mean, he moved *all* of my stuff—my gaming chair, computer, monitor, controllers, headphones, *everything*— into his room and is now in Leokin. He didn't even look up when I came into the room. He wouldn't talk to me, wouldn't stop for even a second."

"Is he…playing…as you?" But unless Aimee had given him her password, that was impossible. But nothing else really made sense either.

"Nope. Made his own account, his own character, the whole thing."

"But…how…What's he doing?"

"Killing a bunch of trolls when I was in there," Aimee said grimly.

Maya turned round eyes to Kiera. "I think you broke the hot guy."

Yes. It did appear so. Crap.

Zach loose in Leokin. With only a basic knowledge of the game. And pissed off at the world—the real world, anyway. This had disaster written all over it.

Kiera set her purse and the car keys down on the table and started for the stairs.

"Where are you going?" Maya asked. "Aren't you going to Zach's?"

"I am," Kiera affirmed. "But I'm going in for the long haul. I'm going to need some more comfortable clothes and some supplies."

"I'll pack some things up in here," Aimee said, heading for the cupboards.

"You're going to *game* with him?" Rob asked with a grin.

"I'm going to do whatever he needs me to do," Kiera said. "But if he wants to game, then yeah, we're going to game."

"What if he won't talk to you?" Aimee asked. "He wouldn't even look at me."

"I can play for *days* without talking to anyone."

"You're going to outlast him?" Maya asked. She looked amused.

"Oh yeah," Kiera assured her. "If Zach Ashley thinks he can escape me in Leokin, he really has a lot to learn."

"He can be *really* stubborn," Aimee said, putting a box of crackers and a couple of apples in a plastic bag.

"Well, I've done gaming marathons with *Pete* and *Dalton*," Kiera said. "Zach will be putty in my hands in a few hours. Heck, he probably thinks he can get through this on energy drinks and Twizzlers."

Rob groaned. He'd made that mistake. Once.

"Be sure you put some bottled water and protein bars in there," Kiera told Aimee. "I'm going in prepared for anything, and I'm not coming out without Zach."

CHAPTER TWELVE

There really was something incredibly freeing about not giving a shit.

And sitting in a dark room alone and worrying about nothing but what animated creature might pop out at him next.

He was receiving messages along the side of the screen. Things like, *Dude, what are you doing?* and *Who are you?* and *That's not how you use the Dagger of Darian.* He assumed they were referring to the little dagger he'd found under a rock along the stream.

He didn't know who the messages were from and didn't know how to answer them anyway, so he'd begun simply ignoring them.

That was also very freeing.

As was ignoring all the calls and texts coming in on his phone. He hated texting anyway.

Zach moved his controller, stomping through the virtual forest with heavy footsteps. For the most part, creatures scattered as he marched through the trees, but every once in a while, some ugly little critter would rear up and snarl at him. He cut their heads off.

He had no idea if that was what he was supposed to be doing, but he had a sword and a dagger and some major pent-up aggression, and hell, most of the time the creature's head would regrow in a matter of seconds and it would go running off.

He liked that best of all. He was able to kill stuff without it being permanent.

He reached a narrow valley filled with some kind of flower. As he stepped forward on the screen a message popped up in the center of the display, unlike the irritated ones running along the right-hand side.

This one said, *You have been summoned to the palace by Princess Kirenda.*

Zach scoffed. He was sure he had been. He was surprised only that it had taken this long for Aimee to tell on him.

He hadn't taken his eyes off the game or removed his headphones when she'd come into the room—it was only fair, considering how many times she'd done the very same thing to him—but he admitted he'd been happy to know she was home. And he'd known she'd go tell Kiera what he was doing.

But he didn't care. He wasn't in the game to get her attention. He was here because...he wanted to get lost. He wanted to play in a fantasy world for a while. He wanted to be the rogue warrior who had no family and no responsibilities, who was unpredictable and maybe even feared. If Leokin had helped Aimee all these months, it was worth a try.

He closed the message about the princess without replying and went stomping down through the wild flowers in the valley.

Fifteen minutes later Princess Kirenda herself moved into the space between the gaming chair he'd set at the foot of his bed and the desk where he'd put the monitor. She was dressed in a pair of cutoff sweatpants and a loose T-shirt. Her hair was tied back, and she had no makeup on. And she was holding a plastic grocery bag in one hand.

She looked a little ticked off and completely beautiful. And he wanted her so badly that his teeth ached.

"What are you doing here?" he asked, grumpily.

"Climbing into your bubble."

His heart stuttered. But no. He was done with bubbles and pulling people in and out of them.

"You're in my way," he told her, leaning to the left to look around her.

"You ignored my summons."

He had no idea how she'd been able to send the summons, since she would have been in the car for the past twenty minutes or so, but he didn't care.

"Yep." He made his warrior climb a steep embankment even as it sucked his energy to a dangerously low level.

Apparently stomping over the flowers—the magical flowers—had depleted his energy, and his warrior was having some trouble staying on his feet. He was looking for a safe place to rest and let his avatar rebuild.

Kiera glanced over her shoulder at the screen. "If you destroy the beauty in Leokin, it, in turn, destroys you."

He sat his warrior down and then sighed, looking up at her. "I didn't think the princess would come looking for a dangerous rebel."

"The princess does whatever she wants to do," she informed him with an eyebrow arched.

"The princess *wanted* to come looking for the dangerous rebel?" Kiera didn't come after people. She was usually the one leaving.

And he could admit, he got it now. It had felt liberating walking out of the hotel. He'd taken control of his part of the situation and how it played out for *him*.

"Well, the princess is in love with the dangerous rebel," Kiera said, crossing her arms.

Zach's heart kicked hard against his ribs, but he kept his expression neutral. Or he tried to, anyway. "The king sent me a message and informed me the princess doesn't get to choose to love anything but the kingdom."

Pete Candon, the creator of World of Leokin himself, had sent Zach a private message. It hadn't been hard to read between the lines of the message from Leokin's king either. Kiera was Pete's friend and Pete didn't like hearing that Zach had upset her. Zach didn't even want to know how Pete knew about his relationship with Kiera or how he'd found out that the relationship was over or that Zach was now in Leokin. Pete had a bit of a God complex. Which was maybe a little understandable considering he had, in fact, created a world. But Zach didn't care about Pete.

He was trying really hard not to care about *anything*.

Not caring about Pete was easy.

"The king is a little full of himself and forgets the princess can rewrite the rules in Leokin at any time as easily as he can. He probably forgets because he gave her that power one night when he'd had too much pomegranate vodka."

Zach almost smiled. Almost.

But he was pissed. He was tired. He was frustrated. And

he'd been honest—he couldn't do it anymore. Any of it. He couldn't worry about his mother and be pissed at his father and nag his sister and butt heads with Kiera.

He just wanted to exist somewhere where everything worked out the way he wanted it to. A place where there were rules, and nobility was rewarded, and bravery and heroism were well defined and applauded.

He wanted to hang out in Leokin. *Ironic* didn't even begin to cover it.

"That may be true," he said. "But knowing the princess as I do, I would guess that she would never rewrite rules to *make* someone do something they didn't want to do."

Kiera seemed to be trying to figure something out as she studied his face. Finally she shook her head. "No, the princess wouldn't force anyone into anything."

"So if the rebel warrior just wanted to be left alone to explore the world and do his own thing, she'd let him do that?"

She nodded slowly. "Yes, she would."

"Okay then." He waited for her to move out of the way.

"But she would also caution the warrior that, if he continues to kill the innocent magical creatures in the forest, he's going to have multiple tribes descending on him, and he won't last through the night."

"The innocent magical creatures that keep hissing and growling at me?" he asked mildly.

"Yes."

She moved out of his way, and he had to resist the urge to grab her and pull her into his lap.

But he did resist. Because she was part of his frustration. He had never been as aware of his shortcomings in his relationships as he had been since he'd met her. He didn't think she was trying to make him feel bad about how he handled things...exactly. But Kiera didn't shy away from pointing out when he was being stubborn or judgmental or just plain wrong.

And it was messing with his ability to deal with his family.

They weren't perfect. At all. And he didn't think he actually had all the answers. But they needed someone to guide them, someone to demand they step up and do better. And until Kiera had come along, he'd been that guy. Confident and firm. But now he was questioning everything, including if they really needed him at all. And how he felt about that. What if they didn't? Would he feel free and happy? Or would he feel purposeless?

He was afraid of the answer.

So he was going to tramp around in a magical world where things worked a certain way every time. Sure, he might have screwed up by walking over the magical flowers that were now sucking his energy away, but at least he now knew that's what would happen every time. In the real world, he was never sure what was going to suck his energy away.

"And just so you know," Kiera said, plugging in another controller—because of course she'd come prepared with her own—and settling down on the edge of his bed with her feet tucked under her like a little kid, "They're not hissing and growling at you. They're upset about the Dagger of Darian."

"Because I'm lopping their little heads off with it," he said.

"No. Well, yes. But their heads will grow back."

"I noticed."

"It's because you can control the black fairies with it." She signed into the game on the split screen she'd brought up.

"Hold on." He looked over at her. "I can control something with this dagger?"

"The evil black fairies. Yes."

"Son of a bitch," he muttered. He made his warrior avatar get up from resting and walk to the edge of the bluff overlooking the flowered valley. He grabbed the dagger and heaved it into the flowers.

Kiera looked at him. "What was that?"

"I don't want to control anything. I don't want to be in charge of anything. I don't want to be responsible for anything."

She nodded. "Okay. Got it."

She pressed some buttons and moved her controller. He noticed that her avatar was in the castle. And looked almost exactly as Kiera had the first day he'd met her.

"What are you doing?" he asked.

"Sending some knights to retrieve the dagger. Don't want it falling into the wrong hands."

"Right." He watched her for a couple more minutes. Then he said, "How would the princess feel about a night of hot sex with a rogue warrior?"

She looked over at him. "Tell you what—if your warrior can find the castle before I leave on my next quest, just have him climb up the south tower."

"Easy." He'd seen the castle about an hour ago. In the far-off distance, but he'd seen it.

"Here, you might need this," she said, handing him a can of an energy drink.

"Thanks. Are those Twizzlers?"

She gave him a dazzling smile. "Indeed they are."

* * *

Zach woke with a nasty hangover.

Considering he hadn't drunk anything but fruit-punch-flavored energy drinks the night before, that was puzzling.

Until he tried to uncurl himself from the position he'd slept in. He was still in Aimee's gaming chair, his legs stretched out in front of him, his head tilted at an angle that was definitely not anything he would have tried if he'd been conscious.

How did someone fall asleep on energy drinks?

But the last thing he remembered was it being three a.m. and Kiera still happily gaming away on some quest with her clan. She'd been drinking water and eating what looked like nuts and fruit and granola.

He'd gone for the caffeine and sugar. And when he'd crashed, he'd crashed hard.

He'd never had a chance of making it to the castle for a quickie.

Slowly straightening his bent spine, Zach groaned and looked around. Kiera was curled up in his bed, sleeping peacefully. She wouldn't have any cramped muscles or sore joints.

He should have known better than to take her on.

He got up and headed to the kitchen for real food. By the time he got back to his room, Kiera was awake and again sitting on the end of his bed. She had her controller in hand and was already moving through Leokin.

She gave him a smile when he came into the room with his bowl of oatmeal but said nothing before she turned her attention back to the game.

She was granting his wish—she was leaving him alone

to do what he wanted. No words about going to work, no comments about the night before, no admonishment for passing out in the gaming chair.

But she wasn't leaving. She was clearly settled in for the long haul.

Zach took a bite of oatmeal and moved to the chair. Great. He didn't want to talk. He didn't want to rehash or be reminded of the things he'd left undone, the loose ends flapping in the wind last night.

He didn't know where Aimee was or how his parents were or how the party had turned out.

And he wasn't going to ask. As Kiera kept telling him, not everything about everyone was his responsibility.

They played for five hours. The only time they weren't sitting next to one another, controllers in hand, was when one of them got up to go to the bathroom or to answer the door for the pizza delivery guy.

Kiera did have her phone next to her knee and would receive and send the occasional text, but otherwise she was as focused on the game as he was.

She shared her crackers, nuts, and apples with him, and he cut back on the energy drinks and drank five bottles of water instead. And he did feel much better.

But damn if she didn't outlast him again.

Zach fell asleep in the chair for the second time, but woke around two a.m. and crawled up into bed next to her. In spite of wanting to be left alone, he wrapped his arms around her and pulled her into his body before falling into a deep sleep.

When he woke in the morning, she was already up. She'd showered and was sitting in her spot on the end of the bed, back in Leokin.

Zach got up and joined her.

He was on the other side of the forest today and was practicing his archery. He'd acquired a bow and arrows yesterday by rescuing a wizard from a carnivorous tree that had wrapped its branches around the older man and would have slowly absorbed him over time.

That seemed dark to Zach. So he'd chopped the tree down after hacking the old man free.

Now, apparently, there were forest dwarves pissed off at him about the tree.

Still, Zach grinned about the whole thing. At least that made sense. He'd chopped down their tree, and they were mad. He could understand that. It was much clearer than many of the things people got upset about in the real world.

He liked Leokin.

The doorbell rang downstairs and he frowned. Pizza at this time of morning?

"I'll get it."

Kiera was up off the bed and across the room before he realized those three words were the first she'd spoken to him in almost sixteen hours.

He'd wanted the silence. He'd wanted to be alone. But he was glad she was there. And he missed her voice.

Not that he'd admit that.

She came back into the room with a thick envelope.

"What's that?" His voice was scratchy from disuse. He'd uttered, "Dammit" and "Seriously?" and "Whoa" a few times yesterday as they'd played, but otherwise he hadn't used his voice box much.

"Something for me," she said, setting it on the bed next to her.

Okay, well, then one more thing he didn't need to worry about. Great.

He got absorbed in the game quickly.

As he was practicing with his bow and arrow—and finding he kind of sucked—a young girl went racing past. She wasn't a human girl. She had long flowing blue hair, and, though she was running, her feet didn't touch the ground. She was, however, being chased. A huge green snakelike creature came slithering past him, not far behind her. It had a snake's body but a rooster's head and wings.

"What the fuck is that?" he asked, swinging his avatar around.

"A bromdike," Kiera answered.

He lifted his bow and arrow. He wasn't a great shot yet, but he had to at least try.

"No, wait!" Kiera said as he drew the bow back. "You can't kill it."

"Why not? It's after that...girl."

"She's a pessal," Kiera said. "She steals from travelers in the woods."

"And the brom-thing kills her because of it?"

"It's only going to retrieve whatever she took. It will bite her, and she'll fall asleep temporarily. He'll take back what she stole."

Zach shook his head. "How am I supposed to keep up with this stuff? He looks like the bad guy."

Kiera smiled. "Things aren't always what they seem."

He rolled his eyes. "Right. Nice lesson there."

Kiera shrugged. "We do what we can. You could read the book, I suppose."

"There's a book?"

"Absolutely. It has all the rules, maps of the world, glossary of terms, and a dictionary of all the creatures. And it's only fourteen ninety-nine."

He shook his head. "No coupon or discount for sleeping with the princess?"

She cocked an eyebrow. "You haven't even made it to the castle yet, Mr. Rogue Warrior. You're too busy doing good deeds along the way."

He sighed. "No matter how bad I want to be, I can't quite pull it off."

Kiera turned back to the game. "That's why I've instructed the guards to let you in and bring you straight to my chambers. If you ever manage to find your way to the palace, that is."

Zach focused on the screen. Oh, he'd make it to the palace. "So Pete and Dalton programmed Leokin so that the characters could have sex?" he asked.

"I texted them, and they're working on it," she said. "I figure by the time you actually get there, they'll have it done."

He stopped and looked over at her. "They're *adding* sex into the game because of me?"

She laughed. "No."

She'd been messing with him. "Really? No sex in Leokin? And I was really starting to like it here."

They both fell into the game. Zach was still determined to make it to the palace, just to prove he could.

Two days later he still hadn't made it out of the woods. It seemed every time he made any progress toward the castle and the princess and the things he really wanted, someone came across his path who needed help. Or he came across their paths. Or whatever. It seemed that there was always someone in need of saving.

And he did it every time. He dropped whatever he was doing and came to their rescue. He was successful each time too.

He refused to think about that as a metaphor for his real life.

Besides, he was having a good time. He had managed to save more people and there was talk through the land of a mysterious new warrior who some people suspected had been a knight at one time. Everyone wanted to meet him, and he had four invitations to join clans.

Which he happily declined. This lone wolf stuff was okay.

So was not going to work, not going to his family's weekly dinner, and not worrying about Aimee and her classes or her social life or her relationship with his mother. She wasn't gaming—that much he knew for sure—and he put the rest out of his head more easily than he'd expected.

Kiera was the only person he wanted to spend time with. Which was a good thing because the girl hadn't left his side in five days.

She hadn't been in Leokin the whole time. She'd had someone bring her laptop over, along with more clothes, and she'd propped herself up on his bed and worked some of the time too. She would also venture into the kitchen once or twice a day and make food that didn't come via delivery guy or convenience store.

She was letting him do what he needed to do. But she wasn't leaving him alone. She wasn't walking away this time.

Zach truly believed that he never needed to leave his room again.

There was a huge banquet going on in Leokin in one of

the villages, and he was the guest of honor, having saved their herd of goats and two little boys from some beast with a lion's body and a dog's head.

After the bromdike incident, he hadn't been sure which things he should fight and which he shouldn't, but his gut had told him the lion-dog was bad news, and he'd been right.

He was a hero in Leokin. He'd even gotten a summons from the king to appear at the castle to receive an award.

He'd declined. He didn't want to give Pete the satisfaction of having him respond to a summons—he still wasn't sure he liked Pete all that much—and, well, he couldn't find his way to the palace anyway.

Zach sat his avatar on a log near the huge bonfire the village had built and set the controller aside, stretching.

It was dark outside when he glanced at the window, and he realized that Kiera wasn't in her usual spot at the end of the bed.

He turned to find her propped against the headboard, two pillows behind her, reading glasses perched on her nose, her attention on a stack of papers.

"What are you doing?" he asked, crawling up the bed and stretching out next to her.

She pulled her glasses off. "Reading about Josie."

The words seemed to echo in his head.

Josie.

His dead sister.

In the real world.

In Leokin he didn't have any family. He wanted to take the sexy, sassy princess to bed, but he didn't have any true personal connections to anyone. No one he was responsible for.

He didn't have a dead sister in Leokin. Only trolls and some other things he didn't know the names of—because he also wasn't giving Pete fourteen ninety-nine for his Leokin encyclopedia thing.

"Oh." He pushed up off the bed and went back to his chair. He needed more fantasy.

He asked one of the pretty village girls to dance at the party and concentrated on the celebration. On his behalf. In the village he would leave behind the next day as he moved on to something else. Somewhere else.

"Have you read the article about the accident?" Kiera's voice was soft and seemed to come to him from a distance. "I found it online."

Of course he'd read the article. And the accident report. And heard about the accident from his cop friends. And he knew what she was going to say. Josie had been dead when the rescue squad arrived. It was likely she'd died instantly. There had been nothing anyone could have done. There was nothing *he* could have done. He knew that. He'd read it over and over, trying to get it to sink in and really *matter*.

He threw back a pint of ale at the party and concentrated on the dancing and celebrating.

He wondered if avatars could get drunk. He decided to find out.

"'I just wanted to tell you that your song "True to You" really means a lot to me. I discovered it at a really tough time in my life, and I listened to it over and over. Thank you for sharing those words with me.'"

Zach frowned. He had no idea what Kiera was talking about. He refilled his glass. Online, anyway.

"'I wanted to let you know that your story about why

you wrote the song "All My Heart" inspired me to write a song too. I sang it for my dad at his birthday party, and it made him cry. We've had a rough relationship, and this really helped us start to heal. Thank you.'"

Zach grabbed another girl from the crowd and began spinning her around to the music in Leokin.

"'Your song "The World According to You" is so beautiful. I hope your brother knows how much you love him.'"

Zach dropped the controller. That meant his avatar stood near the bonfire in the town square doing nothing. Like he was numb. Which was how Zach felt in real life.

He stared at the screen but didn't see it. "What are you doing?" he asked hoarsely.

"Reading comments on Josie's band's website," she said. "There are hundreds. These are from about a year ago. There are some really beautiful things in the past few months."

Since she'd died.

He hadn't even thought about her band having a website.

"Why?" he asked.

He heard the rustle of his sheets and blankets and felt Kiera move in near his left shoulder. "I'm trying to show you that there were good things about Josie's music. I know you wanted her to be a teacher, to touch lives that way, but she did touch lives, Zach. I wanted you to know that."

He dropped his chin to his chest.

"And she loved you so much. I looked up a video of her singing the song about you. It's amazing."

He pulled in a ragged breath.

Kiera put her hand on the back of his neck. The warmth

from her touch soaked into him, and his next breath wasn't as shaky.

She said nothing. She didn't move. She just sat with him.

"What if I told you I didn't care?" he asked after a moment. "What if I told you that I'm still angry about her accident and about her dying and not knowing about the band and that if I had known, I would have tried to stop her?"

All of that was true. He couldn't deny it.

She rubbed her hand across his neck. "Do you mean, would I be mad at you? Would I stop loving you? Would I leave?" she asked. "The answer is no."

He turned his head. "That's the second time you've told me you love me."

She nodded. "I do."

His heart thumped. But he couldn't deal with everything that meant to him. He simply focused on the primary thing he felt because of her words...comforted.

"Then stop pushing me," he finally said.

Her eyes flickered with disappointment, but she pulled her bottom lip between her teeth and nodded. "Okay. I won't tell you that your mom went back to AA and your dad went with her this time. And I won't tell you that Aimee went over there and apologized and has been staying with them since you've been holed up and she's got two A's and two B's in her college classes."

He shook his head. She was pushing.

He was the pusher. He was the one who was always making people face things, hear things, acknowledge things they didn't always want to.

Damn. It really was kind of annoying on this side.

She was supposed to be the one to back off and let people be. And he didn't miss the fact that seeing her do this to anyone else would have thrilled him.

He picked up the controller and returned his mind to Leokin.

He wasn't going to stay in the village tonight. He didn't want to be with people, even virtual ones. He would camp out in the forest again tonight. That was where stuff happened. He was learning the places to be wary of, the things that came out at night, the ways to stay safe overnight.

He had, of course, learned these things the hard way. He'd actually died twice in Leokin and been injured four times. But it turned out that if you were noble and loyal, you were rewarded with additional lives in Leokin, and he'd come across some dragon glitter that healed his wounds immediately.

He loved Leokin. If only fucking up and going on afterward were so easy in the real world.

He shouldered his pack and picked up his sword and headed to the edge of the village.

Three hours later he stared at the screen. He'd just finished a battle with a small army of goblins he'd found attacking a family's campsite. Most of the goblins were dead, their bodies absorbed into the forest. The rest had run off. He'd saved all four members of the family. It had almost been too easy.

As the family celebrated and thanked him and offered him food and gifts, Zach sat there just staring at them. Because, of course, none of it was real.

He had felt the initial surge of triumph. But it had quickly faded. Because...it didn't matter.

He liked Leokin because things always worked out. It

was a nice escape. It was fun to pretend that he was the big hero. And if he messed up, the rules of the world still ensured that everything was fine in the end. It fed into every one of his fantasies. Not the prince, not the pirate, but the guy who saved the day, who knew all the answers, who everyone needed.

But that was all pretend.

Staring at the world where Aimee and Kiera both chose to spend so much time, he knew that they loved Leokin for the same reasons he did—good things happened, they could be who they wanted to be, they could do things they couldn't do in the real world.

The difference was, they knew that. That was why they went to Leokin. To spend time away from the real world.

For Zach, Leokin was more or less an animated version of the real world—a place where he was lauded as a good guy who could be called upon when someone was in trouble...with a few weird creatures thrown in to keep it interesting.

Hell, even in the real world, he'd stumbled across a princess and a wizard and a few hobbits. He'd met a graphic designer whose dining room was a costume shop and whose idea of a night out included little kids dressed as superheroes. Who was to say that the strange and fantastic happened only online?

Strangely, the idea that he really could be the hero, right all the wrongs, and fix all the problems was the true fantasy. All of those things could happen in Leokin. It was in real-world Boston that those things became make-believe.

In the glade in the forest, with the grateful family still gathered around him, Zach turned to look to the east. The castle, where Princess Kirenda lived, was still past a river, several hills, and another dense forest.

He was never going to get there.

He dropped the controller. There was one thing he wanted that he seemed unable to achieve in Leokin— getting to Kiera. Thankfully, the real world was a different story in this case.

He looked over his shoulder. She had crawled into bed and was sound asleep. There for him. For however long it took him to figure everything out.

Zach stretched to his feet and looked at the clock. He took a deep breath. Apparently it had taken him five days, eighteen hours, and twenty-six minutes to figure his shit out. That was probably pretty good.

He stripped out of his clothes and climbed into the bed. As he wrapped his arm around her, she stirred, her big brown eyes blinking open.

"Hi," she said softly.

"I love you too."

She smiled. "I know."

"And I get the leaving."

"Yeah?" She rolled to her back. "Well, I get the staying," she told him. "I get that love can be stronger than the hurt."

He lowered his head and kissed her deeply. He'd never managed to get to the castle in Leokin, but it turned out there were still some things he preferred in the real world.

* * *

Ten hours later Kiera padded into the kitchen.

"Hey."

He looked up from the griddle. "Hey."

She grinned. "Literal pancakes?"

"And metaphorical ones." She looked beautiful, and he realized that these were the most important pancakes he'd ever made.

She slid up onto the bar stool on the other side of the countertop from where he stood. "Does this mean that Leokin's new, mysterious warrior is taking a break today?"

He slid a chocolate chip pancake onto a plate and passed it to her. "It does."

"What will all those people in trouble do without you?"

Zach crossed his arms and looked at her closely. "Yeah, I was going to ask you about that."

She cut off a piece of pancake and took a bite. She moaned. "Oh my God, these are good. So worth waiting for." She gave him a wink.

"I need to talk to you about Leokin. I'm concerned, and as their princess, I would think you'd want to know."

She chewed and swallowed. And frowned at his strangely serious tone about the game. "Okay."

"There are *a lot* of bad things happening in that forest. I could hardly travel for an hour without running into some menace trying to hurt someone."

She took another bite and chewed. Slowly. She was also very intent on studying the edge of her plate.

Zach braced his hands on the counter and leaned in. He suspected that Leokin was not always such a hazardous place, and he thought he maybe knew why his arrival had prompted so many run-ins with the bad element. "Kiera? What is going on in your forest?"

Finally she set her fork down and said, "Pete."

That wasn't the answer he'd been expecting. "Pete."

She nodded. "He loved that you got into Leokin and was trying to give you the hero experience."

He had really expected that the hero experience had been coming from Kiera. Or even Aimee.

Zach shook his head. "I don't know if I like Pete."

Kiera grinned. "You don't like Pete or you don't like that he seemingly knows *you*?"

"He doesn't know me."

She picked up her fork and took another bite. "You're pretty easy to figure out. You love being the hero. He thought you'd get a kick out of it."

"Uh-huh. And did he also purposefully keep me from reaching the castle?"

She swallowed. "Probably."

Zach came around the end of the counter. He swiveled her stool so she was facing him. He noticed that the smudge of chocolate on her lower lip matched the color of her eyes before he swiped it off with his finger and stuck the finger in his mouth. "Well, you can tell Pete that I got to the princess. In spite of all the barriers and problems and obstacles between us." He lowered his head and looked her directly in the eye. "Right, Kiera? I got to the princess, didn't I?"

She nodded. "You most definitely did. Before you ever even picked up a sword, hot guy."

He smiled. "Know what I figured out along the way?"

"What?"

"My real world's been a fantasy—the idea that I can save everyone and always figure it all out."

Her eyes softened. "But don't forget, our fantasies are a part of us. We have to acknowledge and explore them sometimes."

"Well, I've been all about the fantasy. I think what I need to acknowledge is the real world. I need to recognize that I'm *not* a superhero or a pirate or a rogue, loner warrior. I'm just a guy—an imperfect, sleep-deprived, messy, hungry guy who's trying to do the best he can. And that's who I want to be. Because when I'm that guy, I'm also happy, and able to understand and forgive my family, and in love with you, and looking at the world differently, and making you laugh...and making you come."

Her smile was large, her eyes filled with love and happiness. "I'll tell you exactly what you are, Zach Ashley."

"Yeah?"

She nodded. "Gorgeous and kick-ass."

* * *

2½ months later

"Zach, we can't just give the warriors the power to fly," Pete said in the exasperated tone he always used when talking to Zach about Leokin. He bumped the swinging kitchen door open with his hip and went through with a stack of plates and a handful of silverware.

"It's only the nine of us," Zach argued, following with the bowl of potatoes and the gravy boat. "And I have *yet* to get to the castle, for God's sake."

"That's not what I heard about you and Kirenda's castle," Troy said with a huge grin. "I heard you breached that a long time ago."

"You keep getting killed by the trolls," Zach reminded him. "Maybe you need to stay quiet."

"Maybe you need to quit bringing these loner warriors into the forest," Pete griped. "Leokin was always known for the clans and the sense of community until you came along and decided to stay independent. You and these friends of yours don't even answer summons."

"We can't get to the fucking castle," Zach exclaimed. "It's ridiculous the number of things we're called upon to do as we go through the forest."

"And we keep getting lost," Troy added.

Zach kicked him under the table. "We could find our way if we had to. But if there was some kind of spell for flying..."

"I can't just make a flying spell," Pete said.

Kiera rolled her eyes as she set the green bean casserole down in the middle of the table. "Of course you could," she said. "But you won't. Because Zach wants it."

Pete and Zach had a grudging friendship, mostly because they both loved Kiera. But when they were together, they turned into five-year-olds.

"That's not fair," Pete said. "I added the drawbridge, and I made the apples in the north orchard give extra strength after they're eaten. Those were Zach's ideas."

It was true. Kiera sighed. "Just give him a flying spell."

"That makes no sense," Pete insisted.

"Well, I'd like him to make it to the big ball we're throwing at Christmastime at the castle," she said. "I'm not sure how else to get him there."

Everyone laughed.

"Fine. I'll make a one-time potion or something," Pete said. "*If*..." He pointed a finger at Zach. "You stop harassing my customer service people. It's not a game glitch that you always forget about the elves in the lower forest, and if you're going to sleep in the trees, then you have to expect to have birds around sometimes."

"Birds that try to adopt me as one of their own every time?" Zach asked.

Pete chuckled. He'd programmed one bird to fall in love with Zach, and every time Zach ventured into that part of the forest, the bird followed him around and tried to nuzzle him and get him into her nest.

"That bird could come in handy as an ally sometime," Pete said. "And I expect a huge thank-you when that happens."

"Anyone ever tell you that you have a God complex, Pete?" Zach asked.

Pete laughed. "Have you ever read or heard an interview with me? It's pretty well established that I have a God complex, Ashley."

"Clear the way."

Zach's father came through the swinging door from the kitchen with the enormous Thanksgiving turkey and set it on the table next to the potatoes.

They had cleared out the costume shop and were using the dining room in Kiera's grandmother's house as a, well, dining room.

Temporarily. The material, hats, weapons, and mannequins would be back in the morning.

But for now, they were having a traditional Thanksgiving dinner with all of their friends and Zach's family.

Kiera's parents had been invited but hadn't been able to make it. But it didn't bother her. Looking around the room, she realized that her true family was right here with her now.

"Let me get that for you." Dalton shoved his chair back

and went to relieve Aimee of the bowl of stuffing she was carrying.

"Thanks." She gave him a big smile.

But Kiera knew that Dalton didn't have a chance. Aimee was very much in love with Cody.

Cody noticed Dalton's attention on Aimee. He stood and took her arm, pulling her around the table to sit next to him. And as she settled into the chair, Dalton came around and sat on her other side.

Kiera just shook her head and took her place between Rob and Zach. Maya and Sophie pulled out chairs across from her, and Zach's mom and dad were on the end. The table was full. And so was her heart.

"I'd like to propose a toast," Zach said as they got comfortable.

Everyone reached for their glasses and held them up.

"To new traditions, new friends, and new outlooks on the world," he said. Then he looked at Kiera and said, "And to metaphorical pancakes."

Kiera lifted her glass. "And to real-life heroes...and virtual perfection."

Maya Goodwin is obsessed with martial arts, superheroes, and her alter ego. But it's only when she meets Dr. Alex Nolan and his daughter that Maya gets a shot at saving the day ... and getting the hot guy.

A preview of *Forever Mine* follows.

CHAPTER ONE

The answer to his prayer came in bright purple leather.

He hadn't been expecting that.

Alex didn't know if the woman was supposed to be a superhero or what, but he was definitely in need of a little saving.

Along with the leather pants and vest, she wore a black tank top and black boots that went to midcalf. And then there was her big stick.

The guy she was battling had an equally big stick. Of course it was a staged fight, which was a part of a bigger demonstration of the techniques taught in the classes at Active Imagination Martial Arts and Fitness Studio. Still, the strength and skill it took to wield the weapons was obvious.

Even to Alex, who had never give two seconds of thought to what it would take to use a weapon.

A flyer had been thrust into his hand at the mall entrance. When he'd seen the words *kids* and *superheroes*,

Alex had assumed the kids would be the ones playing superhero. But not one of the fifty or so young people gathered around the stage, ranging from about age four to nearly twenty, was dressed up.

The seven adults demonstrating various martial arts, stage fighting, and weaponry techniques were, however. One guy looked like an Indiana Jones impersonator, another was clearly a Superman knockoff, cape and all. A couple others also wore leather, though none as well as the woman in purple.

"Self-esteem is how you feel about yourself, no matter what other people say," the woman said, finishing the battle and addressing the crowd as she had been doing periodically throughout the demonstration.

Alex glanced down at the pamphlet in his hand. Maya Goodwin. She was the owner of the studio and taught a few of the classes. They offered classes to adults too, but it seemed that Maya specialized in working with kids. The Super You class, where the kids dressed up as superheroes, was apparently her specialty.

Which made her exactly the person he needed to meet today.

"It's knowing who you are, no matter what's going on around you," she went on. "It's the person you want to be in good times and in bad."

Her voice was as sexy as her ass in the tight purple pants. And that was saying something. She couldn't have been more than five six or five seven. Her hair was nearly black, with deep-red stripes through it, and stopped at her ears. Her eyes were also dark, shining brightly from swoops of black and purple that looked like a mask but were clearly painted on. She was trim, the pants and her sleeveless top and vest showing off the contours of muscles that spoke of regular workouts. Her outfit also did nothing to hide the jagged scar that ran from below her jaw on the left down her neck, disappearing under a few inches of leather and then reappearing to join three others traveling down her upper arm to her elbow.

Alex could have told himself that it was his medical degree that made him curious about the injury that had caused those scars, but he knew better. That was the kind of disfigurement that made everyone curious about what had happened. But the scars simply joined the list of things he found fascinating about her.

For instance, she seemed so much bigger than she was. Her voice was strong, her smile confident, and the way she moved her body and handled her weapon, though chore-ographed, was mesmerizing. Or something.

Alex couldn't explain it. He'd stopped at the demonstra-tion because it made him think of his ten-year-old daughter, Charli, and her obsession with the huge movie franchise *Galactic Renegades*. Something Alex knew next to nothing about. He'd intended to grab a registration form, ask a few questions, and be on his way. That was twenty minutes ago. During that time he'd found himself moving steadily closer to the raised performance platform.

Now he stood at the front of the crowd, only a few feet from Maya, probably blocking the view of a bunch of little kids, unable to take his eyes off of her.

He'd known when she first noticed him. Their eyes had met, and for just a moment, she'd faltered in what she was saying.

This woman didn't falter. He had no idea how he knew that, but he did. The big-stick battle might have been part of a show, but her passion and confidence were not. And ever since he'd come to the front of the group, she hadn't made eye contact with him again. Alex found that as intriguing as the rest. Did he fluster her? And if so, why was that the best thing that had happened to him in some time?

"You can be anything, but first you have to imagine it," Maya said to the crowd. "And that's what our classes are about. Yes, it's martial arts and self-defense and weapons work, but it's more than that. It's about figuring out what makes you feel strong—not just physically but emotionally. That answer is different for everyone. We all get our strength from different places. Some of the kids will come and find a group of friends. Some will come and find an adult mentor to look up to. Some will come and find their inner strength from doing something that's hard that they never thought they could. And some will come and find their strength in letting go, in having a safe place to play and imagine and pretend.

"Yes, we dress up," she said, with a light laugh that made Alex feel as if he'd just taken a shot of brandy. She gestured to the people in capes and spandex. "And we encourage the kids to become that character in class. We want the character to represent the things they love most about themselves, along with some traits they want to develop."

Maya was moving across the stage, addressing the crowd, talking to the kids as well as the parents. Her enthusiasm was clear and contagious, and she was obviously quite comfortable as the center of attention.

Alex knew what it was like to have a hundred pairs of eyes on him at once. He was a nationally renowned expert in genetic disorders and regularly spoke to groups of patients and caregivers as well as lecturing to medical students and colleagues from multiple fields. But he was never completely at ease in front of a crowd.

Maybe because he was always hiding something.

Maybe he needed a costume.

"We spend the first two classes helping them develop their character," Maya continued. "We have teachers and a counselor on our staff that work with the kids by asking them questions about what things they like about themselves, what they admire about others and why, what powers they most wish they had, and more.

"Then our amazing artist, Kiera"—she pointed to another woman, who was dressed as some sort of warrior princess, and the princess raised her hand and smiled—"sits with each child and helps them sketch how they want their character to look.

"Then one of the top costumers in Boston, Sophie"—this time she pointed to a curvy blonde dressed in a white jumpsuit—"comes in and helps us put the costumes together. Their time and expertise make this program truly unique and utterly wonderful."

If her words hadn't been enough to get people pulling out their pens to sign up and write checks, the smile she gave them would have been.

Damn. Alex shook his head. If she ever turned that smile on him, she could have anything she wanted.

"Kiera and Sophie are going to bring around some sign-up sheets while Ben and I do another bo staff demonstration," she said, as the man she'd been battling before stepped forward. "And then we'll take some questions."

Bo staff. That was what the big stick was called. Alex

pulled his phone from his pocket and made a note. He'd have to look that up later. Right now his eyes and brain seemed unable to do anything but watch Maya Goodwin.

She and Ben positioned themselves several feet apart on the platform. She was on the side closest to Alex, which meant he couldn't see her face. They did a little bow and then they went at it. The sticks clacked against one another as they moved together, then away, thrusting and blocking and turning. It was almost like a dance—if you were constantly trying to knock down your partner while you tangoed.

Alex watched her intently, noticing that there was a limit to how high she could raise the arm with the scars and that she most often swung and thrust with her right arm, perhaps due to a lack of strength on the left. She continued to use the arm, wincing as she did, but not giving Ben a single advantage. They turned in a wide circle and finally she was facing Alex's direction.

As far as marketing techniques went, this was brilliant. Put the hot girl in leather to get the dads to pay attention. Show off her kick-ass bo staff techniques to get the kids' attention. Have her use buzzwords like *self-esteem* and *fitness* for the moms. And then pass out sign-up sheets.

Alex was ready to sign up himself.

His head and heart had been spinning for the past two months, since he'd found out that not only did he have a ten-year-old daughter with a woman he remembered only as "the cute blonde who liked butterscotch schnapps" but that his daughter was sick. Because of him.

Ironically Rachel, who hadn't touched schnapps since that night, had found him only because of Charli's condition. She'd read an article he'd written about hemophilia for a parenting magazine. She'd recognized him from his photo and tracked him down at Boston Children's Hospital with the help of his bio at the end of the article. Otherwise he still wouldn't know his daughter.

And if he could untangle his emotions about missing ten years of Charli's life and the guilt over being the reason for her condition in the first place, he could get closer to her and be a real dad to her.

His first step in showing Charli that she was the most important thing in his life was bonding with her over the things she loved. *Galactic Renegades* and superheroes, to start. He could ask her all about them, of course, but he couldn't deny that a part of him wanted to impress her by already knowing a few things when they talked.

The first time Charli had initiated a conversation with him, it was to ask him who his favorite *Galactic Renegades* character was. His initial reaction had been, *Well, shit.* His second had been to answer Beck Steele, the tough-guy fighter pilot Alex had heard of only because one of his favorite actors played the character. But he knew that she suspected he was lying.

He knew nothing about superheroes or sci-fi space sagas and was apparently no good at faking it. He'd been watching one *Galactic Renegades* and superhero movie after another ever since. He was still unclear about whether the renegades were considered superheroes, but he wasn't sure it mattered. If Charli liked *Renegades*, then Alex was going to become a *Galactic Renegades* expert.

He watched the woman in purple and wondered what she knew about *Galactic Renegades* and Piper, the newest young heroine in the movie franchise. The first three movies had come out about five years ago, but now they were doing a next-generation kind of thing, and Charli was all in. That meant Alex needed to get all in.

Just then Maya pivoted and lifted her staff into the air. But just before Ben struck, her gaze swung to Alex. They made eye contact for less time than it took for him to suck in a deep breath. But it was enough to cause a reaction.

Ben's staff came down swiftly, but instead of blocking with her staff, the woman flinched. Ben's stick hit her on the shoulder, and she went to her knees.

There was a moment of stunned surprise from the audience and the performers alike before she got to her feet and swung to face them with a big smile.

"We work on things like concentration and focus as well as getting up again after you've been knocked down," she said. "And with that, I'm going to let Sophie take my spot, and she and Ben are going to show you some sword work."

The blonde in white looked around quickly, and someone thrust a sword and scabbard into her hand. It seemed obvious to Alex that Sophie hadn't been prepared to step in, which made him think that Maya was taking herself out of the demo unexpectedly and might be hurt.

She moved to the side with the rest of the demonstrators, rolling her shoulder forward and back. But she didn't seem to be in distress, and Alex made himself stay put. He wasn't her friend, and while he was a physician, he certainly hadn't done any acute injury care recently. Or ever. He'd gone to medical school for a very specific reason, and his focus had gotten him the residency at Boston's Children's Hospital. He'd been there ever since.

Though she talked and smiled at her fellow superheroes, Maya was also scanning the crowd—and avoiding looking at Alex again. He smiled. He was either distracting her because she was attracted to him or because she thought he was a stalker. And he'd be very happy to get close enough to assure her he was not stalking her. Which would seem stalkerish.

He should just focus on the whole Active Imagination presentation and staff. Any one of them could probably help him with the plan he'd started forming for Charli's birthday.

But if he'd been thinking about what he'd need to do to keep Charli safe while she took part in a class where she could be the one who got smacked by a bo stick, he would have missed Maya slipping off the edge of the stage and making her way around the side of the crowd of people.

Alex turned and saw two teenage boys talking to a girl about their age. The girl didn't seem pleased. She yanked her arm out of one boy's hold and tried to pass them, but they stepped together, blocking her way. Alex frowned and noticed Maya heading in their direction. He slipped to the side and then headed around the back of the crowd, who were oblivious to any drama unfolding behind them.

The girl finally managed to push past the boys, and she walked quickly down the east corridor of the mall, turning into a clothing store after about twenty yards.

The boys followed. And so did Maya.

Alex headed in that direction as well, picking up his pace. She probably knew the kids or something. Maybe they'd been in one of her classes. Still, something told him to follow.

Or maybe it was just that he wanted a few minutes of time to talk to Maya privately. Or that once she left the stage, the demonstration had lost most of its appeal for him.

Maya made it to the storefront a few strides in front of

him. She glanced at him, startled, as he came up beside her. She opened her mouth, but before she could say hi or ask if he was a stalker, something in her peripheral vision inside the store drew her attention. Her brows slammed together, and she headed in.

Alex was right behind her.

* * *

The last thing she needed was the hot guy from the demonstration distracting her in here. But Maya couldn't take time to get rid of him. She had to make sure the girl she'd seen being harassed was okay. So she headed into the store and tried to ignore him.

The store was deserted other than one young female clerk at the register on the far side of the store. The boys had the girl in a corner behind several racks of clothes. The one in the green hoodie had a hold of her wrist, and she was clearly trying to get loose.

Maya went straight for the kids, but the guy who had followed her hung back. He pretended interest in a table of T-shirts, but he was close enough that he could hear everything. She didn't know what his deal was, but as long as he stayed out of the way, it would be fine.

"Leave her alone," Maya said firmly as she approached from behind the boys.

The boy in the black denim jacket glanced over his shoulder at Maya. "This is none of your business," he told her. Then he got a good look at her. He straightened and turned. "It's not Halloween, babe."

Maya planted her hands on her hips, her feet spread. "I said leave her alone."

The other boy and the girl both stopped struggling and focused on Maya.

The first boy, who couldn't have been more than seventeen, laughed. "You a big, brave superhero or something?"

Maya's eyes narrowed. "Or something. Like Boston PD."

"Yeah, well, everything is fine here," the kid in the black denim said, disdain dripping from his voice. "We're just talking to her. We're not doin' nothin' wrong."

"I saw you stop her outside and then follow her in here. Guessing she's already turned you down," Maya told him. "So how about you back off?"

"I'm not hurting her. We're friends."

"I don't care if you know her or not," Maya said. "No means no."

"Tell her that you didn't say no to me," the kid said to the girl.

The girl winced, and Maya assumed the boy had squeezed her wrist. Maya started to step forward when she heard, "Can I be of some assistance?" from right behind her.

She turned. It was the guy. It made sense that he had a sexy, deep voice. It totally fit.

She shook her head. She could *not* be distracted by him right now.

The boys swung to face him, which drew their attention away from Maya. She took the opportunity to move in closer.

"No, you fucking can't," the first kid said. "You can mind your own damned business."

"How about you lower your voice and let go of the young lady?" The guy's tone was authoritative, and he drew himself to his full height—which had to be at least six two—and his gaze hardened.

She wasn't getting distracted. But damn, he looked good being all big and bad and heroic.

The kid in the hoodie straightened as well and took a step forward, dragging the girl with him. "How about *you* stop harassing *me*?" Green Hoodie asked. He looked at Maya. "I'd like to file a complaint."

"Too bad. I don't have any forms with me, and my memory is terrible if I don't write things down," she said blandly. She also wasn't active duty right now, but he didn't have to know that. "I guess it would end up being your word against mine about what happened."

"I'm not afraid of you," the kid said.

"That's because you're stupid," Maya told him bluntly. "Which is also, no doubt, one of the many reasons that she wants nothing to do with you."

"Okay, everyone relax," her hot hero interrupted, stepping closer. "Do you know these guys?" he asked the girl, who had been standing there, her eyes wide.

She glanced at the boy holding her, but then looked at Maya. Maya gave her an encouraging smile.

"No," she said. "They just came up to me outside."

"And do you want to be with them?" the guy asked.

Her eyes still on Maya, the girl shook her head.

"Let her go." He delivered the words in a tone that should have made the two teens' knees shake. Even Maya felt her eyes widen.

Green Hoodie's hand loosened on the girl's wrist, and he took a step forward. "Who the fuck do you think you are?"

"I'd like to be the guy who's going to make you understand that you can't put yourself into other people's space just because you want to," he said. "But no matter what else, I *will* be the guy who's going to make sure this girl leaves the mall without you."

The girl suddenly jerked her arm and pulled free from Green Hoodie's hold. Maya moved quickly to put herself between the girl and the two boys. "Are you hurt?" she asked the girl.

"No."

"You need help getting home?"

"No." The girl worried her bottom lip. "I still need to buy what I came for."

Maya glanced at the boys. "I'll make sure they don't come with you. If you want, I'll shop with you."

The girl looked at the boys, her expression hardening. "You don't have to." She took a deep breath and looked at Maya again. "But I'll be at Daniel's looking for a dress. If you have time."

Maya relaxed slightly and smiled. "I'll meet you there." There was no reason this girl should have to leave the mall just because these two jackasses had insinuated themselves into her day.

As the girl left the store, the boys started to move too. Maya spun, her smile gone. "No way. You're not leaving yet," she told them.

"The fuck if we're not," Black Denim said.

"You're going to wait until security gets here to throw your asses out of the mall," she told them.

"We're not leaving this mall until we're damned good and ready," Black Denim said.

Maya was unfazed. "I'll follow you around the entire time you're here."

"And do what?" the boy challenged.

"Nothing. Unless you decide to be assholes again."

The kid balled up a fist and took a step toward her.

Maya braced herself, readying to block any attack.

But she didn't need to bother.

"Stop right there." Hot Hero grabbed the kid's shoulder.

The kid swung around and pulled his arm back, but as soon as his attention and center of gravity shifted, Maya moved in. She wrenched his arm behind his back and put him on his knees.

"Goddammit!" The kid started to turn. "I'm going to—"

Maya put a knee in the middle of his back and pushed him onto his stomach. She pulled his other arm behind his back and held his wrists pinned together.

"I'm pressing charges with the Boston PD!" the kid shouted.

"Well, good luck with that. They can't fire me twice," Maya told him.

She hadn't been fired. She'd been given a desk job after her injury. But she simply wasn't made to sit in an office all day, so she'd left and started the studio. But she didn't owe this kid any explanations.

"You're not even really a cop?" Black Denim asked, writhing underneath her.

She put more of her weight onto him. "Well, consider this a lesson in consequences. You mess with someone who doesn't want you, and you could get messed with by someone *you* don't want."

Maya lifted her head to find Hot Hero again. He was talking to the store employee. Maya started to shift, but suddenly there was a sharp pain in her side. "Dammit!" The kid in the hoodie had punched her. The dick. The surprise of it made her let up on her pressure on Black Denim.

He tried to roll, but she leaned on him again, as Green Hoodie turned toward Hot Hero. She opened her mouth to yell at him, but the kid kicked him in the side of his knee before she could make a sound. *Holy shit.*

The guy swore, and his leg buckled. Maya instantly started to move toward him, but Green Hoodie swung around and grabbed her hair, pulling her off his friend. He shoved her, and she went to her butt, her head colliding with the display stand behind her. Stars danced in front of her eyes, and she had to work for her next breath.

Just then two security guards showed up. "Alright, what's going on?" one asked, coming around the racks of clothing.

Hot Hero immediately got to his feet. He grabbed Green Hoodie by the front of his sweatshirt and lifted him onto his tiptoes before turning and shoving him toward the security guards. Then he lunged for Black Denim as the kid spun toward Maya. He got a hold of the denim jacket and started to pull, but Maya drew her leg up, kicking out and sending the kid sprawling.

She scrambled to her feet, and she couldn't avoid gasping and grabbing her side. She started forward, but one of the guards and two other teenagers who'd come into the store were on Black Denim first. The teens helped get him onto his stomach while the guard handcuffed him.

But she forgot all about the kid when the hot guy tried to put weight on his leg and grimaced. "Hey, you okay?" she asked, ignoring the stabbing pain in her side. *Son of a bitch.* She'd fractured ribs less than a year ago at Comic Con, and it felt as if the kid had hit her in exactly the same spot.

The guy opened his eyes. "Yeah. I'm good."

"Doesn't look so good," Maya said. He had his leg straight now, but he had sucked in a quick breath as he'd extended it.

"I'm fine. You could have a concussion," he told her. "Let me take a look."

He was going to take a look at her? She shook her head, then winced at the pain it caused. "No nausea, no dizziness, no ringing in the ears, and I remember everything that happened." She frowned. "Even the first time you distracted me and I stuttered, and the second time you distracted me and Ben got a shot in, and the third time when that kid was able to get a hold of me."

The guy actually smiled. "Those were all my fault?"

She nodded, then winced again. "I never get distracted."

His grin grew but he asked, "You know the symptoms of concussion?"

"I do martial arts," she said. "We fall down sometimes." Her whole staff knew first aid and had experience using it. Working with weapons required it. "How do you know how to do a concussion check?"

"Doctor."

Huh. "What kind of doctor?"

"Pediatrician. So yes, your head is bigger than the ones I'm used to dealing with." He gave her a cute smile. "But it's basically the same thing." He glanced around, then took her by her upper arm and pulled her to a chair that sat outside one of the changing rooms.

"You're kind of grabby," she complained, but she found she didn't really mind. He had nice hands. Big hands. Strong hands. And he had, after all, jumped into the fight with her.

"Yeah, the Hippocratic oath is so inconvenient at times," he said drily.

That amused her. "You just can't take my word for it?"

"Sorry."

He put her in the chair and then started to kneel to look her in the eye. He frowned as he bent his knee, however, and stopped with his hands on his thighs instead, putting his face right in front of hers.

He was really good looking—sandy blond hair, cut short; deep green eyes; a deep voice that rumbled right through her.

And she was suddenly just fine with him taking a look at her. She'd show him whatever he wanted to see. "I'm not familiar with this concussion test," she said softly as he continued to just look at her.

"This is turning out to be more of a test of my willpower than of the condition of your head," he told her.

Oh, she liked that. "I thought maybe it was some kind of medicinal magic."

"Not being able to take my eyes off of you?"

"Well, my head suddenly doesn't hurt anymore." Wow, she hadn't flirted like this in a long time.

They just paused there, smiling at one another in a way she couldn't remember ever smiling at someone. Just smiling. For several long seconds.

"What about that?" he finally asked, pointing to where she was pressing her hand against her side.

She sighed. "A rib, I think. He punched me in the side."

Big Bad Doctor's eyes hardened. "He *punched* you?"

He straightened and turned toward where they'd left the kids with the security guards. Maya had the distinct impression he wanted to go after the kid who'd hit her. And that did funny things to her stomach. Security was on the way out the door with them, though.

"Let me check your rib," he said, focusing back on her.

"You're not in great shape yourself, Doctor Wonderful." She gestured to his knee, which was clearly bothering him. "I've had cracked ribs before. And worse." She indicated her shoulder with a small smile. His gaze followed along the line of her scars. "Besides," she said, dropping her hand from her side and straightening in the chair. "I have a dress to shop for." The girl was probably waiting for her in Daniel's Boutique.

"That was really nice of you to offer."

She shrugged. "A girl shouldn't shop for a dress alone. I don't know where her friends or sisters or mom are, but the least I can do is be sure she looks for something in red."

"Red?"

"She'll look great in red," Maya said.

"And you're also going to talk to her about being safe? Not shopping alone?" he asked.

Maya frowned. "No. There's no reason she can't shop alone. That's crap. Those guys had no right to harass her."

He nodded his agreement. "But you're not just going to shop and blow it off." He said it as a statement, not a question.

She had no idea how he knew that, but no, she wasn't just going to shop with the girl. "I'm going to talk her into coming in for a few free self-defense classes," Maya admitted. "Next time she'll be the one with the knee in the guy's back."

"Not worried about her cracking a rib?"

"The only reason that happened was because a certain

good-looking doctor distracted me," Maya said. "As long as she stays focused, she'll be okay."

That got her a big grin. He almost looked smug. "Maya, I—"

He was cut off by a chorus of "Oh my God!" and "There you are!" and "What happened?" as Kiera and Sophie swept into the store.

But she didn't miss that the guy knew her name. She had no chance to say anything else to him. Or to find out *his* name. Or to even say thanks. Or good-bye.

By the time she'd been hugged by her friends and looked around for him, he was gone.

ABOUT THE AUTHOR

Erin Nicholas is the author of sexy contemporary romances. Her stories have been described as toe-curling, enchanting, steamy, and fun. She loves to write about reluctant heroes, imperfect heroines, and happily-ever-afters. She lives in the Midwest with her husband, who only wants to read the sex scenes in her books, her kids, who will never read the sex scenes in her books, and family and friends who say they're shocked by the sex scenes in her books (yeah, right!).

You can find Erin on the Web at:
  ErinNicholas.com
  Twitter @ErinNicholas
  Facebook.com/ErinNicholasBooks

Fall in Love with Forever Romance

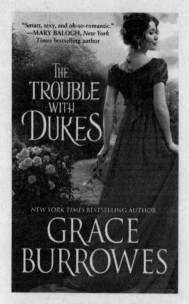

"Smart, sexy, and oh-so-romantic."
—MARY BALOGH, *New York Times* bestselling author

THE TROUBLE WITH DUKES

NEW YORK TIMES BESTSELLING AUTHOR
GRACE BURROWES

THE TROUBLE WITH DUKES
By Grace Burrowes

USA Today bestselling author Grace Burrowes brings us the first book in her new Windham Brides series! The gossips whisper that Hamish MacHugh, the new Duke of Murdoch, is a brute, a murderer, and even worse—a Scot. But Megan Windham sees something different, someone different. She isn't the least bit intimidated by his dark reputation, but Hamish senses that she's fighting battles of her own. For her, he'll become the warrior once more, and for her, he might just lose his heart...

ABSOLUTE TRUST
By Piper J. Drake

When Brandon Forte left to serve his country without saying good-bye, Sophie Kim tried to move on. Now he's back, and she can't forget what they shared. When her life is threatened, Brandon uses his specialized skills to protect her.

Fall in Love with Forever Romance

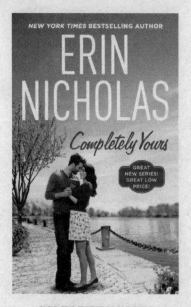

COMPLETELY YOURS
By Erin Nicholas

New York Times bestselling author Erin Nicholas kicks off her new Opposites Attract series! Zach Ashley is an EMT who lives to save people, while Kiera Connolly is a graphic designer who prefers to hide behind her computer. When disaster strikes and Zach must rescue Kiera, there's an instant attraction. The two don't agree on much, but despite their differences, they have one very important thing in common: They are crazy about each other.

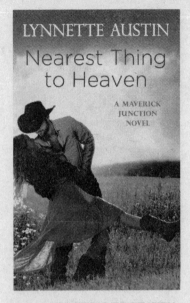

NEAREST THING TO HEAVEN
By Lynnette Austin

Ty Rawlins had a soul mate—and lost her. Now, the young widower refuses to love again. But when he meets Sophie, the cowboy suddenly finds it difficult to control his desire to wrangle the gorgeous city girl.